LITTLE HAMPTON

John E. Poulson

LITTLE HAMPTON

DOUBLE DRAGON

ISBN 978-1-78695-606-4

Double Dragon
is an imprint of
Fiction4All

Published 2021
Fiction4All
www.fiction4all.com

Chapter 1 - The Crime

"Nigel, how good of you to come," Andrew said as he opened the door to his guest.

Nigel smiled back at Andrew and held his hand out. "It was good of you to invite me after the recent, erm, unpleasantness," Nigel replied.

"That's all in the past now, surely. Caroline, darling, lovely to see you," Andrew said, greeting Nigel's wife.

"How could we possibly refuse the invitation? What was it you said on the invite, something about burying the hatchet?" Caroline asked.

"Indeed, yes, I have decided to retire, so old enemies should be the first to know and be conciliatory," Andrew said.

Nigel and Caroline entered. They said their hellos to Andrew's wife who was stood just behind him taking their coats and handing them to the servant to put away.

"Introductions are not necessary for Brian and Colin. Allow me to introduce Susan and Wendy, their wives respectively. What can I get you to drink?" Andrew asked.

"G and T, please," they both seemed to say in unison.

"Two G and T's coming up. Find a seat," Andrew said, indicating the arm chairs.

The waiter served Nigel and Caroline with their drinks and then they began to converse with the other guests, avoiding the past troubles when the men all vied for the control of the company, or to get their plans passed by the company. Arguments had been heated and they had left scars which would take time to heal.

These boardroom debates were usually just that, debates, but these men were far more aggressive and at times it felt more like a war zone than a boardroom.

At one point Nigel and Andrew had actually come to blows; there was no love lost between any of the men and their women folk stood by their man. This made the initial meeting strained, but the position of Managing Director, the COE of the company was about to be put up for grabs, which meant that it was in their interests to be there and pretend to be friends, and convivial.

At seven thirty on the dot, the waiter entered and announced that dinner was ready; Andrew led the way into the dining room and indicated the seating arrangement. Andrew sat at the head of the table with Caroline to his left, then Nigel. Wendy sat next to Nigel and then Brian, Susan came next, then Colin and Sophie on Nigel's right.

This arrangement put Colin as a good contender for the post, being sat on Nigel's right, indicating his right hand man, but at the other end of the table sat Brian. Was this an indication that he was a good contender, or that he was at the opposite end? He sat opposite Nigel, but then again at the bottom of the table, indicating that he was the least probable candidate.

These men all played the psychological game of position and drew their own conclusions of the positioning of the guests.

With the first course there was a very nice light white wine, the butler offered it to Andrew, who smiled and told him to allow his wife to taste it.

The waiter went to Sophie who smiled, accepting the offer graciously. She had been studying wines as a hobby and was now used to tasting the wine for dinner. The waiter poured a small amount in her glass and she sniffed it, swilled it around and then took a sip, rolled it around her tongue and swallowed it.

"Very nice, dear, an excellent choice, slightly nutty, but full flavoured and an excellent nose," she said and took another drink, draining the glass ready for a refill.

The waiter left her and poured wine for the guests, going around the table, leaving Andrew till last. The waiter was just about to pour the wine into Nigel's glass when Sophie collapsed onto the under plate in front of her. Sophie's eyes were wide open and her mouth agape.

Andrew jumped up and rushed to his wife, feeling for a pulse, but there was none.

"Someone ring for an ambulance and the police, Sophie is dead," he said, shocked and alarmed. He bent down, tears in his eyes as he caressed the lifeless form of his wife.

Chapter 2 - Assigned

The shrill tone of her phone brought Julie back from her relaxed state as she watched, rather dozed, an old episode of 'The Sweeny.'

"I don't know why you insist on watching it, you usually fall asleep half way through," Julie's latest male friend commented.

"Obviously, my dear, that is the reason," she replied and laughed with him. "Detective Chief Inspector Ashton," Julie said into the mouth piece, it had a nice ring to it.

"Ma'am, the Super asked me to ring you. We have a high profile death in suspicious circumstances. Sorry to spoil your evening, Ma'am," her sergeant said.

"OK, give me the address, I will be on my way in ten minutes," Julie said, picking up the pen by the phone to make a note of the address.

She went to the toilet and splashed water on her face to help wake her up. She took her dressing gown off, put her dress and her shoes on and she left the house within the ten minutes, after kissing her visitor and smiling at him.

"The joys of being a police person, get used to it, or don't come back," Julie said, being her pragmatic self, adding, "You will probably have left by the time I get home." She gave him a kiss and left the house.

Julie arrived at the address and began to look around the outside; it was her way of getting the feel, as she put it, of the scene.

"Sorry, Ma'am, this is a crime scene. You are not allowed inside. Can I ask you what you are doing here?" a police constable on the door asked Julie.

"Quite right, officer, do not allow anyone to enter, apart from police officers, I am Detective Chief Inspector Ashton," Julie told him, showing him her warrant card.

"Sorry, Ma'am, I-I didn't know," he apologised.

"Seeing as I have just arrived, I didn't expect you to and you were right to challenge me," Julie said.

She made her way up the steps to the front door and acknowledged the officer on the door, then entered. She again stopped and looked around before making her way up the entrance hall of this mansion, in the direction of all the activity. Julie would nod to the officers, showing them her warrant card as they acknowledged her.

Upon entering the room she saw a Detective standing by the table with the figure of the dead woman still slumped on her plate, with the doctor in attendance.

"What do we have? I am Detective Chief Inspector Ashton and you are?" she asked, showing him her warrant card and having made her own mind up already on the circumstances.

"Detective Sergeant Collins, Ma'am, The deceased is Lady Sophie Mac Adams; the wife of

Sir Andrew Mac Adams, the chairman of Mac Adams Construction. There was a rumour that he was in line for a peerage in the Queen's birthday honours. There were eight diners, including the Mac Adams. The dinner was for him to announce his retirement tonight and he was going to announce his successor after the dinner. There were two candidates for the post and they were both here.

"The doctor has pronounced and we have the time of death at nineteen forty pm, the doctor's initial findings indicate that she was poisoned; Ma'am, but he will know more after the post-mortem.

The Mac Adams had brought in a chef and waiting on staff for the dinner and they were all catering students from the local technical college. They had pre-dinner drinks in the lounge and then at seven thirty, sorry nineteen hundred and thirty hours, they came in here for dinner. Sir Andrew Mac Adams asked the waiter to pour the wine for the first course, after asking his wife to taste it.

"Apparently she was studying wines as a hobby and when they were having dinner she tasted the wine, not him, unless they were out and then he tasted it, being the host. She took a sip then another and then collapsed dead, Ma'am," Sergeant Collins said.

"Hum, so we have how many suspects?" Julie asked.

"There is Sir Andrew, then six guests and six students, unless we include the victim as a suspect," Sergeant Collins asked her.

10

"Your wit does not suit the occasion," Julie said formally.

"No, sorry, Ma'am, but it is usual for the host to taste the wine, Ma'am and I wondered if it was meant for him, which would mean that his wife would have to be a suspect and this is poetic justice. Sir Andrew and Lady Sophie Mac Adams; were in the middle of an upset, Ma'am, which may have resulted, in divorce. I learned this from one of the diners, things were not as rosy as they appeared, Ma'am," Collins told her.

"Interesting. She tried to poison her husband, but when he offered her the offer to taste, she had two options; she gave herself up and showed her hand, as it were, or drank the poisoned wine and committed suicide, rather than admit to trying to poison her husband. Is this a distrust common among the wealthy?" Julie asked him quietly.

"They are the ones who do the honourable thing, Ma'am, or is that, just on the films?" Collins asked, smiling at her.

"That is the question, but it usually applies to the upper classes, not the ones who have dragged themselves up by their boot laces as it were. For now we will begin looking at the case as if she was the intended victim, but I will bear in mind what you said.

"The other option is the opposite, was it him trying to kill his wife and succeeding? Who had the most to gain? The other question is, how many people were the intended victims? I assume they were to all, be given a glass of that wine, even Sir Andrew? So who was the intended victim?" Julie asked Collins as a rhetorical question and walked out of the dining room into the lounge, where all the people had been gathered.

"Ladies and gentlemen, I am Detective Chief Inspector Ashton and we do thank you for your co-operation by waiting for us. We will now need to interview you all and we will be as quick as possible so that you can go home as soon as possible," Julie informed them.

"Inspector, can't this wait? It has been a very distressing night for us all, especially our wives. I mean we were all supposed to drink from the same bottle, had she not dropped dead in front of us so quickly, you may have been investigating a mass murder," a guest asked.

"Sorry, no, we need the events to be fresh in your minds, we may need to ask you some more questions at a later date, as the investigation continues, but we need to speak to you now. Sir Andrew, is there another room we can use to speak to you all individually?" Julie asked.

"Yes, yes you, you can use the study, erm, and the library, I presume there will be more than one doing the interviews?" he asked.

"Yes. Sergeant, will you go with a DC in the study and I will take a PC with me into the library," Julie suggested.

Collins took a female Detective with him into the study, taking one of the female guests with them, and Julie took Sir Andrew with her and a police constable into the library.

"Sir Andrew, may I first of all express my sympathy for your loss. We will try and be as quick as possible; do you have a friend you can stay with, for tonight, Sir?" Julie asked him.

"Inspector," he said in a belittling tone.

"Chief Inspector, sir," Julie said, correcting him.

"Chief Inspector, sorry, it was common knowledge that I was estranged from my wife. We have not shared a bedroom in six months, so although I regret her death it is not as traumatic as if we were still in love. I will be fine sleeping here tonight. To get to where I am in business, you make enemies and if it was one of them trying to get at me, then they failed.

"My wife changed over the years, as we all do, she was not the same woman I married. Her good taste had become her greed, she was no longer happy with good clothes, she wanted top of the range, designer dresses, shoes and even her underwear had to be designer. It had become an obsession with her that she had the very best of everything.

"I am rich, but not that rich, we were going to Spain next month for a week's holiday to see if we could resurrect the marriage and she wanted to hire a private jet to take us there. We had a row about it. I am sure someone will tell you, so I won't hide it.

"She wanted to live the life of a billionaire, I am just a millionaire. I will want for nothing, a new car whenever I want, holidays whenever I want and for as long as I want, but there is a limit, a butler, servants, private jets are as much a dream to me as they are to you. I will not fret over the fact that I don't have them; I will have a very good life from now on with my investments. Six months in the Bahamas, maybe even have a house there, I can afford it, but butlers and servants live in? No. A daily to keep the place clean and tidy is all, I will need," he told them.

"I presume that your wife got on with all your guests, they were friends?" John asked.

"You couldn't be more wrong, Chief Inspector. The guests were enemies; they would fight like cat and dog. The difference in pay from their earnings now to being made CEO, is about twenty five thousand a year plus bonuses of a million a year perhaps. The person will go from being wealthy to being rich.

"Last year, my bonus was two million, this year I am expecting three million as my bonus. By retiring now I will also get a golden hand shake of about five million, but the construction industry is heading for a down turn. So what should I do, wait and watch as my income drops or go now at the height of the trend, with millions, in an off shore account? Or wait and watch as all my hard work is destroyed by a down turn in construction? Leave waving a merry good bye to the workers, secure in their jobs, or appear down hearted, as I make half of them redundant to save the firm, knowing the effect the downturn will have on my finances?

"No, Chief Inspector, the time to go is now and allow my successor to struggle, not me; to allow them to make the hard decisions and necessary redundancies" he told them.

"Who stood to gain from your wife's death, excepting the loss you suffered, so who stood to gain or who wanted to hurt you?" Julie asked him.

"My wife had no enemies, she helped out at the local hospice and served on the committee, organising functions to raise money. She was a very caring person and everyone liked her. As for me, well I am successful and inevitably there are people who feel aggrieved, but I would hate to say that I had the kind of enemies, people who would want me dead.

"My wife and I have had a very happy time together and settling a million on her in a divorce would not be unfair, or hinder my future life, erm, living standards. It would be a damn sight cheaper than staying married, but kill her rather than divorce? Never, I still loved her very much," he told them.

"You said a million; I presume you have a prenuptial agreement?" Julie asked.

"No, we married before I had attained the position of CEO. My wife was a secretary, and I was an up and coming business man with a degree in business studies. Landing the job with Mac Andrews construction, and the potential it offered, was pure luck. I took a small, localised building firm and turned it into a national company with a turnover in billions and excellent profits. But the tide has turned and the building industry is set for a poor period, during which lots of firms will go under, not only the small or medium sized firms. We are set for a recession and it may not be a small one. I doubt it being as bad as the Wall Street crash of the twenties, but tighten your belts now, it will be bad," he told Julie.

"Thank you for the warning. So you cannot think of any reason for someone to kill your wife. Does this mean that you think you were the target, or someone else at the dinner?" Julie asked.

"Like me, my dinner guests have enemies, but not nasty enough to want them dead. There is one other thing, it is usual for the host to taste the wine, not their wife and definitely not a guest. Had it not been for my wife's interest in wine, I would be the one tasting the wine. I therefore must assume the target, was me," Sir Andrew said factually.

"We cannot ignore that possibility, so I will leave an officer here for the night, although I doubt anyone trying again tonight, having just failed, if, you are the intended target," Julie said with compassion.

"I agree, so it will not be necessary to leave an officer here for the night. Their time may be better spent finding the bastard that murdered my wife," Sir Andrew said.

"Thank you for your help. Please don't leave the area, we may have to ask you some further questions," Julie said, and nodded to the officer who escorted Sir Andrew out of the room.

"You don't suspect me, do you?" he asked.

"I suspect everyone to some degree, so my first job is to eliminate several suspects. Once we find out how the poison was administered, I will have a better idea as to who I can eliminate. Once again I am sorry for your loss and thank you for your help," Julie said, ending the interview.

Julie had another guest brought in and again the story was the same; his wife was a pillar of the community and well liked. He had inevitable enemies, but none they thought would stoop to murder. He was a fair man but strict and ran a tight ship, as the saying goes.

Julie left the house and headed for the hotel she had booked into, after telling Sergeant Collins to join her there.

"Sergeant, what are first impressions?" Julie asked as they sat in the bar of the pub/ hotel with a beer in front of them.

"She was well liked, he had enemies, but none of the guests I interviewed could point a finger at anyone who would murder him," Collins told her.

"That is what I understand, but it seemed too pat, a beautiful wife loved by everyone, a handsome husband who still loves his wife but wants a divorce because she spends too much, does seem a bit odd," Julie said thoughtfully.

"Yes Ma'am and a big business man who has ruffled feathers, but hurt no-one; that also seems odd to me," Collins said.

"I think we need to get back to basics, Motive, Means and Method. The Method is right in front of us, she was poisoned by the wine. What the actual poison was we have yet to find out. Means, again obvious the wine, but how did the poison get in the wine, so the means is mysterious and finally Motive, there isn't one. So question, was Lady Sophie the intended victim?

"Tomorrow I want you to go to the firm and get a profile of how Sir Andrew was viewed and his wife. Try and probe for skeletons in their cupboards, no-one is without them," Julie told him.

"Ma'am, I was told to get a senior person on board at the start, because of it being a Sir and Lady involved, I know you have as yet not handed the paper work in, but I had already been issued with your mobile number, so I felt it important enough to call you. I hope you don't mind," Collins said meekly.

"Well let me put it like this, I like to hit the ground running and I most certainly have here. I have yet to register at the pub. I was just pulling into the car park when you rang me, so I may have to wear the same clothes tomorrow as today," Julie lied and smiled at him.

"Sorry, Ma'am, I'll go now and let you get some rest," he said and stood up, about to leave, then turned to face her again. "Ma'am, can I ask you if it is true that you took out four assailants single handed?" Collins asked.

"Shall we get one thing straight? It serves no purpose to ask if you can ask and then ask, anyway? If you have a question, just ask it. In answer to the question, my Sergeant at my last station was being attacked by six assailants, what would you do; stand by and let him be beaten to death or help?" Julie asked him.

"Call for back-up and get stuck in," he replied.

"That is exactly what I did and, to save further questions, yes, I put four of them in hospital, because I could not hold onto them, so I took them out and got a reprimand for being overzealous, police brutality. It earned me a promotion, but in a

18

quiet corner of England, supposedly, so that I can cool my heels, helping aged people across the empty streets," Julie said, part joking and smiling.

"Ma'am, they made a big mistake. This area is more like Dodge City, where accidents happen in retribution and where we meet a wall of silence. Last year a local farmer employed a local lad to plough his field, the tractor over turned and the lad was killed, The farmer's barn caught fire when it was full of straw and no-one saw anything. The farmer had just gone in for a coffee, otherwise he would have been caught in the fire," Collins told her.

"Really, and what happened? Did you investigate either accident?" Julie asked.

"Can I say the old Chief Inspector has retired, under mysterious circumstances? Personally, if I can, between you and me, I believe he was warned off and rather than ignore it, he retired," Collins told her.

"I appreciate your comments and it is logged and noted. Does this have any bearing on our current case, even remotely?" Julie asked.

"I never thought about that. The farmer is a tenant farmer on the Lord's land, so perhaps, remotely. Sir Mac Adams is reportedly to be made a lord, Ma'am," Collins said.

"Noted, now go home. I have had a hard day and expect to have another one tomorrow, so I am going to bed, after registering and unpacking and … well, I am sure there are more things I need to do before sleep, good night," Julie said and gave Collins a smile, thanking him.

Julie had registered and didn't want to tell him that she had just slept with an old friend. She looked around the room and stripped off, took a shower, made a coffee after putting her dressing gown on and sat by the window, gazing out over the tree tops as the sun slowly sank.

Julie didn't see the amber glow or red sky, her mind was on recent conversations. She didn't notice the scurrying clouds that drifted by, or the slowly sinking sun casting rays of light between the tree tops. She saw nothing, yet saw everything as she turned over and over in her mind what Collins had said and what the witnesses to the crime had told her.

By the time the sun had fully set and the moon had taken over lighting the area, her eyes had closed as she sat in the comfortable arm chair and she had drifted off to sleep.

Chapter 3 - A New Station

Julie woke, still sat in the chair, the sun was rising. It was still early. She watched the sun rise and then took a shower and got dressed, taking clean clothes out of her suitcase. She hung a few dresses up, 6ogether with trousers and tops and then put her underwear in the drawers and make-up on the dressing table before going down to breakfast.

After breakfast, she checked her watch again. It was still too early to go to the station to check in, so she went for a walk along the main road.

The hotel was in the centre of the town with an open aspect at the back where her room was located; She smiled at several early risers as they made their way to work and the postman closing the garden gate after delivering their mail.

"Morning, I'm Detective Chief Inspector Ashton and I'm new to the town. Do you deliver the mail to the big house?" Julie asked him.

"Yes Ma'am. I deliver the mail to all the houses. Since the advent of computers there isn't as much mail, except bills, so I suppose I'm now not the postman, just the bill delivery man," he said with irony.

"Yes, I suppose you are, I hadn't thought about that. So what mail does the big house get? Is it as you said, just bills?" Julie asked him.

"Mainly, but there has been a few brown envelopes, recently," he said with meaning.

"Do you ever talk to the residents, have a conversation on your rounds?" Julie asked.

"I don't have time; it's all rush and push, these days, being on my own, like. Not that long ago there were four of us, when people got mail, letters and the like, now I can manage it on my own. Did you say you're new to the town? Where are you living? I can't think of an empty house in the town. There are a few for sale, but they are still occupied," he told her.

"No, yes, erm, sorry, I am not fully awake yet. I'm new and staying at the Market Hotel. Thank you for stopping to chat, if you hear of an empty house, please let me know, or leave a message at the hotel. I only have a month there before I'm supposed to have found a house, rented, until the sale of my house goes through, so if you hear of anything; I would appreciate you letting me know. Bye," Julie said, and continued with her walk.

The sun was out and it promised to be another nice day, warm and cheery. She looked in the shop windows as she made her way down the high street, they hadn't open yet, it was only eight o'clock.

She reached the far side of the high street, turned around and made her way back. She heard a noise and then a patrol car sped past her, going up the high street, lights flashing and sirens blaring.

'This was supposed to be a quiet country town for me to think and calm down and as I arrive we have a murder- and now what?' Julie thought, *'Couldn't they at least allow me to sign in, first?'*

She called in at the newsagents and bought a paper.

"Hello, I'm Detective Chief Inspector Ashton. The Mail please. What can you tell me about the Mac Adams, did they buy their newspapers here?" Julie asked him.

"Morning, Chief Inspector, yes they did, it is terrible what happened, she was such a lovely lady, the hospice will miss her terribly; she literally kept the place running. Sir Andrew had the Mail, Telegraph and FT delivered, we also delivered Woman's Own and Country Life when they came out. Lady Sophie had a sweet tooth; she would call in and buy a quarter of Liquorice Allsorts most days, rather old fashioned, she never asked for two hundred and fifty grams, it was always a quarter. Harry, the butcher, told me that she was just the same over in his place, a pound of this or that, always imperial measure, never metric.

"She told me that Europe had ruined England, robbing us of our identity, I must say I agree with her sentiments, what was wrong with the good old English King Edward, you could roast it, boil it, mash it and chip it, an all-round potato, but we now have foreign rubbish and not one that is as good tasting, or robust as the good old King Edward," he told Julie.

"What was Sir Andrew like, did he shop here?" Julie asked.

"Not that much, Lady Sophie, did all the shopping and paid the shop bills, but occasionally he would call in and buy a box of cigars. That was the last time I saw him actually, two, no, three days ago, when he bought a box. I presumed it was for the dinner party, Lady Sophie ordered them the

23

week before, but he was the one that collected them and paid for them. Lady Sophie said they were dirty, nasty things and would have nothing to do with them. Be with you in a moment, sir," he said to another customer.

"Please," Julie said, indicating he serve the customer, "I need to be on my way, thank you, oh and order me a Mail for tomorrow, please?" Julie asked.

Once again this saintly persona of a good, friendly and helpful woman was being portrayed. So why did she have to die, who hated her that much? According to the shop keepers and everyone Julie spoke to said the same, she was well liked, the heart and soul of the hospice.

A car pulled up beside her and she looked at it, then bent down and smiled.

"Collins, I wasn't expecting you just yet, it isn't nine o'clock yet, is it?" Julie asked.

"No Ma'am, the Super is up at the police station and she wants an update, so I thought it wise to collect you early. Are you ready, Ma'am?" Collins asked.

"I don't suppose I have any option," Julie said, laughing, and got in the car, "Then again you saved me from a soaking," she added as the cloud that had rolled in, burst.

'Typical, my first day at a new station and the cloud bursts,' Julie thought, remembering her first day at the London station.

Collins drove her to the station and introduced her to the desk sergeant, then they went through to the Super, who was in the briefing room.

"Good of you to join us, Sergeant, and you must be Chief Inspector Julie Ashton, pleased to meet you. Now what about last night? I am sure the new Detective Chief Inspector wishes to be brought up to speed," she said.

"Not really," Julie said, smiling at his look of shock, "Sergeant Collins had the wisdom to contact me, even though I had not formally joined the station, because of the importance of the case.

"There isn't much just yet; Lady Sophie Mac Adams was killed last night, presumably by poison, but we are waiting for the autopsy report to be sure. We also need that report to find out exactly how the poison was administered. We have four guests, two chefs and two waiting on staff, a pot wash, a wine waiter and Sir Andrew. As yet we do not have a motive, but are pretty sure of the method and means.

"My first job is to ascertain what the night officers have found out, they were doing background checks on the guests and staff and I have asked Detective Sergeant Collins to visit the firm this morning, to carry out checks there, all standard procedure, Ma'am," Julie told her.

"Very good, I will take this opportunity to introduce you to the station as the new Detective Chief Inspector. You have met Detective Sergeant Collins, so all that remains is for me to wish you a long and happy time with us and remind you that this case is high profile and takes precedence over all other cases. Sir and Lady Mac Adams were very influential, pillars of the community, Lady Mac

Adams will be sadly missed, very much so," the Superintendant said.

"That is what I have been hearing, Ma'am, not a bad word has been spoken about her, Ma'am," Julie said.

The Super introduced Julie to the officers and stepped to one side and indicated that Julie now take the meeting.

"Good morning and hello everyone. You now know who I am and I am sure I will soon get to know each of you. As the Super said, this is a high profile case, so we cannot afford to slack. I want all the reports I asked for by tonight. Do not allow anyone to delay your enquiries, any problems tell me about them, and I will light a fire under them.

"I hit the ground running, keep up, I will not slow down, it will be up to you to keep up with me, so get to work," Julie said, and turned to leave the area.

Collins showed her to her office and left her to settle in, Julie hung her coat up on the rack and sat down to a clear desk. She picked up the phone and rang a number.

"Hello, Sergeant Williams, please?" she asked the operator.

"Julie, sorry, Chief Inspector Julie, come on, tell me how many parking tickets have you given out?" Williams asked her, joking.

"None, I've been too busy catching a murderer. I drove into the hotel car park and my mobile rang, I hadn't even booked into the hotel before I have a high profile case. How is London?" Julie asked.

"Just the same, I leave tomorrow, they did recognise the work I've done and I'm to move to a Manchester station as the new Inspector. I passed the exam six months ago and I've been waiting for a vacancy," Williams told her.

"Anybody else? They all deserved some recognition." Julie asked.

"Evans is coming with me as a Sergeant, Hastings has also been promoted to Sergeant and is going to Humberside, for some odd reason they liked him. The others have also been promoted and are moving to new stations over this month. We had an excellent team, Ma'am," Williams said.

"We did and I'll miss them, keep in touch and give my regards to Alex," Julie said, and hung up.

Julie sat back and allowed herself a few moments to reminisce about her last case with Sergeant Williams, and her team.

A man dressed as a woman walked up to prominent people, shot them dead, and walked away - in a public place. They nicknamed him the Illusionist, because he wanted to be noticed but not seen. He used a gun, yet no-one heard the bang, the wound was as if from a distance, but it was close range, everything they knew about the case was contradicted. A meek and mild man who assassinated several politicians in several countries and no-one saw or heard anything, yet they all saw him do the deed and didn't realise it. Confusion haunted the case from start to finish. Literally hundreds of witnesses and no-one saw anything.

Well that is in the past now and she had a new case to solve, hopefully not as ridiculous or complex, but only time would tell.

Julie put her coat on and again went for a walk in the town. She felt she needed to get to know the town and people and where and how Sir and Lady Mac Adams fitted in.

The butcher was again helpful and spoke freely about Lady Sophie's obsession with imperial measure and her generosity, buying legs of lamb for Sunday lunch at the hospice last Easter and turkeys for their Christmas dinner.

Julie began to think that Lady Sophie was too good to be true, she didn't believe anyone was that good. There is always dirt; no-one is that perfect.

So she liked designer clothes and spent more than she needed to, according to her husband and she had high ideals, wanting a private jet to take them on holiday. Was that enough to kill her? According to her husband, no. He would have been quite happy to divorce her and give her a million pounds in the settlement, just ten percent of his bonuses over the last three years, but would she be happy with that? What if she wanted half the estate? Now that was surely a different matter and without a prenuptial agreement that was what she could expect.

Julie entered a café and ordered a coffee then pulled out her phone and rang the office.

"Sergeant, the students that served the meal: which college did they come from? Was it the local one?" Julie asked him.

"I don't know, Ma'am, I presume so; would you like me to check?" he asked.

"Yes please, ring around the local colleges to find out, don't ask Sir Mac Adams. I am sure the head of department will know," Julie said.

"Your coffee ,Madam," the waitress said, Julie looked at her and smiled.

"Hold on a moment, please, do I-" Julie paused, recognising the young lady. "You were at the big house last night, waiting on, weren't you?" Julie asked her.

"No, Madam, sorry. That was my younger sister, she's at the local college studying hospitality management, she hopes to become the manager of a hotel," the waitress told Julie.

"You could be twins, sorry to have hindered you. You do seem to be very busy." Julie looked around.

"Wait till the summer comes fully, this is quiet, then we have tour buses and coaches pulling up," she told Julie, smiling.

"Sorry. I'm Detective Chief Inspector Ashton, that's why I was asking about last night. I need to ask your sister some questions. I thought it was too good to be true meeting you like this," Julie said, smiling back at her.

"She usually gets home about six o'clock. I don't know if I should ask you this, but will she get paid for last night? As a student she needs the money," she asked.

" 'm sorry I can't answer that. From what I hear they are genuine, so I suppose so," Julie said.

"Lady Sophie was generous, but him, Sir Andrew; well he has been compared to ducks, but tighter. The last dinner he had, the students worked quarter of an hour over their time, instead of finishing at ten o'clock, it was quarter past. The guests all complimented them for their efforts, but he paid them till ten and seemingly begrudged that. One of the students heard him telling his wife that she could have done the dinner and saved him forty eight pounds. Two chefs, four hours' work; even so that's only six pounds an hour, when the minimum wage is eight. Madam, he got them cheap and still complained. Yes, sorry, Alice, coming," she said to the other waitress.

"Like I said, sorry to keep you, thank you," Julie said.

Julie picked up her phone and rang the desk Sergeant. "Hello again. One of the waitresses does go to the local college, she's doing Hospitality Management. Contact that college and find out if they all came from there." Julie told him.

Julie was quite pleased with her walk, it had introduced her to the town, she had met several people and was beginning to build up a picture of Sir Andrew and Lady Sophie, him the miser, the controller, whist she was generous and kind. A

brawl erupted onto the street from the local pub. Julie was quick and grabbed the nearest combatant, pulling him behind her, facing the other as the one behind her made to continue the fight. She stuck her arm out, hitting him in the chest, winding him, whilst she glared at the other who seemed frozen to the spot.

"I have two options, walk away because you've stopped, or arrest you both for disorderly conduct and causing an affray. Now which is it to be?" Julie asked them.

"I don't know who the fuck you are, bitch, but he started it. He spilled my beer, pushing in," the one facing her said angrily.

"I'm Detective Chief Inspector Ashton and I want you to be careful what you say. I don't like swearing. Did you spill his beer?" Julie asked the one she had winded.

"How the hell should I know? I was pushed from behind; it's market day and the pubs are packed as usual. If I did, it wasn't my fault, as I said I was pushed from behind, but I didn't lash out, he did," he said.

"So it was an accident, what do I do, take you both in for causing an affray, or watch you shake hands? Where would you like to spend the next twenty four hours, in the pub, or a cell?" Julie asked them.

"OK, you win," the one facing her said, and made to go back inside, followed by the other.

"If we're called back, you two will be arrested. Heed my warning, I do not make false promises," Julie warned them and continued on her way.

Julie chuckled to herself as she made her way back to the police station; she knew that in the old days, when pubs were only allowed to open certain hours, in these small country side communities, they were allowed to open all day on market day. With the introduction of unrestricted hours, it wasn't quite the same, but the influx of market stall holders and local farmers selling their crops and the influx of people from outside the community, the town bulged at the seams.

The main street was all but closed off, with numerous stalls filling one side of the street and the market square and traffic had to be diverted around the back streets. This also led to scuffles. Julie, not aware as yet of the situation, had acted correctly, the police tended to turn not so much a blind eye to these troubles, but were perhaps more tolerant of them and moving people on, rather than arresting them.

Julie was amazed at the throng of people as she weaved her way between the customers and stall holders.

"Bloody hell, Sergeant, it's worse than London, what's going on?" Julie asked the desk Sergeant.

"Market day, Ma'am, it happens once a week; all the outlying villages pile into the town with the farmers who probably have farm shops, but turn up here with their goods. The last Chief tried to stop it, because there is always trouble and it causes congestion. The town hall vetoed his efforts, because they're shop keepers and cafe owners and trade is increased by so much that they wanted it to continue. It gives us a headache, but the pub can take as much today as it does the rest of the week," he told her.

"So it is a tradition and by royal charter, is it?" Julie asked.

"Interesting you should say that, tradition yes, but they say it is by royal charter, but can't produce the document," he told her, smiling with meaning.

"I won't interfere unless it becomes a problem. I broke up a fight on my way back, something of nothing really, so I suggested they make up, or I would arrest them. They made up. I was thankful, it would have meant a lot of paperwork for me, had I arrested them," Julie said smiling at him.

"That is what we try to do, keep the peace," he said, also smiling, "I passed your request on to Constable Everet and she rang the college for you, Ma'am. You'll find her in the break room, Ma'am," the desk sergeant told her.

Julie left the desk and made her way to the break room. Half a dozen officers were sat in there, drinking tea or coffee. Julie looked around.

"Ma'am, who are you looking for?" an officer asked her.

"Constable Everet," Julie replied.

"She's sat over there, Ma'am, the blonde," he told Julie and she thanked him.

"Constable Everet, I believe you have some information for me?" Julie asked her.

"Ma'am, all the staff were from the college, they supplied two chefs and two waiting on staff. The chefs were to arrive at six o'clock and the waiting on staff at six thirty. Dinner was to be served at seven thirty and expected to last till nine o'clock, four courses with wine. The chefs were to finish, having cleaned up at nine thirty, and the waiting on staff at ten o'clock, Ma'am," Constable Everet informed her.

"Good work, Constable, you didn't by any chance ask what the menu was, did you?" Julie asked her.

33

"I did, it was soup, followed by a fish dish, then sorbet, the main course of beef with vegetables and then Crème Bruleè and coffee. To be correct, Ma'am, that is a five course dinner, because cheese, biscuits and fruit were to be served with the coffee and port, but it never got that far," Everet told her.

"Well done, a comprehensive report, thank you. My Sergeant is occupied this morning looking at the firm, not knowing the area I will need a guide for a couple of hours, it will mean missing your break, because I need to go now, before they break for lunch," Julie said.

"I'm finished, Ma'am," Everet said. Julie smiled; she liked to encourage junior officers to go for promotions and move up the ranks.

They took a car and made their way to the college.

"How long have you been an officer?" Julie asked her.

"Two months now, Ma'am, I wanted to be a chef and attended the college for a year, before changing direction and becoming a police officer. No, I didn't like it, that is usually the next question. As they say, 'if you can't stand the heat, get out of the kitchen,' and that is exactly what I did. A solid top stove produces as much heat as a central heating system, it was a mistake and didn't suit me," Everet told Julie.

"Not everyone knows what they want for a career when they leave school. I trained as a nurse before joining the army, it isn't a mistake, just an experiment to find where you fit in. The average person is looking at spending the next forty five to fifty years doing that job, eight hours a day of misery or enjoyment, so you do need to try things before deciding," Julie told her.

"Ma'am, do you remember an officer named Hastings? I believe you were both at the same station a few years back somewhere in or near Manchester?" Everet asked Julie.

""Hastings, that does ring a bell with me," Julie said and laughed. "I'm not mad, just annoyed at myself. I never forget a face and I knew I recognised him, but couldn't place him. Just you wait till I get my hands on him. My last case before moving here was a very difficult one and Hastings was drafted in to assist on the case, so yes I know him. I was with him a month ago in London. Why, do you know him?" Julie asked.

"He's my brother-in-law and it was him who suggested I join the police because I like sports and the outdoors. I have a blue belt in Judo and Karate, so I can look after myself," Everet said.

"Do you plan on taking the brown belt?" Julie asked.

"I'm booked in for the test next month," Everet told her.

"Excellent, let me know if you pass, won't you?" Julie asked her.

"Yes, Ma'am, here we are, the catering department is on the second floor, Ma'am," Everet told her, and led the way.

They entered the building and made their way up to the second floor. They turned left and stopped at the first door, the Principal's office where Julie asked to see the Principal, after introducing themselves as police officers.

The secretary showed them in, introduced them, then left.

"Mr Starkey, pleased to meet you. I'm investigating the murder of Lady Mac Adams and I believe four of your students were there to cook and serve the meal. I have a few questions I need to ask them," Julie said.

"A terrible thing to happen to such a lovely person, we are all shocked. Sir Mac Adams used my students quite a bit, it gave them experience putting into practice what they had learned," he told them.

"It is a terrible thing. Now is there a room we can use? I would like to speak to them before they break, for lunch?" Julie asked.

"Yes, please follow me," he said.

"Mr Starkey, were there any problems with payment that you know of?" Julie asked as they made their way to the room.

"Payment?" he questioned, "Indeed not. All the students were paid as they left. No-one has ever questioned their honesty. All the students were paid as agreed, why do you ask? I find it offensive," He asked Julie.

"It just completes the picture; I sometimes need to ask offensive and difficult questions, it is just part of the job, like their marriage just how stable was it?" Julie asked.

"It was the epitome of how a successful marriage should be, they were a very loving couple," he replied.

"Just before you get the first student, did they contribute to your department in any way?" Julie asked.

"In time, yes, Sir Andrew often gave the prizes away at prize day and Lady Sophie did as well, but not fiscally, if that is what you mean, Inspector?" he told them.

"Thank you; can we see Sandra Gee, please?" Julie asked him.

A few moments later Sandra knocked on the door and Everet opened the door for her. She was dressed in whites, having been cooking in the kitchen.

"You wanted to see me? Will this take long? I'm in the middle of a lesson and had to leave the lecturer looking after my meal," Sandra asked.

"I'm sorry about dragging you out of a lesson, but this is a murder enquiry. We need to know what you were doing, were you a chef or waitress?" Julie asked her.

"I was in-charge of the kitchen, Ian Sanders was my assistant, being a year below me," Sandra told them.

"I see, so Clair and June were the waiting on staff: that helps us. Had the serving of the meal started?" Julie asked.

"Yes, they had the soup and then with the Sole Bon Femme there was a light white wine. The dirty soup plates came back and I sent out the Sole, it was silver service. Claire served the Sole, whilst June was serving the wine, she put the plates down first, then served the wine as Claire began to serve the Sole," Sandra told her.

"I see you saw June serve the wine, did you?" Julie asked.

"No, but that was the plan and seeing as Claire was in the kitchen collecting the flat of Sole, I presumed June was placing the plates in front of the diners and opening the wine," Sandra said.

"A logical assumption. Tell me: the soup, what was it and how did you serve it?" Julie asked.

"I made a cream soup, cauliflower and stilton, which I poured into the soup tureen and June took it in. This time it was Claire who put the soup bowls out on the under plate and then whilst June held the tureen, Claire served the soup," Sandra told them.

"I see ,so you made the soup, did Ian help you?" Julie asked.

"Obviously he was there to assist me, he crumbled the stilton in whilst I stirred it, he also cut the florets off the head for the garnish and chopped up the stalks, but I cooked it and made sure the garnish was al dente to give the soup texture, as well as being creamy," Sandra said.

"Once the soup left the kitchen, was it ever out of your sight?" Julie asked.

"Why all the interest in the soup? I tasted it and Ian had some. I thought it was the wine that had killed her?" Sandra asked.

"We have not got the autopsy report back yet and seeing as we believe Lady Sophie was poisoned and she had only had a sip of wine, we need to make sure. Now, was it ever out of your sight?" Julie asked.

"Yes, but June wouldn't kill anyone," Sandra said, shocked.

"I didn't say she had. Did you put any poison in the soup?" Julie asked her bluntly.

"I did not," Sandra said just as bluntly, giving Julie an angry stare.

"I'll need the recipe you used for the soup," Julie said and Everet opened the door for her to leave, then Ian was asked to enter.

The interview followed the same pattern, with him assuring them that he only assisted Sandra and again confirmed that once the soup left the kitchen, it was out of sight for a short period, before entering the dining room. Claire was next.

"You served the soup whilst June held the tureen and then served the wine whilst June collected the fish course, is that correct?" Julie asked her.

"Not quite. I put the plates out and opened the wine whilst June collected the fish course and as she served the fish, I poured the wine," Claire said.

"Who collected the wine?" Julie asked.

"I have no idea, on the side there was the wine cooler with the wine in it, and beside it the red wine for the meat dish and once I had removed the white wine from the cooler, I put the desert wine into the cooler; it had already been chilled. There are only eight glasses of wine in a bottle on average, so with eight diners the wine would not be going back into the cooler," Claire informed them.

"Eight diners, I thought there were six, Sir and Lady Mac Adams and four guests?" Julie asked.

"Sorry, that is correct, but we were told eight. I presume two didn't turn up," Claire said.

"I see, so there was some wine left over, you didn't pour it all if there were only six diners?" Julie asked.

"Yes, erm, there must have been," Claire said.

"Was there some wine over, or not?" Julie pressed her.

"Y-yes, not much, the average is six to eight, depending on the size of glass and how full they are," Claire said.

"Claire, I am not interested in averages, I do not need a lesson in wine; I need facts. Was there or wasn't there any wine left in the bottle?" Julie asked, pressing her.

"Y-yes, there was," Claire said.

"How much wine was left?" Julie asked her.

"N-Not much, just about a glass," Claire said, embarrassed.

"What happened to it, the bottle was empty when we collected it," Julie pushed her.

"I-I took it into the kitchen after serving them, Lady Sophie was still alive then and Ian drank it, only when I got back did I find out that Lady Sophie was dead after drinking it. I-I dashed back into the kitchen, Ian was being sick in the sink. June had told them and Sandra had stuffed her fingers down his throat to make him sick," Claire admitted.

"Thank goodness for Sandra's quick actions, it probably saved his life. Thank you. Get Ian and bring him here now. Everet, call an ambulance, please?" Julie asked her.

"You've seen him, he's fine," Claire told her.

"We don't know what the poison was, which means that we don't know the long term effect, and the steps we can take to stop him from dying six months from now; go and get him, now," Julie told her firmly.

Claire brought Ian back to them and he was taken to the hospital for a check-up, and to give blood for analysis.

"Ma'am, do you think he could die, in six months?" Everet asked her.

"It is very doubtful, but it is better to be safe and it may give us the poison a lot quicker. The mortuary is overflowing after that multiple car pileup on the motorway," Julie said.

"Shall I send June in, Ma'am?" Everet asked her.

"Might as well, she is the only one left to shed any sort of light on this," Julie said as if dismayed.

June's statement was the same as Claire's statement, or very similar, apart from confirming that she had run into the kitchen as soon as Lady Sophie had collapsed, warning Ian and alerting Sandra.

"So the only person not to touch the bottle was Sandra?" Julie asked June.

"No, when I put it on the table, Sandra, picked it up and handed it to Ian, saying that she was driving," June told them.

"Great, so everyone, including the murderer, if it was the wine, handled the bottle and they were probably the only person not to leave finger prints," Julie said.

"Unless it was Sir Andrew, then he would not worry, because he presumably brought the bottle from the wine cellar," Everet suggested.

41

"Good point," Julie said. "We still don't know if it was the wine or not and what the poison was. I hope Collins has had better luck," Julie said as they left the college.

"We do know that the students set the table and they polished the glasses s it could not have been in a glass, and they would have been set randomly, which is not a good idea if you wish to poison someone. You cannot be sure that the glass will be placed where they were to sit," Everet said.

"Again a good point, but just illustrates what we don't know. Turn around, and go back," Julie said suddenly.

They went back and Julie this time entered a class room and asked Claire to come outside.

"Was the dining room left unattended at any time after you set the table?" Julie asked her.

"Yes, Sir Andrew greeted the guests and showed them into the lounge where June served then with a pre diner drink, whilst I was in the kitchen getting ready for service, polishing the serving spoons and clearing the central table ready for service. I also washed some of the pots to save time later. The pot wash had yet to arrive, Sir Andrew timed everything, she was due once there were plates to wash, he timed it too precise and she hadn't arrived as some of the prep dishes were at the sink, that is how tight he was," Claire said.

"How long was that for and were all the guests visible at all times?" Julie asked her.

"I was in the kitchen, so I can't answer that," Claire said.

Julie went to June's class room and, after asking her to come outside; she asked her the same question.

"Sir Andrew, told me that the white wine was in the cooler and the red was beside it, which I already knew and that the desert wine was next to that and that I was to serve them in that order. He told me this in the corridor outside the room, so everyone in there was out of my sight whilst we spoke. He was obsessed with perfection and repeated it, so I would say for five minutes I could only see him, all the others were out of my sight," June told her.

They left, and returned to the police station.

"So the only person who knew that Lady Sophie would be tasting the wine, was Sir Andrew, which makes him our chief suspect, if it was the wine," Julie said.

Chapter 4 - Deadly Nightshade

Julie returned to her office, and sat down just as Collins entered.

"Well Collins, what did you find out?" Julie asked him.

"On the surface all appears well; but once I began to dig down, things were not quite so cosy. The company has taken a ten percent decrease in trading figures over the year, which confirms Sir Andrew's convictions, but the construction industry as a whole has dipped only four per cent, which means his company is not fairing as well as it should be doing.

"Profits are down even more and this is because of slight irregularities in the accounts. Sir Andrew's expenses are far higher than usual and his wife now has an expense account, as his PA.

"Ma'am, he is creaming off the top, I believe he is making fraudulent claims and several of the employees are owed wages. There are cash flow problems," Collins told her.

"Interesting, that is very interesting, apart from one thing. How did a disgruntled employee manage to poison his wine?" Julie asked.

"It doesn't, apart from the glowing picture of a rich, very successful business man and a generous wife may not be quite so rosy; especially if one of the people at the table knew more than they said and wanted to stop him bleeding the company dry, but got the wrong person?" Collins asked, cocking his head to one side, querying his comments.

"All avenues are open at this moment in time and that is a possibility, they all had the opportunity, including Sir Andrew, before the guests arrived and whilst he was making sure the staff knew what was expected of them," Julie said thoughtfully, "It also begs the question who was the intended victim. If we assume it was Lady Sophie, then the spotlight falls on Sir Andrew, being the only person who knew she would be tasting the wine. It is normal for the host to taste the wine, so did they kill the wrong person?" Julie asked.

"Apart from the staff," Collins suggested.

"No, even they were not seen all the time, so we cannot exclude anyone at this moment. I still have a question mark over who was to be the victim. The poison was either meant for all of them, being in the wine, which, I very much doubt; or the person sat at the head of the table who tasted the wine, being Sir Andrew. Assuming the killer did not know that he would ask his wife to taste the wine.

"We will not know that until forensics have completed their tests. How long does it take for forensics to send results here?" Julie asked.

"We do not have our own lab, Ma'am, samples are sent to Oxford for testing and they have all their own crimes to complete tests on, so we tend to get put to the bottom of the pile, depending on what crimes they have on their books," Collins informed her.

"Ah, the joys of a country copper. Get me the lab, please?" Julie asked him.

"Good morning, Detective Chief Inspector Ashton speaking, I need the results of the samples we sent over. As you may have noticed our case has hit the headlines and is considered by the force as being high profile, so if you don't mind, a quick reply would be appreciated before I have to make serious waves," Julie said, emphasising the importance of their findings.

"Chief Inspector, we do realise the importance and I have put a rush on the tests, but our local police also have had a serious murder to investigate so we have a lot of samples to examine. I should have your results by the end of the week," the voice on the phone said.

"Thank you, I would appreciate the results as soon as possible and that will save me having to make another phone call on Monday if we have them by then. Saving us both time to continue our work rather than speaking on the phone; wouldn't it?" Julie asked the person on the phone, the head of the lab.

"Ma'am, there has been another death, one David Morris; he was one of the guests at the dinner party, but did not arrive. He was out walking with his wife when he fell. He tried to get up, but was unsteady and she went to help him, being a few yards behind him when he stumbled again and fell over the edge of a quarry, two hundred feet to his death," PC Everet told Julie.

"That sounds accidental, death by misadventure, why was he so close to the edge?" Julie asked, thinking aloud.

"Shall I bring the car around to the front, Ma'am?" Collins asked.

"You need to ask? Why are you still here; get the car!" Julie said, and left her desk, going to the front of the station.

"The autopsy report and some of the forensics reports, Ma'am, have just been delivered," the desk Sergeant told her as she passed his desk.

Julie thanked him and had a quick look at the papers and then went out as Collins pulled up in front. She got in and began to study the papers.

"Interesting, all but one of the glasses were clear of poison, the heaviest concentration was in the base of the glass, presenting with the poison, cyanide. We now know what poison was used and how it was administered. One of the glasses had some in the bottom. Claire polished the glasses, which would wipe some of the poison off, unless it was sprayed in after she had polished them. After we have been to the scene; I want you to speak to Claire and find out how long before the meal she polished the glasses and if every guest was in sight between her polishing the glasses and the guests, sitting down for the meal.".

"Here we are, Ma'am, but it is now a good half hour trek to the actual site, the other side of the hill," Everet told her.

"I hope you enjoy the walk, go and bring back the Land Rover. Heels are not and were never meant for fell walking, remind me to get a pair of sensible shoes to be kept in the office. In London I could kick my shoes off when chasing villains, here it is not, so simple," Julie said.

"Yes, Ma'am, I have a pair of wellingtons in the boot, more often than not, fields are involved in an investigation, being out in the country and soggy fields," Everet said, and laughed.

"Saved by the bell, Sergeant, a police Land Rover has just arrived, leaving the scene, I presume," Julie said.

Everet stopped the Land Rover, they climbed in and were taken to the site.

The Land Rover stopped on the top of the quarry face and they got out, telling the driver to stay where he was.

"Ma'am, we have ordered a crane with a cage to lower us down to the actual scene. It is a long way down, isn't it?" Everet asked Julie.

"What are we doing up here, Everet, when the crime scene is down there?" Julie asked her.

"Last year, Ma'am, the floods washed away what was left of the wooden bridge they used as an entry and we cannot get across the river. This is the only access, Ma'am, down the face of the quarry," Collins informed her.

"Then bring the Land Rover over here and I will abseil down," Julie said.

"Ma'am, is that wise? I mean, it is a very long way down," Everet queried.

"Sergeant, I have abseiled down a lot longer faces than this, I will use the winch on the Land Rover, either that or I will climb down. We need to be down there, not up here, the body is down there. So unless you have any more suggestions, bring the Land Rover over here, preferably before it goes dark, Everet," Julie said forcefully.

"Yes, Ma'am," she said and indicated that the Land Rover comes nearer the edge.

Julie pulled a length of the wire from the winch and put it between her legs, around the top of her thigh, back between her legs and around the other thigh then under the wire and up around her waist and back to the wire and clipped it on creating a form of cradle, then backed up to the edge.

"OK, lower me down slowly," she told the officers and they switched the winch on as she began her descent, walking as it were down the smooth quarried face.

Once at the bottom she began the meticulous task of looking around at the debris and the body.

"OK, Everet, haul me back up," she said and again apparently walked up the face of the quarry, aided by the winch.

"Ma'am, what did you find out?" Everet asked.

"Being glib, a dead man at the base of the quarry face, what else? From what I know. accepting that I am not a doctor, I would say he is dead and was not pushed, lying at the base of the face, too close to have been pushed," Julie said adding a smile at the futility of the question, "I now wish to speak to his wife," Julie said.

"Hello, I'm Chief Inspector Ashton, I wish to express my regret at your loss and that I need to impose on you, by asking you some questions at this time. What was the state of mind of your husband, prior to his fall?" Julie asked the distraught woman.

49

"You-you don't think he jumped, do you? I mean he just stumbled and fell over the edge," she said.

"That is not for me to say, Madam, at the moment we have a deceased male and I am trying to find out why. What was he doing so close to the edge to fall?" Julie asked.

"David wanted to look down; he felt that the quarry was worth investing in and re-opening it. He made his way closer to the edge to look down and take photos to study later, but I am sure I saw him wobble; he looked unsteady and was flushed. He had complained earlier that he felt sickly. I suggested that we go home, but he insisted on coming here to check and get evidence to present to the board as to the viability of re-opening, the quarry. Well, to make them investigate it further, a few photos would not be enough to re-open it, but he decided that they would show that it warranted investigating further," Caroline his wife informed them, through a veil of tears and sobs.

"I am sorry to have to ask these questions, but they are important. Was the quarry the cause of the argument prior to the dinner, the other night?" Julie asked.

"Yes, Andrew's dad was the manager when the deaths occurred and Andrew didn't want it re-opened. David and Andrew had argued, a real coming to blows sort of argument and Colin supported David, as did Andrew's wife, but Brian sat very securely on the fence, he was always indecisive. The dinner was really to erm, cement, re-build the good rapport they usually had and appoint a successor to Andrew, who had decided to retire. Nigel was the front runner; he was the Managing Director and had helped build the company.

"David knew he would not get the job, so we decided to come here; he wanted to use the stone for the business as facings for their buildings, to give the upmarket buildings class. You don't think, no, it can't be, he just stumbled, didn't he?" Caroline asked, shocked at the idea.

"I have to ask this, why if he fell yesterday, did you only report it, today?" Julie asked her.

"David was unsteady and kept asking for a drink, complained of a headache and I was the same. I fell and banged my head, I spent the night here. Do you have any water? I am so, so thirsty." she asked Julie.

"Officer, escort Mrs Green to the hospital, will you?" Julie asked a nearby female officer, who guided Caroline to a police car and took her to the hospital.

"Ma'am, you didn't answer her question, do you suspect foul play? If so, how? I don't believe she pushed him, so if not her; when they were the only people here, who?" Everet asked her.

"Suspect no, but I am not ruling anything out until after the autopsy. I find it very odd that a fit, late forties male stumbles just as he reaches the edge of a two hundred feet drop. The position of the body tells me that he did indeed fall and was not pushed, but why did he fall?" Julie asked.

"So the wife didn't do it then," Collins asked.

"What makes you say that?" Julie asked.

"Obviously he wasn't pushed and she was the only other person here, so she didn't push him," Collins said.

"Collins, there is more than one way to skin a cat; there was enough of him whole to be able to see a rash, add to that his unsteadiness and his constant requests for a drink, the headache he complained of. Everet you heard the whole interview, have I said anything she did not comment on?" Julie asked.

"Not that I can recall, Ma'am," Everet said.

"If we take symptoms like headache Arsenic and Bella Donna come to mind, both can cause headaches and were used widely in Victorian times as cosmetics. The famous Sherlock Holmes took morphine as a recreational drug. It's a derivative of heroin. Not all poisons kill immediately. Used in smaller doses, they kill over a period of time, like Lead, Arsenic, heavy metal poisons. Although apparently she didn't push him, she could have poisoned him. Deadly Nightshade in small doses causes headaches, a desire to drink a lot, a rash, diarrhoea, being unstable, unsteady. Does that ring any bells, with you?" Julie asked him.

"Yes Ma'am, those were what she said he was suffering from, but she also said that she was suffering from them as well," Everet said.

"So, I am not saying that she poisoned him, just that it is possible that he had been poisoned, by whom, we need to find out, perhaps? Always keep an open mind until the evidence gives us a pointer. I also find it convenient that two people who wanted the quarry re-opened are now dead, don't you?" Julie asked.

"I would say that it was very convenient and points the finger in Sir Andrew's direction, but how did he manage to poison David, if that is what it was?" Everet asked.

"Before we waste many man hours on a wild goose chase, shall we make sure it was a case of poisoning?" Julie asked, with a smile.

"How do we get the body to the mortuary? Using the crane as they suggested?" Everet asked.

"We could do, but that will take time and I want the body examined now so, we build a breeches buoy and winch them across. We can have one set up in say an hour or two and save a lot of time. What was it, twenty four hours to get a crane and cage here?" Julie asked.

Julie, with Everet, made contact with a builder's yard and organised scaffolding poles and a length of wire. Julie used the Land Rover's winch again to abseil down, along with two volunteers and the poles. They built a tripod as Julie directed, facing the one being built on the other side of the river and fixed pulleys and fired the wire across.

The doctor was the first across to confirm that he was dead, a formality, and then they loaded the body onto a stretcher and carried it to the breeches buoy and winched it across, followed by the doctor. Then they dismantled the breeches buoy, as Julie used the Land Rover winch before returning to the police station in the Land Rover.

She met Collins and went to the college to speak to June.

"Once again I end up taking you out of a lecture, I hope this is not affecting your studies too much? Tell me about the room and your instructions. How was it set up when you arrived?" Julie asked.

"The central table was clear and we laid it, he wanted it to be correct as per Victorian standards. When the place was set to be correct, fully correct that is, each setting was placed between each course with the place setting wiped down in between each course. He wanted them set less formally, so we covered the table with the table cloth and then set each place.

"You begin with the last course next to the plate and then move out with each course so on the side plate we put the dessert knife for buttering the break cobs furthest away. Then next to the under plate we put the dessert knife on the right, and the dessert fork. It was a gateau for dessert and then cheese and biscuits on the left, then the joint knife and fork next to them, fish knife and fork. Next came the teaspoon for the sorbet on the right and finally, on the outside, the soup spoon furthest out on the right. The nearest setting was to be quarter of an inch in from the edge of the table and every setting quarter of an inch further in.

"The wine glasses were to be the same, with white wine for the fish nearest the setting and then the red wine glass and then the dessert wine glass going out at an upward angle. Finally we put the rolled up napkin in a gold napkin ring and lay it diagonally across the under plate," she told them.

"You learned this at college?" Julie asked.

"Yes, it is part of the restaurant sessions for formal dinners. But I don't know who she was, the cleaner I think, she showed us, as if we didn't know," June told them.

"Oh, you never mentioned her, before?" Julie asked.

"Well I mean, we are in our final year; I mean it was embarrassing, to be told by a cleaner what we had to do, when we have studied it for three years now. We know all the various settings from the formal to the informal settings, to the greasy spoon settings, when it isn't set, shall we say. The classical very formal setting is rarely used these days, where you crumb down between every course, but we still learned it, the history of dining, you could call it," June told them.

"Interesting, but I am more interested in the woman. You didn't get her name, did you?" Julie asked.

"No, sorry, she just showed us where to put the wine glasses. We smiled and thanked her, cursing her under our breath, we already knew," June said.

"I see and where was the place setting she put the glasses? Did she remove them, afterwards for you to re-polish them?" Julie asked.

"Erm, no, she left them in place, to show us in case we forgot, I think. Let me think now, so much has happened since then. Yes, it was Sir, no, Lady Mac Adams' place setting. She, yes, she was to sit on his right hand side, so yes, it was her place setting, she showed us on," June said.

"Thank you, that is very helpful. When do you start your finals?" Julie asked.

"Next week, I am currently revising," June told them.

55

"Good luck with your finals," Julie said, smiling at her and turned to leave. "Sorry, just one more thing. Was she in the room when you entered and if she was, where was she stood?" Julie asked.

"Yes, she was in the room, by the table where the glasses were," June replied.

"Thank you," Julie said and left.

"Ma'am, we have the autopsy report. He did have high levels of Atropa belladonna in his system, whatever that is," Collins said next morning as she entered the office.

"It's a poison from a plant, a bush, commonly known as Deadly Nightshade. Or Belladonna. It is fatal, but in relatively high quantities, the symptoms include disorientation, dry mouth and tiredness, as a start. There are more. The berries are sweet-ish and, along with the leaves, are poisonous, but the most poisonous part of the plant are the roots, especially as the plant ends its season.

"It got its nickname from its use as a cosmetic, Bella, pretty, Donna, lady, or Pretty Lady, but it is very toxic. At the end of the season, when the bush is dying back, the roots are the most poisonous. In days gone by it was used as a beauty treatment, anaesthetic and poison. The course I took on poisons was very interesting and at the time I thought it not of much use. It just goes to show you never know when it may be useful.

"Our accident is now murder; he goes to the quarry to have a look, then moves to the edge to make some notes and survey the quarry, he starts feeling unsteady, stumbles on a rock and falls to his death; accident or murder?" Julie asked Collins.

"Erm, well, seeing as he had been poisoned, but how did the murderer know he would stumble?" Collins asked.

"They didn't; that part was perhaps just luck, but it would have killed him slowly, so, it is murder. Apart from the point that the fall was induced by the poison, disorientation is another symptom. Either way, it is murder," Julie said.

"Now what, Ma'am? I assume we need a list of suspects who wanted him dead; Sir Andrew to me tops it, his wife perhaps. What was their marriage like?" Collins asked.

"That is what I want you to find out. I am going to put my feet up," Julie said and plonked her feet on her desk, smiling at Collins.

"Yes Ma'am, what about Sir Andrew?" Collins asked.

"The Quarry belonged to his wife's parents, she wanted to reopen it and is now dead, Sir Andrew didn't want to reopen it, David was pro reopening it and he is also dead. The wives were, shall we say, neutral, but one Brian Khan, a heavy investor in the company and shareholder was also in favour of reopening it, so perhaps we should have a word with him before he ends up dead," Julie suggested.

"Yes Ma'am, but there are now two to one. Sir Andrew has got his way, there is no need to kill Brian Khan, is there?" Collins asked.

"No, if that is the motive, do we know for sure that the quarry was the motive for the murders?" Julie asked him.

"We don't, well, not for certain, Ma'am, it is an assumption," he replied.

"Think, Collins, how many cases have been won in court by offering assumptions as evidence?" Julie asked him, smiling.

"Point taken, Ma'am. You rest your feet and I'll get the answers we need," Collin said, smiling back at her.

"Collins, I got to be DI by using my brains, not my feet, although I used them as well. The Quarry is at the moment the obvious link, but be prepared to change direction at a moment's notice, as it may not be. Do not get so entrenched in one idea or avenue that you miss a new direction when it appears. Keep an open mind.

"Now you go and see Sir Andrew with a uniform and keep in mind that his wife may not have been the intended victim. Then again, she may have been. She may be the mistake that link the quarry, far better if the intended victim was Sir Andrew to perhaps get the quarry re-opened? I will visit the builder's yard, also with a uniform," Julie said.

Chapter 5 - Autopsy

"Morning, Sergeant. The autopsy is to be performed this morning at ten o'clock, so I don't have long before I need to leave. How did the interview go with Khan?" Julie asked.

"Very well, he confirmed that the quarry was owned by Lady Sophie's father, with her husband as the general manager, before taking over the builder's yard, one of Sir Adam's expansion plans. The company grew from that beginning to a big company. When her father died, the quarry was part of Lady Mac Adam's inheritance.

"It was at this point that there was a terrible accident, they were blasting a new face. A small boy was spotted after the warning siren; one of the men took a chance and raced to save him, but it was too late and he was killed along with the little boy.

"There was an enquiry and it was put down to accidental death. The little boy did not know about the warning siren, being too young; he had sneaked in, The worker was praised for his bravery. The fence was not secure, there was a breach, so the firm was made to put it right, but there was no further action. As required it was checked every month and it was assumed that at the last check it was missed.

"Money and power were blamed, because no further action was taken, but Sir Mac Adams did close the quarry down and concentrated on the building firm.

"His wife did not want it closed and it has been the main point in their arguments. She asked David to make a case for re-opening it and Khan had said that he would support the re-opening of the quarry, along with Nigel. He said he had the support of several members of the board, but Lady Mac Adams was the principle person involved and she was determined to get it re-opened," Collins told her.

"Interesting. That puts Sir Mac Adams right in the frame, doesn't it? He had the reason, erm, motive, means and opportunity, very convenient. But it begs the question as to how did he poison David? His wife, easily, by adding the poison when he was selecting the bottle and being served last, he was the least likely to drink the poisoned wine, before she collapsed and died. It also occurs to me that it is usual for the wine to be poured to everyone, before you take a drink, ensuring that she was the only one to be poisoned.

"We have him," Julie said, but not enthusiastically, "Or so it would seem. Don't you think it is very convenient? It still begs the question as to how he poisoned the Morris's? I also question the woman, erm, cleaner who told the staff about the wine settings. She was alone in the room so had opportunity and the fact that she set Lady Mac Adams place, ensuring the glass was placed where she wanted it, very convenient, don't you think?" Julie asked, raising her eyebrows in question.

"Do you think that the quarry is the motive?" Collins asked.

"Unless we can find a different motive or reason as to why three people would need to be killed? Yes, I do," Julie said, "And why Mrs Morris. She was not involved in the question over the quarry, so why poison her?" Julie asked.

"By accident," Collins posed.

"I am not happy about this. Who but Sir Andrew stood to gain from their deaths, or wanted the quarry not, to re-open?" Julie asked.

"Ma'am, you had better go, or you'll be late for the autopsy," Collins said.

Julie got Everet to drive her to the mortuary for the autopsy, it was something she would need to do if she was to progress through the ranks.

"Is this your first dead body, Everet?" Julie asked.

"Yes, Ma'am," she replied.

"There will be more, we always hope not, but there will be. Stand by the sink; it saves a mess on the floor. As I always tell officers for their first autopsy, on the table lie's a slab of meat, the spirit, or soul has left the body, it is no longer a human being. It may seem crude, but it helped me at first. Death is a part of life, we all try to avoid it, but inevitably, we all fail at some point," Julie told her.

"Yes Ma'am, I am not squeamish, Ma'am," she informed Julie.

"Blood and guts on the television or cinema is quite different to it being in the flesh, as it were," Julie said and smiled at her.

"The body of a well-nourished male of about mid-forties, weighing about one hundred and twenty pounds. The injuries are consistent with a fall from a height. There are several broken bones again consistent with a fall from height and abrasions where the body hit the face of the quarry on its way down.

"The facial injuries suggest that he didn't try to defend his impact with the ground, suggesting that impact with the face caused him to be unconscious, or dead, at the time of impact.

"A linear fracture to the Temporal and Parietal bones of eight centimetres suggests impact with a small ledge on the descent and probably the cause of death. I will confirm that when I open up the skull and see the full extent of the damage to the brain.

"Chief Inspector, unless you wish to stay for the full examination, it would appear that he stepped off the edge and was definitely not pushed. He was close to the face, close enough for his head to collide with a ledge and unless something else crops up; that collision was the cause of death. He was not dead prior to the collision from the blood around the wound, his heart was still pumping," the medical examiner said.

"Thank you, doctor, but I will wait until you remove the skull before leaving and I need the toxicology report as soon as possible, please. I suspect not suicide as you indicate, but poison, causing him to fall," Julie said, adding a smile for him.

"There are grass marks on his hands, and the knees to his trousers, so it is possible that he stumbled, landing on his hands, and knees, and then rolled, as it were, over the edge, again consistent with being close, to the face," he replied.

He picked up the scalpel, and pulled back the skin to the victim's head, and that was it for Everet, who now ran to the sink, relieving herself of her breakfast, Julie smiled. Even the toughest of police personnel failed at their first autopsy at some point. The best way was to get it over and done with. She returned as the doctor picked up the electric saw and removed the skull and brain for closer examination. Again she visited the sink.

Outside, Julie smiled at Everet. "Best to get it over and down with. This was perhaps a nasty one, removing the brain, but it served a purpose. His head colliding with the ledge was the cause of death from the fall, but was it assisted by poison, as I believe?" Julie posed as a question.

"Is it always like that? I have watched some of the bloodiest movies on the screen and not had that reaction, carving up victims in horror movies and enjoyed it," Everet said.

"Have you hunted and killed a deer, say, skinned it and gutted it?" Julie asked.

"No," she replied.

"I have and as I said that, is what lies on the table, as long as it is once removed. Then I can cope with it, just my way, crude maybe, but it helps and as time and the number you attend goes on, it ceases to be as bad," Julie advised her.

"I don't think I could do what the doctor does, it would turn my stomach," Everet said.

Julie smiled, "Neither could I, at the end of the day it is human and I could not get over that fact. Remember it is a legal requirement that I attend and as you progress through the ranks at some point, it will be a requirement you cannot avoid," Julie told her.

"Ma'am, did you, well, erm," Everet asked.

"After two tours in Afghanistan with special services, no. I have seen it, moved it and collected parts of it for the doctors to hopefully put it back together for burial and then I did. I am human and when it is the bits of a friend and colleague after a roadside bomb, then it really gets to you," Julie told her sadly.

"Now you are hardened to it," Everet said.

"I wouldn't say that, more that I just learned to accept it as a fact of life. That's enough about me, every job has a part we wish was not part of it, but in every case there is dirty work to do, a job we dislike," Julie told her. "I enjoy collecting all the pieces of the jigsaw puzzle, putting them together to make a clear picture, followed by the satisfaction of the arrest. In this case we have perhaps the corners, but even that is doubtful and some of the edges," Julie told her.

"Sir Mac Adams is very much in the frame for the murders, isn't he?" Everet asked.

Julie smiled at her novice's assumptions. "If it was just Lady Mac Adams then he would be, but what if it is connected to the quarry, now where does David fit in? How did he administer the poison, if that is what caused him to fall? You will learn we do not assume, we collect all the pieces and then discard ones that do not fit, leaving us with a probable picture, which we then verify with evidence.

"There are far too many ifs and probables as yet to begin to follow one avenue. Keep an open mind until something begins to make sense," Julie told her.

"Sorry, Ma'am, I assumed as you said that the quarry was the link, but I again suppose that they may not even, be linked. But it does seem strange that we have had two deaths so close together, without a link," Everet said.

"I do not believe in coincidences, so the assumption that they are linked I would agree with. Just posing a situation shall we say; what if say Sir Andrew was having an affair with David's wife? Now what do you say?" Julie asked her.

"I had not considered that and they both killed their partner so that they could be together and has nothing at all to do with the quarry? That is the red herring, throwing us off the scent, a possibility I suppose," Everet said, considering the idea.

"Neither had I until just now. To show you the problems with assumptions, it is a possibility, but very improbable, because David's wife was also affected. Then again, could that be just to throw us off the reason? It was a much milder dose, if it was poison, which is why I am not assuming until we have the evidence from the autopsy that he was poisoned. Then we have a coincidence, the quarry and adultery to consider. The waters are getting very muddy, aren't they?" Julie asked.

"Indeed, Ma'am, very muddy," Everet said.

Collins arrived back at the station just as they did and he stepped to one side to allow them to enter.

"Not many of them left, hey, Everet, a gentleman?" Julie asked glibly.

"No, Ma'am, then again you are the senior officer, Ma'am," Everet said smiling.

"Go on, spoil my nice thoughts. Well, Collins, what did you find out?" Julie asked.

"In the early days everyone knew everyone else, but as the company grew, the directors came in from various towns, and villages and they did not socialise. Sir Andrew decided it was time for the wives to meet for some odd reason not known by the dinner guests, as if he wanted to assess the wives before making his decision," Collins told her.

"So he had never met the wives of his directors, is that what you are telling me?" Julie asked.

"Apparently, which seems odd, to me. I mean, did they not meet at the annual general shareholders meeting?" Collins asked.

"A point, but that depends on whether or not they were shareholders. get me a list, will you?" Julie asked him.

A short while later, Collins handed her the list, "Hum, not one of the wives were shareholders and not all of the directors were, nothing unusual there, shareholders and directors are not necessarily one and the same person. Do we know which of the shareholders and directors are in favour of re-opening the quarry? Find out, will you?" Julie asked.

"Ma'am, we know why the quarry closed and now, seeing as two supporters of it re-opening are dead, then it looks like Sir Andrew has got his way, doesn't it?" he asked.

"Hum. Everet, go to the hospital and interview David's wife, erm, Caroline Morris, you know why, and be tactful?" Julie asked her, then turned to Collins.

"Ma'am she is a bit, well, too inexperienced, isn't she?" Collins asked.

"Not really, we posed another possibility, it will be good experience for her, how else do we learn unless we do the job? Now you, what if he was having an affair with Caroline and they decided to dispose of their partners? I agree very thin to non-existent, so good experience for Everet and an avenue we need to close, but I do not believe that was the case so her visit will not interfere with the investigation," Julie said.

"Ma'am, you did not tell her who to take with her, for the interview," Collins posed.

"No I didn't, shall we see of she has the gumption to take someone? I believe she will, inexperienced she might be, but not green. She has a good head on her shoulders. Now, Sergeant, who is this woman in the dining room, have you managed to find that out?" Julie asked.

"Yes, Ma'am, she is the daily that cleans for them, she was asked to do extra hours to make sure the house was perfect," Collins told her.

"Great, so who is she?" Julie asked.

"She is Mrs, Angela Jones, Ma'am, she lives in the village at fifty two, high street, Ma'am. She said that she was asked to work extra to make sure the house was clean and knowing that the staff for the night were students she decided to help them, to avoid them being shouted at by Sir Andrew. He was a tyrant when things were not precise and it was to avoid the students being shouted at. He had a vicious tongue," he told Julie.

"They asked her to ensure the place settings were accurate, did they?" Julie asked.

"I wasn't so blunt, Ma'am, rather accepting that she knew how nasty he could be and being youngsters she offered advice to help them, Ma'am, a kindly gesture," Collins said.

"I do not believe in coincidences and the only other link to both murders is the quarry, which puts Sir Andrew right in the frame. That to me is too convenient. He is not stupid and to kill his wife in front of six other people is brazen and too obvious. We are missing something; the affair angle again I discredited immediately, and serves as a good opportunity for Everet to gain experience. I am sure she will come back agreeing that it is not the case, which leaves us with the quarry and coincidence, of which the quarry is to me the motive, but why?" Julie asked, considering all the possibilities.

Chapter 6 - Confusion

"Ma'am, there's been another death, it has just come through. I was just about to ring you, but you're here," Collins said as Julie entered the station the next morning.

"Here I was hoping to get some more clues to the previous two and now we have a third one. Who?" Julie asked.

"One Brian Tindall, the company's managing director," Collins informed her.

"I don't suppose you know which side of the fence he sat on, do you?" Julie asked.

"No Ma'am, just that he committed suicide, apparently," Collins said.

"Then we had better go and look at him, hadn't we? Collins, don't make assumptions even if you try to hide it later. All we know at this point in time is that he has been shot. Now has the doctor confirmed that he's dead? Courts deal in facts only and it will serve you well to do the same," Julie told him.

"Ma'am, he's dead, shot in the head. I have yet to meet the person still alive after being shot in the head, Ma'am," he said, hurt at the apparent telling off for assuming.

"Then remind me later and I will introduce you to someone. He is a vegetable, but still very much alive." Julie said, getting out of the car at the scene.

She walked slowly down the path to the front door and Collins directed her to the back garden and the shed at the bottom of the garden.

"Morning, doctor," Julie said as she entered the shed.

"Morning, Chief Inspector. He has been shot in the temple, at close range. My initial findings are that he committed suicide at or about midnight, say between eleven o'clock, and one in the morning, again I will know more after the autopsy," he told her.

"Is there a suicide note?" Julie asked.

"We haven't found one," the Doctor told her.

"Was he ambidextrous?" Julie asked.

"How would I know that? Later. from the muscular structure. I may be able to tell, but not now," the Doctor said.

"Sorry, I didn't mean to ask it openly, but when we interviewed him after the dinner he signed his statement with his left hand, but the entry wound is right handed. Rather odd, don't you think?" Julie asked him.

"Now you mention that fact, then yes, but not uncommon for a person whose predominant hand is their left to use some tools with their right hand, ambidextrous, as you said. Most tools are designed to be used with the right hand, so they train themselves to use both hands, possible?" he mused.

"Possible, but not probable. Prior to the act he would not be thinking clearly so instinct takes over and he would automatically use his main hand, his left, an assumption I agree, but more probable than using his right hand," Julie suggested.

"Again from the height of the blood spatter, he was leaning against the workbench when shot and facing a blank wall. Not impossible, but odd, the last thing you see is planks of wood, why not the immaculate garden, a pleasant sight?" Julie posed.

"Like you said, not thinking clearly, perhaps?" the doctor asked.

"Thank you, doctor, how soon can I have the autopsy report?" Julie asked.

"Give me a day to recover, three autopsies in three days is not heard of in these parts, so I perform the autopsy at eleven o'clock the day after tomorrow, after surgery," he said.

"Sorry, doctor, I am still getting used to the differences between London and the country. I am used to having the report by the next night at the latest, usually the same night, but then again that is all the coroner does in London, we get so many deaths," Julie said.

"I do appreciate how urgent it is, but I do have patients to attend to as well. If you wish you can call in a medical examiner, I will not be offended," he offered.

"No, that won't be necessary; I have several lines of enquiry to follow, but as soon as possible, if you don't mind?" Julie asked.

Julie left the shed and went to the house to interview his wife.

"Mrs, Tindall, I am sorry about your loss. I believe you found your husband this morning and I need to ask you a few questions, if you don't mind?" Julie asked her.

"What questions? I mean, he shot himself, didn't he?" she asked, weeping.

"That is how it appears, even so I need to ask, was he depressed at all and if so over what?" Julie asked.

"No," she said emphatically, "I mean, he had days when things didn't go right, we all do, but it didn't depress him. He was a half full type of guy, there is always tomorrow, more pragmatic. He did worry that opening the quarry would be upsetting for the village, ten years seems a long time, but the child's mother still lives in the village, I think? He seemed to believe she did," Mrs. Morris said.

"So he was against re-opening the quarry, because he was more worried, shall we say, about the effect it would have on the village and that effect on the company than the economics, of re-opening the quarry?" Julie asked.

"Yes, I suppose so, in a business sense, it was viable, but at what cost for the village? None of the men were keen to go and work in the quarry, it had a bad feeling. Four deaths in four years leaves a nasty taste in your mouth, not all the directors were here during that period and some have short memories," she told them.

"I am, as you know, new around here and I didn't know there had been two previous deaths, just the man and the child. When were the other deaths, and who died; do you know?" Julie asked.

"No, it was before we moved here, but I have spoken to the villagers who say the quarry is cursed. Lady Mac Adams father, Bill Lightfoot, was as tight as a duck's, excuse me, but he was. When the health

72

and safety laws came in for harnesses and the like, he said he would have to reduce the staff or wages to pay for the equipment. Shortly after that, a man fell from the top on a sling type thing they used.

"I don't know his name, or the next man to fall the same year. We can't prove it, but so they say, money changed hands. A year passed and then a loose face collapsed. It was reported that he had been told not to go there and ignored the advice, but Alan Jackson was not stupid. He would not go there unless told to," Caroline said.

"Sorry, but you said four, that makes five and not in the last four years, I understood it has been closed longer than that?" Julie asked.

"Sorry, four in the four years prior to the two deaths you know about, the last one, again a fall from high up was in nineteen ninety one, one year before the health and safety regulations came into force. Then the two you know about, twelve months prior to that accident Bill had died.

"Sir Andrew does not have money, you do know that, don't you? It's his wife's money, or was, he used the quarry profits to build the building firm. I'm not taking anything away from him, he made that firm successful, but without the funds from the quarry it would never have begun. He is the major shareholder in the building firm. Lady Sophie does not have a share in it, but she owns sixty percent of the quarry. Sir Andrew, along with the other shareholders, own five percent each and I do not see Sir Andrew taking orders from a woman, he is sexist, very sexist," she told Julie.

"Please excuse me, but I need clarity on this. Sir Andrew started the building firm, when?" Julie asked.

"In nineteen eighty nine, after the second death at the quarry. He wanted to move away from the quarry. He invested the year's profits and used the quarry as security for the loan for the building firm," she told Julie.

"I must presume with the owner's consent?" Julie asked.

"That remains to be seen, it was as Bill died, so we do not know. He had been married for two years by then to Sophie, so knowing him as sexist I would say he never asked her, being beneath him, to ask," she told them.

"Thank you Mrs. Tindall, that was very helpful. History sheds light on the present and you told me a lot, thank you. Where are you staying if I might ask; in case I need to ask you some more questions?" Julie asked, getting up to leave.

"Martha, a friend from Cambridge, is coming over to stay with me for a few nights and then I may go to her for a bit," Caroline told them.

"That's my personal number, please; if you think of anything, contact me and if you decide to go to Cambridge," Julie said, handing her a card.

"Sergeant, what are your first impressions?" Julie asked him back in the car.

"Confusion, if it is to do with the quarry then why commit suicide? He was on the winning side, that has me confused," he said.

"Very simple really, he didn't. One: he was left handed, so why use his right hand? Two: and this is something you will not be aware of, you do not make a hole that size with a nine millimetre bullet at very close range. There was a lack of tearing from such a close range shot, it was fired close by, but not touching, perhaps as close as I am to you, but not touching. Come on back to my hotel and I will show you, not properly," Julie said.

"OK, here, see? Always check the clip is out, the barrel is clear, now to commit suicide usually, but not always, the barrel is pressed against the skull, like so. Now can you see how awkward it is to pull the gun away for the shot? You also need to realise that the person is shaking, it is not natural to kill yourself; it goes against our natural instincts of self-preservation. Here, feel the weight of the gun and now imagine that you are about to die. See, your hand is shaking, you could very easily miss. No, he definitely did not commit suicide, but the gun was very close by, so how did the killer get so close?" Julie asked.

"His wife; you didn't ask where she was last night," Collins said.

"You're right, also I didn't ask if he owned a gun. He does, but it is not that gun," Julie said.

"Are you telepathic? How did you work that out?" Collins asked.

"The gun safe under his bench was locked," Julie said.

"Was that why you moved the shavings under his bench?" he asked.

"The floor had been swept, but not that little bit, missed perhaps, or to hide something. I didn't check, but I'm willing to bet it's embedded in a block of concrete. A shed is not considered a secure place to hold a gun, unless it can't be removed. Check with licences and local gun clubs, he'll have a licence for a pistol or revolver, apart from the trophies on the shelf which depict a marksman having won them," Julie informed him.

"I wondered what they were for, but didn't like to ask, not believing them important enough for now," Collins said.

"The name rings a bell with me, like an Olympic contender in the British squad. Out of interest, check the medal winners in the British pistol squad, it shouldn't be too difficult. He was forty five and say he started at fifteen, thirty years divided by four so, the last seven Olympics and just the pistol class," Julie said.

"Ma'am, you said that was not the gun used, how did you know if it wasn't?" Collins asked.

"It may surprise you to know that people who commit suicide don't want to hurt themselves, so usually they are sat down, so they do not fall and hurt themselves, it's psychological, they probably aren't thinking about it, but that appears to be the case. I have yet to encounter a suicide where the victim was standing when using a gun.

"The entry wound was to the right temple, when he was left handed and the gun drops, so it is close by the victim relatively, that gun had been tossed in. It was too far away, a rather clumsy attempt at making us believe it was suicide and at one hundred and forty five decibels, why did no-one hear it?" Julie asked.

"A silencer, Ma'am, simple," Collins said, being clever.

"You mean a suppressor. Are cars silent? No. why? Because they use a muffler or suppressor in the exhaust, baffles, which reduces the noise, but does not silence it. That gun fitted with a suppressor would still bang, some one hundred and fifteen decibels, a reduction in noise of just thirty decibels. Yet even his wife did not hear the bang," Julie said and slammed the brakes on. "I'm forgetting myself. Where was she? We never asked." Julie asked.

"Visiting her friends at the local pub, Ma'am. It was a girls' night out. She found him this morning when she realised he was not in bed with her and went to look for him. He often worked late in his shed. She arrived back at eleven o clock and went to bed, assuming he was still working. He also repaired guns for the local gun club and serviced them," Collins told her.

"I assume he would test fire a repaired gun, or one he had serviced, hence the water tank and the neighbours not being alerted by the bang. Then again, did he often test fire a gun at almost midnight? I very much doubt it.

"The gun was on the bench and, as he fell, he knocked it onto the floor, which was why it was not close by him. The gun has nothing to do with his death, but will be full of his fingerprints pointing us in the direction again, of suicide. After test firing it, he would automatically clean it, gunshot residue on his hands, all leading us to believe it was suicide. Causing a delay in our investigation before the autopsy when the examiner would alert us to the

77

fact that the wound was caused by a forty five and not the nine millimetre lying on the floor," Julie said as she thought through the scene.

"Ma'am, can I add another anomaly? He wasn't in favour of re-opening the quarry, he was opposed to it," Collins asked uneasily.

"Collins, why waste time asking when you ask anyway? Just ask or inform me, I don't bite, well, not much," Julie said and laughed.

"There are more anomalies: poison is a woman's weapon, a gun is more of a male weapon, so apart from working as a director at the building firm; there is no connection to the previous two murders and this one, excellent. I like a simple case, easy to solve, one where all the jigsaw pieces fall into place," Julie said, being glib.

"So you think they are still connected and this is not a new case?" Collins asked.

"Keep an open mind. I have yet to decide if the other two are connected. They appear to be, but is the re-opening of quarry the connection? It's an obvious link, but is it the actual link, especially now, when a member of the opposition, has been murdered?

"We have been busy and not so much neglected the basics but have yet to find time. So let's do the background checks on the victims first thing tomorrow, make it all the directors, to see if there is any other connection between the victims and other directors," Julie said and moved off.

Chapter 7 - Reports

Julie left the office with Everet again to watch the autopsy, leaving Collins to organise and do the background checks with a few other constables.

It was just a country station and had limited personnel. Julie missed the large number of officers she had to call upon when in London.

When investigating the 'Illusionist,' she had a team of fifty officers at her disposal, here that was the contingent based at the station to cover three shifts, seven days a week.

"Everet, I have not had chance to talk to you about the interview with, Mrs. Morris. How did it go?" Julie asked as they drove to the mortuary.

"I thought very well, she made lunch, sandwiches and a flask of coffee. They walked for some time enjoying the views and then made for the quarry. It was a day out, as well as work. She made corned beef sandwiches, her husband like HP sauce with his corned beef and she had run out, so she bought a new bottle from the local shop. She had also made salmon and mayonnaise sandwiches, mainly for her. They stopped to eat the sandwiches on the outskirts of the quarry, admiring the view. They estimate that there is at least five years' worth of stone still to be quarried. It was about a mile from where they ate lunch to the actual face.

"The doctors told her she is lucky to be alive, from the poison, the fall and being out overnight all combined, she is very lucky.

"She always made far too much to eat when out and as the survey progressed, her husband wanted longer, so they had more of the sandwiches there as well and it was going dark before he decided it was time to go home. One last look over the edge and that was when he stumbled and fell. She ran to him, but she also stumbled and fell, banging her head on a stone, knocking her out. David was working and he was hot, so gave his coat to her, which she put around her shoulders. That prevented hypothermia, his action helped save her life.

"I went to her house, got the bottle of HP and handed it to the forensic people who had the remnants of the sandwiches and flask.

"The poison was in the HP sauce," Everet told her.

"Well done, Everet, good work; now, do we know how the poison got into the sauce?" Julie asked.

"Not yet, Ma'am, I've been in touch with the manufacturer. They're tracing the batch number and its movements for us," Everet told her. "But to me it still looks like the wife did it. I didn't know how many checks these products go through and the bottle is sealed so how could anyone poison it prior to her buying the bottle?" Everet said.

"Excellent, case closed, all you need now is evidence or had you forgotten that part? Judges are not too happy about guilty verdicts just because you can't be arsed to get proof, or that manufacturers do loads of tests and have security procedures in place. They tend to like proof, evidence. Your work is good, your conclusions are terribly flawed, do not jump to conclusions. Eliminate all possibilities and then what is left is the fact and then you have to prove it before you show it to me. The facts were what I asked for, not conclusions, it is far too early," Julie told her.

"Yes, Ma'am, sorry," she said sullenly.

"Don't sulk, passing out doesn't make you a good copper, experience does and you have just learned a valuable lesson, absorb it and learn from it, but never sulk. What's the next step to prove your theory?" Julie asked her.

"To bring her in for questioning," Everet suggested.

"And how do you propose to question her, without a shred of evidence?" Julie asked.

"Oh, wait until we have the forensic results," Everet said.

"Much better, get the evidence first, prove or disprove her probable actions, what if there is a tiny hole in the neck of the bottle?" Julie asked.

"Erm, well, could the poison have been injected into the sauce?" Everet asked.

"Good, yes it could have been, now you have a weeping woman sat facing you who has just lost her husband and you have accused her of killing him when, she may not have, because of the hole in the neck of the bottle. How does that make you feel, happy or like crawling into the hole you have just created?" Julie asked.

"I see, Ma'am, as you said a lesson learned; have something to at least indicate she was the person of interest first. How did the killer know she would buy that particular bottle, couldn't she have injected the bottle to throw us off?" Everet asked.

"We are here so you think about that while we watch him carve up this victim. It shouldn't affect you the same, but stay close to the sink, just in case," Julie advised her.

"Morning, Chief Inspector, we started without you. I hope you don't mind?" the coroner said.

"Not at all; I know he is male, well-nourished and forty five, I also know he was shot with a forty five but need the bullet, to prove it," Julie said.

"Why attend if you know all the answers?" he asked.

"Duty and a requirement to have viable proof, like the bullet," Julie answered.

"So the fact that he had stage three cancer doesn't interest you?" he asked.

"Did it kill him, if not, then no," Julie said bluntly.

"You amaze me; I mean surely it's reason for the apparent suicide, isn't it?" he asked.

"I'm glad you said apparent. I've never seen a nine millimetre bullet make a hole the size of a forty five bullet, close quarters as it was, but there was no muzzle mark from being pressed against the skull, minor indications that he did not commit suicide. As a ballistics expert I do know the effects and causes. So If I can have the bullet, please?" Julie asked him.

He nodded to an aide and she handed the bag containing the bullet to Julie.

"Everet, see a forty five bullet, with rifling, feel the weight of it and now hand it back so that it can be sent to ballistics," Julie told her and made to leave.

Everet drove them back to the police station.

"Everet, I want you to write up your reports, list the evidence, state what was said, but do not draw any conclusions, although you can suggest actions and I want it by lunch time," Julie told her, "Collins, how did it go?" Julie asked him on entering her office.

"Ma'am, very interesting, very interesting indeed. It appears that there is another connection between the three men. We know that Sir Andrew was the general manger at the quarry at the time of all of the accidents, with his wife as his secretary and office manager. That also was how they met, but did you know that Brian Tindal was the production manager and that David Morris was the sales manager. All three were working at the quarry at the time of the accidents and gained promotions as the new company grew, Brian becoming the managing director and David the developments director," Collins told her.

"I was not aware, not being in the area at the time, but thank you, Collins. Are you implying that it was a promotion to help them keep quiet, because the accidents were not actually accidents?" Julie asked.

"No, Ma'am, I think they were accidents, but perhaps the safety issues were not what they should have been, more of a cover up about safety. Just a suggestion, I have no facts as yet, but say that the hole in the fence was known about and nothing done about it and they knew children were entering

83

the quarry through the hole. Now the accident is negligence and the quarry could face several compensation claims, so they hushed it up." Collins offered.

"I like your thinking and it is a possibility, so the motive could be the re-opening of the quarry, or revenge for covering up prior accidents, but why wait, ten years?" Julie asked.

"I don't think they did as such Ma'am; I think the re-opening of the quarry is still the case, but to get at the people responsible, and that the first victim was to be, Sir Andrew," Collins suggested.

"Hum, possible, but he would be sat at the head of the table, so how come the poisoned glass was put by his wife', place setting?" Julie asked.

"I have no idea, except that the person wanted him to feel the loss they felt, perhaps?" Collins posed.

"A good suggestion, so why kill the others if they wanted them to feel the loss? Why not their wives or children?" Julie asked.

"They almost got Mrs, Morris and Mrs, Tindal was out, which they may not have known," Collins suggested. "One more thing, Ma'am, the shed is double lined and sound proofed, erm, a shed within a shed, Ma'am," he added.

"That explains the lack of noise. I did think the door rather thick for a shed," Julie said, "So the person entered the shed and closed the door, which also means that he knew the person, rather suggests that he did," Julie now suggested.

"Then again, Ma'am, if they wanted the victim to suffer, being not the person killed as it were, why poison Mr. Morris's sandwiches, surely they got that wrong as well?" Collins said confused.

"Again a good point, but they have removed the principle people, the main players in the game and his wife, making Sir Andrew vulnerable?" Julie posed as a question.

"He is now, or should be, in fear of his life, a good point, Ma'am. Do you think we should put him under police protection, being the next victim?" Collins asked.

"I doubt it, but put an officer at the front door to preserve the crime scene. Let's not draw attention to our theory, because it is just that. We know that Brian Tindal and David Morris were the intended victims, which follows that Sir Andrew was the other intended victim, but his wife was the actual victim. So either we have two crimes, as we have always said, or someone made a mistake and missed the intended victim," Julie said, walking up and down her office, thinking.

"Ma'am, the forensic report on the HP sauce bottle, there was a tiny hole in the neck of the bottle," Everet said, handing her the report.

"This is interesting, they took three samples, one from the neck, half way down and from the bottom. The highest concentration was in the neck, and they suspect that it was not evenly dispersed, but during travel it got mixed in, ensuring that the first dollop out, had the highest dose, enough to kill him," Julie read out.

"Does that let the wife off?" Collins asked.

"I don't believe she did it, but to keep an open mind, she could have injected it into the bottle to

85

throw us off the scent. Allowing for the fact that she had ingested some of the poison, her reactions were what I would call normal for that situation. Everet, do we know how she managed to be poisoned?" Julie asked her.

"Not definitively, but she said that they were enjoying the view sat on the hill side overlooking the valley and she spotted a falcon hovering. She pointed it out to David and dipped into the wrong box. She only realised after she had taken a bite. His were corned beef and HP sauce and hers were salmon mayonnaise with salad on both.

She was too polite to spit it out, but then handed the rest to her husband. 'How you can eat that, I'll never know,' she told him.

'Corned beef butties, the staple diet when I was growing up. We didn't have any money then and corned beef was cheap, so we had it stewed, corned beef hash, on butties, with salad and fried, it was very versatile,' he apparently told her," Everet said.

"It is and you can eat it out of the tin, as we did in Afghanistan, when out and about. I always carried a can in case of emergencies, along with my. 'C,' rations. I also agree with him, HP sauce lifts it.

So his wife ate just one mouthful hence the minimal effect, which could again be just to put us off, knowing that one mouthful would not kill her, but he ate what, two rounds of sandwiches?" Julie asked.

"I didn't ask," Everet said.

"I would like to know and how long between ingestion and the effects taking hold. Usually ingested poison reacts quickly, which is why I need to know how close to the quarry face they were at that point." Julie said, "Most of the studies I've looked at are about its use as a drug, a means of a cure, which obviously uses limited doses and the acceptance of the side effects. Here we have a large dose intending to kill, so how much and how long?" Julie asked.

"His wife didn't need to kill him with it, just enough to bring on the delirium and instability and then push him over the edge," Collins suggested.

"Collins, if that is the case, then she was lucky, he was not pushed, he fell," Julie said, "Everet, did you ask how their marriage was? We know the Mac Adams marriage was less than happy, she was about to go for a divorce," Julie asked.

"Yes, they were very happy. I also asked a neighbour and she told me that was the case. They had disagreements as all people do, but she cannot recall an actual, argument," Everet said.

"Follow up on the Tindall's marriage, as well, will you?" Julie asked her and Everet left the office.

"Ma'am, I also find it odd that the first two were poisoned and the last one shot. Has the perpetrator run out of poison, or am I reading too much into this point?" Collins asked.

"Again a good point, Collins, and poison is a female means of committing murder, but shooting is male, as I said. This means that there are two murderers, or our killer is versatile. The only shooting was in a sound proofed shed, which speaks volumes to me. Now consider this, as an ex Special Forces person; I have killed with a gun, so although shooting someone is predominantly male, do not close your mind to it being female, because if I were the killer; I would use a gun," Julie told him.

"Does that mean that I need to question you, Ma'am?" Collins asked with a glint in his eye.

"Apart from the fact that I was otherwise engaged, when the first murder took place, as I said I am adept at both knife and gun, but not poisons. To be honest I wouldn't know where to begin with poisons," Julie told him, smiling back. "Then again the course did teach me quite a lot, like the first poison used was quick acting, less than a minute from ingestion to death, the later one was slower, but just as effective. This could be because he didn't eat all the sandwiches at the same time, but what has me confused is why he continued when he must have felt, ill?" Julie asked, looking confused at Collins.

"Could it be because there was a time limit on the investigation and he needed to complete his investigations by that day to prepare for his presentation?" Collins asked.

"It's possible. Where are we with the woman at the big house, Sir Andrew's cleaner?" Julie asked.

"I've been back and he knew nothing about her. His wife employed all the extra staff and obviously we can't ask her. All we know is she comes from the village. He remembers seeing her arriving and she was walking, so she didn't need a car and he assumed she was local. She was not a regular cleaner there, the daily help was off ill and Lady Sophie engaged two cleaners to be sure the place was cleaned properly.

"I also spoke to the June, the waitress, and she gave me a description, are you ready for this? Female, about her height in low heeled shoes, black, rotund, her hair had a perm, you know curly, but she couldn't remember the colour. From my time here seeing the females of this area, it fits about eighty per cent of the female population, of her age group, say, fifty to sixty years old," Collins told her.

"Not really, as long as I got it right she is black, there aren't that many black women here, are there?" Julie asked him.

"Sorry, Ma'am, her shoes were black, not her skin colour," Collins said, accepting his mistake.

"So let me get this right, she's Caucasian, about five feet six, to five feet eight inches tall and between one and six stone over weight. Her hair is done as a perm, at a guess I would suggest salt and pepper for her hair colour, but I could be wrong and between fifty and sixty years of age. Not that hard a task to find her, surely? I very much doubt that eighty percent of the population is over fifty, let alone the female population. Use Everet. She's good with computers, ask her to find the name and address of every female over fifty, obviously she needs to be local if she walked to the house," Julie said, thinking.

Chapter 8 - Visitors

Several weeks passed by as they interviewed every female over the age of fifty, with nothing coming from it. They all had a rock solid alibi.

"Now it is a needle in the proverbial haystack, Collins. There were two cleaners at the house, one was the one we need to interview the other was mid-thirties, and has been interviewed. She also was not around the dining room, she concentrated on the reception rooms, whilst our female cleaned the corridors, toilets and dining room and they both cleaned the upstairs, which is not part of our crime scene.

"Mrs. Morris did make a relevant comment, but she said it as a throwaway that she was handed the bottle of HP by a woman she didn't know and had not seen previously. This female also fits the general description we have of the one we wish to interview. Who is she?" Julie asked.

"Ma'am, how did this female, assuming she is the woman we are wishing to speak to, know Mrs. Morris would be buying HP sauce when she did? I also need to ask, how did she know he liked HP sauce and that they would be having corned beef sandwiches with HP sauce on that particular day? Don't you think you're grasping at straws that don't exist, Ma'am? Collins asked.

"Yes, perhaps I am, but think about it; the only people to touch those sandwiches in any way was the victim, his wife and that woman, although she did say, according to your report, that Mr Croft was bending down as if going to buy the bottle," Julie said.

"And the shopkeeper who stocked the shelves to keep it local and not going to extremes with regard to who had handled the bottle," Collins put in.

"Point taken but the shopkeeper was not at the house and Croft, although invited, did not attend. His wife was ill, but our mysterious woman was, probably?" Julie asked.

"OK, I have to agree, but we are assuming now she is not local. When Mr. Morris is working on the guns he locks the door, yet he must have opened the door for the killer to shoot him. So he must have known the killer to open the door when he had a gun out, which we know because of the nine millimetre on the floor." Collins said.

"That has me confused as well, he was meticulous about safety and would not unlock the door unless he knew the person, so we start there," Julie said.

"Ma'am, do you want us to re-interview everyone, he knew?" Collins asked.

"No, I want the transcripts of the interviews and then we'll select any weak links. Damn, again straws, they all had rock solid alibis. Are we sure, absolutely sure, they are rock solid?" Julie asked.

"His wife was at the local with the women from both sides of their house and three more friends. Most of the males he knew were at the Rotary club dinner. His wife and her friends saw several other friends at the pub. I am sorry, Ma'am, it would appear that all his friends were out that night with other friends, so unless it is a conspiracy between several of his friends, then yes; their alibis are rock solid," Collins told her.

"Ma'am, there is a man in reception wishing to see you, he just asked me to tell you some sort of surprise, perhaps, he seems to know you," Everet said, entering their office.

"I don't have time for this," Julie said, frustrated, and left the office.

"Dan, I'm rather busy, it is lovely to see you, but, what the hell, come here, you big hulk," Julie said, surprised and delighted.

"The wife and I are on holiday, touring around, and I couldn't come here and not see you, miserable as ever," Dan said, laughing.

"The wife, what do you mean the wife? Where is Alex?" Julie asked.

"In the car it is lunchtime so, I thought we could buy you lunch at the local pub. What is the food like?" Dan asked.

They hugged and then Julie turned to Collins who had followed her out.

"Detective Sergeant Collins, this before you is Inspector Dan Williams, my ex Sergeant and I'm taking the rest of the day off. If anyone wishes to contact me, I will be incommunicado," Julie said.

"Alex, lovely to see you, but did you have to bring that with you?" Julie asked, laughing.

"Yes, I needed a driver, he is quite good," Alex said, laughing.

"Well, Inspector, what news do you have for me?" Julie asked, getting into the car.

"Manchester is a challenge, but I am enjoying it there, we bought a house in Worsley, a ten minute run to the office," Dan told her.

"Dan, I used to live in the area, I know damn well that unless you use blues and twos, it's more than ten minutes to the main station in Manchester. Still full of it, isn't he, Alex?" Julie asked.

"Too right he is, but he's working hard, not as hard as you made him work, but hard enough," Alex said.

"Now you know why I never married, I suppose I am married - to the job," Julie said.

"Did you know that Jones moved to Manchester as well, he's now Detective Sergeant Jones and I fear for my job, he's that good," Dan said, jokingly.

"He had an excellent teacher, so what can you expect?" Julie asked, laughing.

"Yes, I taught him everything he knows," Dan said laughing with her.

"You, ha, I was the one; he did look sweet when we had him dress as the killer. Has he got over it, yet?" Julie asked.

"Do you honestly think I would allow him to? Yes, he's forgiven you for that. He's married now last weekend, she is a lovely girl, a PC," Dan told her.

"Quaint. Is the beer any good?" Dan asked.

"Camra think so, they gave it five stars, direct from the barrel and Alex, the food is good, as well," Julie told them.

"Are all Inspectors alcoholics?" Alex asked her.

"Only the male ones, they can't cope with the pressure," Julie replied, laughing.

"Ladies, stop the insults, or I'll become less of a chauvinist and make you pay," Dan said, laughing.

"He's been going on and on about getting a decent pint ever since we left," Alex told Julie.

"Beer is a live drink and should be stored at fifteen degrees centigrade and served at that, not this modern idea of freezing the stuff. They have to, it has no taste, or body, it's just alcohol, water and chemicals. Brewing beer is an art and science joined in perfection," Dan said.

"Two white wines, that's still your drink isn't it, Julie?" Alex asked, Julie said it was, "And half a pint," Alex told Dan, who went and got the drinks, returning with half a pint for himself.

"I think Alex was just joking, Dan," Julie said as he put the drinks on the table.

"I know that, but a taste first and then a full pint," he said, and took a drink, "Wow, do they have rooms here?" he asked.

"Yes, and they're decent, not up to the Ritz standard, but better than the average hotel today. This is where I'm staying until I find a house," Julie said.

"Book us a room. Another three pints of this nectar and I may be over the limit," Dan enthused.

"May be? Well over is the term, Dan. Do you want to spend the night here?" Alex asked.

"It will give us time to catch up with Julie and the beer is the deciding factor, six hand pulls to taste. I am in heaven and obviously not forgetting the two loveliest females on the planet, for company," Dan said.

"Flattery will get you no-where, apart from a room," Alex said, laughing at him.

Alex left them to book a room. Dan leaned in close to Julie.

"What is this I hear about you and Hastings? I believe he took two days off before moving to Humberside and was last seen at Little Hampton," Dan said.

"That's correct and he spent the night here with me. I'm not the marrying type, but that does not mean that I am a virgin, then again, he could change that. Don't book any wedding venue, just yet. How are the girls?" Julie asked.

"Both well, Samantha is in France again; I think she may move there at some point, she likes it. Janice is doing her GCSE's this year and wants to be a copper, like her dad," Dan told her.

"Booked in, what room are you in, Julie?" Alex asked.

"Seven, next to the exit for a quick get away," Julie said, laughing.

"Next door to us then, so Dan can keep you awake with his snoring as well as me," Alex said.

"From what I can remember; he can keep the whole hotel awake. I spent just two nights with you and didn't sleep a wink," Julie said laughing.

"Nothing you can say will upset me. I am in heaven with this pint," Dan said.

"Dan said you had a problematic murder enquiry, you can find them," Alex said.

"Yes, three dead and not one suspect as yet," Julie said.

"That was why I picked this corner, Julie, can I help at all? Would you like a sounding board say, we can go to our room if you like?" Dan asked.

"Is Manchester too boring for you?" Julie asked.

"No, not at all, it is quite a challenge, as I said, but we are old friends and know how each other works, sorry, it was just an offer," Dan said, a little upset at her comment.

"Sorry, Dan, I didn't mean it like that, lunch - great, and then we can have a chat. This is unlike 'the Illusionist,' where I knew who I was looking for, albeit an illusionist, but I had a focus. Here I do not have even that. Lady Mac Adams was poisoned, the suspect, her husband, linked to a disused quarry, next David Morris, the suspect, his wife and finally Brian Tindal, again, the suspect, his wife, but we have ruled out all three suspects. The only link is the quarry, but every time we find a link something happens to challenge that link. Two deaths were against re-opening the quarry and then the next one was for opening the quarry, which puts doubt on our reasoning," Julie told him.

"You said re-opening the quarry, why did it close? Would that be the reason?" Dan asked.

"It closed some six years ago, so I discounted that, why wait so long?" Julie asked.

"Because re-opening it brought it back to, the forefront?" Dan asked.

"Now I know why we cracked the last case, it is the quarry, but not the re-opening of it; that's just the catalyst. Someone in the village has a score to settle and all this has brought it back. Dan you are a marvel, then again without my lead, where would you be?" Julie said laughing.

"Probably just a PC, Ma'am," he said, laughing with her.

"Julie, in the last case you were seconded to Manchester. What if you seconded Dan here, would that help? I wouldn't mind spending a few days here while you solved the case, it is a lovely village," Alex said.

"Ha, I have three days to find more suitable accommodation. What they mean is they are no longer willing to pay my, hotel bill. It follows that they will not be willing to pay for Dan as well," Julie said.

"What's the problem?" Dan asked.

"The old story, the houses are too expensive for the locals so when a property comes on the market it is snapped up, at excessive prices, for holiday homes. The local council has now put a stop to holiday homes, but the prices have not dropped," Julie told them.

Her phone rang and she answered it.

"Everet, I said I was incommunicado, is it important?" Julie asked.

"That depends, Ma'am, on how important it is to find a house for you," Everet said.

"Then it is vitally important, please continue," Julie said.

"An old friend has just told me that her uncle has died. He lived in what was a tied cottage to the estate, when it was one of the ones owned by the lord of the manor. It is the one that looks lonely, you said; if you remember, to the north of the village with the thatched roof. There is about a third of an acre with it and it has yet to be put on the market. My family owns it. I 've spoken to my dad and he is willing to rent it to you at the same rent with a view to you buying it," Everet told Julie.

"I did like it, if it is the same one, how many bedrooms?" Julie asked.

"There are only two, but you live alone, don't you, I mean no children?" Everet asked.

"Correct, Everet, so as you imply I will only need one bedroom. When can I see it?" Julie asked.

"As soon as you want to, I have the key, so any time," Everet said.

Julie looked at Dan and Alex, wondering, "We've almost finished lunch, so now would be a good time and if you like it, Dan and I can help you move in," Alex said, smiling at her.

"Where are you?" Julie asked Everet.

"At the station, but I am due my lunch break in ten minutes," Everet said.

"Then we will pick you up from the station in ten minutes," Julie said, Everet agreed and Julie hung up.

Chapter 9 - New Home

Dan drove them to the station where they picked up Everet. She got in the car and Julie introduced everyone.

It was only a five minute run to the house. It was situated just outside the town and, as Julie had described it, it looked lonely stuck there like an intrusion into a field of hay. Facing it was a field of corn and there was a wooded area at the edge of the field of hay between the town and the cottage.

To look at, it seemed run down, neglected, but as Everet said, the rent was very low, so her family had completed their obligation, repairing faults, but they had neglected the upkeep. The last tenant had stopped paying the rent a few months before he had died, he was old and they had felt sorry for him, so they had not chased him for the rent.

"Dad has told me that he wants to sell it, it has been a source of problems ever since we bought it as an investment and if you can hand over say ten thousand pounds as a deposit, he is willing to lend you the balance, all legal of course, an agreement drawn up by a solicitor," Everet told her.

Everet opened the front door and Julie entered into a corridor with the stairs facing her. She opened the door on her left into the sitting room; off that room was a door to a room at the back, the kitchen and dining area. She went through a door back to the front and into a bedroom and then back into the corridor and upstairs. Up here there was the bathroom and a second bedroom, both within the eaves of the cottage, with windows built into the eaves, back and front.

"It is beautiful, I like it very much, but that is the feel, it does need a lot of work. Out of interest, does the farmer mow the grass on the roof?" Julie asked, being glib.

"Ma'am, things like that are the reason my dad wants to sell it, the rent over the last twenty years does not cover the cost of a new roof, which it needs. The price of a property like this in the town would be in excess of one hundred and fifty thousand pounds and I am sure the buyer would argue the fault, and get it reduced to about one hundred and twenty thousand pounds, maybe less. If we now take into account estate agent's fees and the time it would take to find a buyer when we have to pay the rates on it, being empty... He is a builder and has estimated the repairs at forty thousand pounds so he will let you have it for one hundred thousand, leaving a bit in it for you," Everet told her.

"I like it and I am very interested, but I need a day, say, to work out if I can afford it," Julie told her.

"My dad said that you would say that and he has agreed to not put it on the market until next Monday, to give you time to consider his offer.

"Ma'am, he is no fool, he knows the problems he will have selling it and he will do well at that price, it will have been a good investment, so he is happy," Everet told her.

"You said that I could rent it, what would the rent be?" Julie asked considering her options.

"He rented it for four hundred a month, but that does not include repairs and as I said he will let you have it for the same," Everet said.

"Hum, I will give him my answer tomorrow, I couldn't see any wet patches on the floor so I am presuming the roof does not leak," Julie said.

"No, Ma'am, it does not, but it will not be long before it does. It needs renewing," Everet said.

They took Everet back to the station and then went back to the pub, so that Dan could start sampling all the draught beers on sale.

"Alex, what is the market like in the area where my house is?" Julie asked.

"Well, Julie, it is excellent at the moment, in fact I have a list of people wishing to buy in that area and with your record of paying on time. I am sure the mortgage company will transfer the mortgage to the cottage. You borrowed sixty thousand, so taking that amount, but it will be less and with a sale price of one hundred and twenty thousand. We now off set that against a cost of say one hundred and forty thousand and this means that you need eighty thousand, which comes well within their requirements for security.

"I would advise you to say offers over one hundred and twenty thousand, the market is that buoyant. I would like to see you transfer the mortgage with no increase," Alex told her, smiling.

"Seriously, you mean a straight transfer, with no increase in my mortgage?" Julie asked, surprised,

"I have just received an offer on the one in the next street, of one hundred and fifty thousand, the day we came away and the owner refused the offer. He is a fool. Let me show them your property, I still owe you that much, for saving Dan's life and save the estate agent's fees," Alex said.

"I will leave it in your hands. To help you; I want the one hundred and twenty thousand you originally said, with a ten percent variance shall we say, so you can reduce the price by ten percent, if you need to, for a quick sale."

"Alex, I am so entrenched in this murder that I really do not want to be distracted by selling my house. Will you deal with it, send papers that need to be signed, but apart from that I will leave it up to you to do the best for me," Julie said.

"I will get you more than the original price I quoted, so when do you move into the cottage? You are very smitten by it, aren't you?" Alex asked.

Julie smiled at her and picked up her phone. She rang Everet, and told her that she would buy the cottage and she was willing to rent it until the deal was done, as long as she could move in no later than Sunday.

That evening she signed the rental contract and paid Mr Everet for one month and engaged him to do the work, she already knew he had a good name in the town.

"Julie, you are lucky in that an estimate usually has a ten percent prime cost added, because there is always something not accounted for, an anomaly unseen, but I know every inch of that property, so I'm sure the price will come in below the estimate," he told her. "The price is for re-wiring, re-plumbing, central heating and plastering as necessary, oh, and a new roof, but not decorating. When I bought it; I put a damp proof course in and treated it for woodworm, dry and wet rot. So you do not need to be concerned about them; I have the certificates and I have not put a price in for a new kitchen. I thought that was a personal requirement," he told her.

Dan and Alex left the next day to continue their holiday and within a week Julie's house had been sold to the couple who had offered the one hundred and fifty thousand for the other house. They wanted to move in, so Julie asked Alex to organise the removal of her furniture and to put it into storage. Mr Everet began work on the cottage the next Monday and by the end of the month, Julie was the proud owner, as she put it, of a building site.

All that remained was for the Police Superintendent, Julie, and the pub owner to come to an arrangement for the extended stay, while her cottage was being repaired.

Chapter 10 - Catch Up

Julie entered the police station after her day buying the cottage with Dan and Alex, to a mountain of reports.

"I will never take another day off, the paperwork once you return is just not worth it," Julie said, looking at the pile of papers on her desk.

"Ma'am, there isn't much there really, just confirmation of what we already knew, all the forensic reports are in and there is one interesting thing, they found a hair and it does not belong to anyone we interviewed. I suspect it belongs to the mystery woman, the cleaner we cannot find," Collins told her.

"You may have a point. I ask, did you check with the data base to see if she is known?" Julie asked.

"I did, Ma'am, and drew a blank," he said.

"So she doesn't have a criminal record. Quite a leap from being a law abiding citizen to a multiple murderer, don't you think?" Julie asked.

"It depends, I suppose, on her motives, the one thing we are not clear about is that it isn't love or money, the two main reasons, because if it were, then we would have to be looking closely at the wives and husband," Collins said.

"Love takes many forms, how sure are you that it isn't love?" Julie asked remembering her conversation with Dan.

"So you think they were having an affair, Ma'am?" Collins asked.

"I said, 'Love takes many forms,' do you not love your children, your parents?" Julie asked him.

"I see, sorry, yes I do, but it is a different form of love. I mean I would not sleep with my parents or children, apart from it being illegal," Collins said.

"Now consider this; if your dad was say, killed in one of the accidents at the quarry and it was brushed under the carpet, could it drive you to kill the owners?" Julie asked.

"No, it would not, I am a police officer, but I do get the point, but why wait so long before acting?" Collins asked.

"That could be, because it needed, to be planned? Then again it could be, because the re-opening of the quarry brought it to a head. Four accidents within four years is a very bad record and with five deaths, yet no action was taken, speaks volumes to me. I am convinced the deaths are linked to the quarry, that is the link, but is the re-opening the trigger, or the reason? It feels odd that someone would murder to stop it re-opening, it's not unknown, but too weak I believe, then again as a trigger, a reason to act out their feelings, has legs. It gives them a cause to seek revenge, closed brings a finality to the incidents, open it invokes deep set feelings, for revenge.

"Find out the names of the people who died; their relatives and addresses. I believe we had the right motive, but the wrong angle. Thank you for the précis of the reports, but I need to read them," Julie said, and sat down to being the marathon task.

Julie knew that it would take her most of the day to read and digest the reports on her desk. They included forensic reports on three crime scenes, autopsy reports on the deaths and reports from her team on the work they had been doing, investigating the crimes.

Alex's words about Dan being seconded to the team played on her mind. Collins and Everet were both good and worked well together, but her rapport with Dan, the fact that they were a team and seemed to know how each other's thoughts, had played a big role in the last investigation.

"PC Everet, just because his hobby was working with guns does not mean that his wife also was as capable with guns. She was more into needlework," Collins was saying as they entered the office.

"Why is that, because she is female? Don't be so bloody sexist. Women are just as good as markspeople as men," Everet was saying in an angry tone.

"Sexist? That was not sexist, it's an observation, there was needlework on the side, she had been sewing before we interviewed her," Collins came back at her.

The argument continued as they entered the office.

"Sewing on the side does not mean that she was the one sewing. I had a boyfriend who, knitted, that does not mean that he was queer, in fact the opposite. He's happily married and still knits for his three children, you sexist prig, join us in the twenty

106

first century. To shoot a gun all you have to do is pull the trigger, not hard," Everet said angrily.

"And if you do that you will miss the target. Now, children. Shall we get one thing straight? If you do not have enough work to do solving this crime, then I will find you extra work. Sexist arguments can come once we have found the killer, until then concentrate on the crime, not personal feelings.

"To fire a gun, is easy, to hit a target is not. The recoil from a forty five means that if you are within say three feet of the target and aim for the head, an amateur will miss the target, which is why police forces tell their officers to aim for the mass, the body.

"Whoever fired the gun that killed Brian Tindal; has had training. I have here a request for you to be put forward for training in firearms, DS Collins. I have signed off on it and you go for psych evaluation next Wednesday. If you are to pass the evaluation, then I suggest you learn very quickly how to control you mood, shouting at a fellow officer is not a good start, is it?

"Everet, sewing on the side is an indicator, not the whole story, did you ask who did the sewing, or assume?" Julie asked them in a quite controlled voice.

"No Ma'am, sorry," Everet said.

"Brian Tindal has been dead now for two days and I presume the house was clean. Seeing as he is not there to do it; I must presume his widow cleaned the house, which she may have done in the past, but because there were two of them, do not assume that it is her job. They could share, or he could be the house proud person in that household or she could be. We do not know and a copper's worst enemy is assumption. We never assume, we collate facts and come to a calculated conclusion, based on facts and evidence. If for any reason you are not able to do that; then I do not want you on my team, is that clear?" Julie said, telling them off quietly, to make her point.

"Yes, Ma'am," they both said in a contrite way and sat at their desks.

Julie smiled to herself as she retook her seat, she knew they were not a bad pair, they just needed direction.

The reports didn't shed much light on her case, they did confirm the cause of death, which she already knew and the time of death, so she put the autopsy reports to one side after a quick glance and concentrated on the forensic reports.

It didn't surprise her that the only fingerprints on the glasses were from the person drinking from them. The staff had to wear gloves when setting the table, as is correct and proper, in those circles. From arriving to leaving almost, the waiting on staff had worn white cotton gloves, even the cleaner when she showed them, according to June, had worn gloves and then removed them, to avoid any finger prints on the glass spoiling the effect of class.

It had been dry for a few days prior to Brian being shot so the ground was hard and there were no foot prints. Julie had to break her own rule and assume that because the gun shot was not heard, the door must have been closed when Brian was shot.

This meant that the person had been known and invited in.

Again in the David Morris case, the fall was the cause of death, rather hitting his head on the rock face, which was the actual cause, but she knew if he hadn't hit his head then the fall would have killed him.

Also the fall was caused by being unstable, because of the atrophy poisoning in the HP sauce, it did tell her that the only bottle in the store damaged by being injected was that bottle. She could rule out the animal rights people. It begged another question, how did the killer know that they would kill the right person. Was David Morris actually the person they wanted to kill? It seemed rather random, to say the least.

Julie got up and walked up and down the office as she considered the murders. Her hand went to her chin in deep thought. The glass at the dinner; how did the murderer know the glass would be placed where they wanted it? Was Lady Sophie the intended victim? It was yet another rather random killing, or apparently so? The only victim that she could definitely say was the victim was Brian Tindal, the other two were left to chance and she did not believe they were, so how did the killer know that they would kill their intended victim?

On the other hand the whole bottle of wine had been poisoned, so again was Lady Sophie the intended victim, or Sir Mac Andrews, because he should have been the one to taste the wine. He would be dead not the rest of them, because the poison was fast acting and before all the glasses had been poured, he would as Lady Sophie had, collapsed and died. So who was the intended victim?

The other main question going around and around in her head was why? What was the motive? She was sure it was the quarry, or the quarry was the link, but was it the motive, or something about the quarry that was the motive?

"Collins, any luck in finding out who our mystery woman, is?" Julie asked.

"No Ma'am. The description fits a lot of females from around here, but the shop keeper recognised the description as a woman in the shop at the time Mrs. Morris was. He added that she was not a regular, so probably not local. Not my assumption, the shop keeper's comment," Collins added quickly.

"I am pleased to hear it, but a reasonable assumption, don't you think?" Julie asked, "There are two, no three grocers in the town, erm, general stores as they are now called. Has she been seen in any of the other stores and is that particular shop where Mrs. Morris usually shops?" Julie asked.

"Yes and no, as with most of us, she does her weekly, erm, monthly, her big shop at the super store, but that is the shop in town she usually uses for emergencies, say." Collins posed.

"So the killer would perhaps know this and be in place when she entered, simple. But how did the killer know she would need to shop that day and for HP sauce at that particular time? That is what is baffling me. Collins do I need butter today?" Julie asked him.

110

"I have no idea, Ma'am," he said, confused.

"Exactly, so how did the killer know?" Julie asked.

"Like the glass, was Lady Sophie the intended victim, or Sir Andrew and if she was, how did the killer know she would taste the wine?" Collins asked.

"If the victims were the intended victims, then it is so random that it is brilliant," Julie said.

"Ma'am, soft thinking if that is permitted?" Everet asked.

"It is, go ahead and soft think," Julie told her.

"I have had a theory, but it as yet has not jelled into a solid theory. When the accidents happened, three of the managers stroke bosses at the quarry have now been killed, could it be revenge?" Everet asked.

"You have a point, a very good point apart from one thing: why wait, what is it, six years since the last death, and now you act? Why?" Julie asked.

"What about the controversy over re-opening the quarry?" Everet suggested.

"Again a point, apart from there was no public controversy, so how did the killer know about it?" Julie asked.

"Not publicly, but locally and friends have friends, so people who have left the town know people still living in the tow, and got to know via them, perhaps?" Everet suggested.

"I can accept that as a reason, Collins, work with Everet and find out the names and addresses of everyone who has left the village since the last death in the quarry," Julie told them.

111

She left them to go for a drive to think. Several new avenues of investigation were opening up, but as yet she had not been able to close current avenues down, which meant that it was dividing her team. A single avenue concentrates the team's efforts, diverse avenues divides it, a situation she did not like. Without a single focal point she knew this case could drag on and become one for the unsolved files.

The sun was shining, brilliant and blinding, as the early spring sun usually was and it was raining a typical April shower, a time for short, and a raincoat as the air warmed up ready for the summer heat.

Work had progressed steadily; the roof had been removed and was now covered ready for the thatch to be put on. Julie watched the thatcher as he began his work. She was mesmerised by the ease and grace of him working, she had never considered building workers as graceful people, yet this operation seemed so graceful.

The bundles of thatch were dumped and nailed with hooks into place, but then came the grace as he tweaked each bundle tapping the edge into a slant, for the rain to run off. More bundles were nailed in place by his assistant, as he skilfully, but more artistically, created the angles and evenness of the ends.

Inside they were hammering and banging as they installed the new wires and plumbing, accompanied by scraping sounds as the plasterers coated the walls.

Unusually for Julie, she was excited about the following Monday, when she would be moving in.

Mr. Everet the builder had told Julie, it would take about four to five weeks. The weather had been good to them, staying dry. They hadn't lost a day to the weather, so three weeks later he had called her to say they would be out the following Monday finished, just one month from purchase to completion.

Her new kitchen was due on Wednesday, she had gone for a cottage styled kitchen and Dan and Alex were due on Sunday, ready to help her move in on Monday, this was after they had helped her decorating, one job the builder had not quoted for, as agreed.

The shower passed, steam rose from the pavements, as the early sun burned it away.

Julie got back into her car, and drove back to the office. It didn't surprise Julie that the five minute drive to her cottage and the five minute drive back had had a calming effect and brought some clarity to her thoughts.

"Meeting," Julie said as she entered the office. "The quarry is the key, Lady Sophie was the owner's daughter and private secretary to the general manager, but I feel that her connection to the owner is the reason, Brian Tindal was a manager, David Morris was also a manager, who else is left from that period?" Julie asked them.

"Sir Andrew, erm, Colin Underwood, he was the works manager and is now purchasing director, erm," Collins said.

"Angus Mc Tythe, he was the explosives expert, he pushed the button when the boy was killed," Everet added.

"Yes, I had forgotten him, stupid, he was the cause of the accident, he should have double and treble checked the face before pushing the button," Collins said.

"Someone has to press it and when they are happy, which I presume he was, everything was in place," Julie said.

Chapter 11 - Focus

"Ma'am, it doesn't make sense, I would hold Angus as the responsible person and if I were to kill anyone it would be him and Sir Andrew. Not minor managers; they were the principles, the ones responsible as the general manager and the person who pushed the button. So why kill lower ranking managers? They were not even present at the time; they were working in their offices," Everet asked.

"Can I throw a wobblier? Who covered up the cause of the accident? Could it be that they aren't after the people responsible say, but the people responsible for, the cover up?" Collins asked.

"Even so, wouldn't Sir Andrew be at the top of your list? He cut costs by reducing the security on site and then was the main person involved in, the cover up," Everet said.

"No matter how we look at it, Sir Andrew has got to be on the killers list and is in danger, as is this Angus feller. I am going to need to draft in troops, we don't have enough feet on the ground to do our jobs and protect those two. I'll ring the Chief Super. Meantime I want you two to make a list of all the managers of the quarry at that time and the managers employed by the building firm. Two different lists, and then to make a list of the managers on both lists. Look for promotions as an indicator of those involved in, the cover-up," Julie told them.

Julie went to her office and rang the Chief Super, "Ma'am, we now believe that because of the controversy of re-opening the quarry the killer is out to kill the people responsible for the accidents, or the cover-up, perhaps both. With the limited force available to me, it would be impossible to mount a twenty four hour protection on Sir Andrew and the explosives expert at the time; one Angus Mc Tythe. I will need a dozen officers to mount the protection required, Ma'am," Julie told her.

"I see, so two people for three shifts is six, why twelve?" she asked.

"They need days off, Ma'am," Julie explained.

"Then you cover that contingency, I will have six extra officers drafted in for two weeks only. This case has dragged on for two months now, Chief Inspector; and you appear to be no further on. You have two weeks to offer me something positive or it will, in all probability, remain unsolved. Not a good start to your new posting, is it?" she asked and hung up.

"We have six officers for two weeks; we need to get our fingers out. Next week I'm on holiday, so that I can move in to my cottage, obviously I will not be taking it; I'll have to cancel it. Collins, this mystery woman, how are you doing with that?" Julie asked.

"Not very well, sixteen females have left the village since the accident. I'm now going through the list to see if any are connected to the quarry and or the accidents," he told her.

"Good, I agree that is the right action to take, it has to be someone with a grudge. Everet, what news on the list of victims involved in the accidents?" Julie asked.

"Again, I have the list, and I'm now checking it against the list of females who have left the town, to see if any names come up on both lists," Everet said.

"Good work, I suppose I had better ring Dan and cancel his holiday," Julie said, dejected.

"Why, Ma'am? He is a good friend from what I have seen and he will not need you to tell him what is needed, will he?" Everet asked.

"No I suppose not, but I can't just abandon him and Alex; that would not be right," Julie said.

"I accept that, but we now have a focus, the partners did not kill the victims so that avenue is closed and the re-opening of the quarry is not the point any more, but is the reason. It is the trigger that caused the events and I believe the killer is not living in the village, but is someone who was here and has left, from what you have said. Do you need to be here twenty four hours a day, with phones, computers and visits?" Everet asked.

"PC Everet, for all I accept your concerns and appreciate your sentiments, there is a difference between need and requirement. I am happy that you will not slack if I am not here, but I am required to be here to direct and investigate. Thank you for the sentiment, but unfortunately, it is invalid, the move in, is postponed," Julie said and rang Dan who argued with her, but she was adamant, it had to be postponed.

"Sorry to disturb you Ma'am, but a regular check on gun safety has revealed that a gun is missing. The farmer keeps shot guns, but also has a licence for hand guns, he is a member of the local gun club and is well respected in firearm circles. This is Brook Field Farm, Ma'am," the desk officer said.

"Why bring this to me?" Julie asked.

"The missing gun is a forty five, Ma'am," he told her.

"I don't suppose we know how long it has been missing, do we?" Julie asked.

"No Ma'am, he has been ill, a stroke and has not touched his guns for months. It is very doubtful he will ever touch one again, it has affected his right side, Ma'am," the officer said.

"Collins, you're with me," Julie said and they drove to the farm.

"Mrs Bancroft, I am Chief Inspector Julie Ashton, and this is Detective Sergeant Collins," Julie said when she opened the door, "I am sorry to have to disturb you, but I need to ask your husband some questions relating to his missing gun," Julie said.

They were invited in and shown into the lounge area where Mr. Bancroft was sitting.

"Mr. Bancroft, I believe you recently lost a gun, a forty five, can you tell me when you last saw it?" Julie asked.

"I am sorry, but it has taken his right side and his speech is slurred, I am beginning to manage to understand him," his wife told them, "He hasn't seen his guns in over three months. He collapsed in the field, luckily I was taking him his lunch, he liked to eat in the field when the weather was fine and it was his favourite, a ploughman's lunch. He is a great traditionalist really, or old fashioned. He ploughs the one acre field with a Shire horse and plough and seeds it by hand. He has won medals for traditional farming methods at fairs and the like, but no longer, our son is the farmer now, and he is keeping up the tradition," she told them.

"Yes, interesting, but I really need to know about the gun. Where did he keep it, do you know?" Julie asked.

"Yes, we have a brick built lean-to as a work shop for the farm equipment. His gun safe is in there, the door is kept locked. He was always very careful about his guns," she told them.

"Would it be possible for us to see the guns?" Julie asked.

"I don't have the key, our son has it and he is out in the fields, we are planting a late crop. He wanted to finish in the day, so he took sandwiches with him, I am not expecting him back till dinner time, six, seven o'clock tonight," she told them.

"It is important so ask him to stay in tonight and we will come back, we need details of the gun," Julie told her.

"I am not sure we can help you there; it wasn't our gun, we were just looking after it for someone," Mrs, Bancroft told them.

"Oh, who? Do you know who your husband was looking after the gun for?" Julie asked.

"Yes, Reginald Green," she told them.

"Do you have an address for Reginald Green?" Julie asked.

119

"No, he's dead, his wife asked us to take it after he died," she said.

"I see. What about an address for her?" Julie asked.

"No, she moved away, a long time ago. I kept asking John what he intended to do with it, seeing as Reginald was dead and she had moved away. John just said that it was not his and he was responsible enough to ensure it was safe until she told him what to do with it, as he had promised Reginald. They were good friends and were both members of the gun club; my John was the better shot, but Reginald was very good," she told them.

"Thank you, Mrs. Bancroft, we will come back tonight, I need as much detail as possible about the gun. I know from the reports by the investigating officer that you are not in any trouble. I just need information; does your son live with you?" Julie asked.

"No, he is married, he lives down the road a ways," she told them.

"I see, so can you ask him to wait here for us after work, please, we will come back for seven o'clock, tonight," Julie told her.

"I'll ask him, is he in any trouble?" she asked.

"No, no, definitely not, we just need information about the gun," Julie reassured her.

They left and went to Julie's house for her to have a look around without the builders being there, and got a surprise.

"Dan, what are you doing here, you're not due till Sunday!" Julie said.

"We had a break in the case, he walked into the station and gave himself up, case closed and I was able to leave early. Alex suggested that we paint the outside, I presumed you would want the wood varnished?" Dan asked, holding his varnish brush over the tin, "I would have gone for UPVC double gazing," he added.

"What, on a two hundred year old farm cottage, it would not be in keeping," Julie said, astonished.

"I agree, but a damn sight warmer," Dan said.

"Dan, dear, dear Dan, the windows are double glazed and fitted, there will be no draughts, the porch I had added stops draughts from the door. Next year I will have a conservatory added at the back, then I can gaze out onto my beautifully manicured lawns, a weekend job for you, while Alex and I, sip our pink gins," Julie said and laughed.

"Julie, I am the gardener, he planted some pansies last weekend and they all died," Alex said, smiling at him.

"You should have told me to water them after planting them," Dan offered, as if hurt.

"Last weekend, when we had a heat wave and most people were watering their gardens anyway and he did not even water new plants in?" Julie asked shocked.

"My fault, I should have told him; being male, they need to be told when to wipe their; well, you know what I mean," Alex said, laughing.

"What are you doing Alex, isn't Dan varnishing the roof windows?" Julie asked.

"I don't have a head for heights," Dan said sheepishly.

"Dan, they are only just, ten feet off the ground, well, perhaps twelve feet, but that isn't high," Julie said.

"Julie, I have never had a pair of boots with a Cuban heel. You don't mind if we set up camp, do you? We thought we might as well make it feel like a holiday and we brought the girls' tent, for you," Dan told her.

"Alex, you are booked into the pub, aren't you? It is a fifteen minute run to the pub and I do not see Dan waiting that long for his pint," Julie shouted up to her.

"Dinner, bed and breakfast, we had to call in to book in, which necessitated the requirement of a pint, while I took the bags to the room," Alex said as if miffed.

"Dan, I am surprised at you, I thought you were a gentleman," Julie said as if shocked.

"What she means is she took her handbag to the room, leaving the suitcases for me," Dan said aggrieved.

"Leaving me naked, wrapped in a towel after having a shower to freshen up, whilst he tried to drink the bar dry," Alex said.

"One pint, that was all I had, it is nectar, and needs to be savoured," Dan said, emphasising the point.

"One pint, took over an hour, to drink, I don't think so," Alex said ,coming down the ladder, "Have you not finished that window yet?" Alex asked him.

"I've been discussing the case with Julie and she's distracted me," Dan said.

"Then I will go, I would hate to be the cause of your demise at the hands of Alex," Julie said, laughing.

"We should be able to finish the front by six o'clock, how about dinner at seven o'clock?" Alex asked, refilling her paint tray.

"Sorry I have an appointment at seven; you eat, and I will join you later," Julie said.

Julie took Collins back to the station and picked up the ballistics report.

It told her nothing new, but did confirm her earlier thoughts that the bullet was not fired from the gun on the floor, being a nine millimetre calibre gun; the bullet was a forty five. It also interested her that the missing gun was a forty five calibre gun. The bullets were a standard make and sold by the thousand, they could also be bought in any gun shop.

Julie was happy that they now had the connection@ it was the quarry, but that raised a second question as to why, what was the actual reason. She didn't believe it was the argument over the re-opening of the quarry, yet that was the reason. She was moving to believe that the re-opening had sparked the murders, but was not the actual reason. She believed the re-opening had brought back anguish and grief, to the perpetrator, forcing their hand, and so was not about the actual argument.

"Collins, if we discount the argument as the reason, but the catalyst, it reduces our suspect pool down considerably, track and trace all the victim's families. What if the murderer is not for or opposed to, the re-opening, but was a family member of the victims, of the accidents and this is revenge against the owners and managers, at the time of the accidents?" Julie asked.

"Ma'am, we discounted that because of the time that has elapsed, it is not, erm, usual can I say; that revenge attacks happen several years after the event. Incited and enraged, those people attack there and then, Ma'am," Collins suggested.

"I agree, but what if say you, and I were married, heaven forbid," Julie said, and laughed, "No, and I say had a calming influence over you stopping you acting, then years later we divorced and then you heard about the discussion about re-opening the mine that had killed our son, say. What reaction could that invoke?" Julie asked.

"The calming influence gone and it brought back to the forefront of my mind and then possibly it could relight all the emotions and anger that has lain dormant all these years. It has legs, but I am not convinced, so can I suggest we leave Everet working on the quarry angle while I start this line of enquiry?" Collins suggested.

"Yes, I am not convinced this is the motive, but a line of enquiry I believe we need to follow, before discounting it," Julie said.

"Evening, Mr. Bancroft, and thank you for waiting to see me," Julie said by way of introduction.

"I didn't feel I had an option from the way my mother put it," he replied.

"I need to speak to you, had it been urgent then I would have come to you in the field, but one way or another; I would have spoken to you and this is the most pleasant way. Thank you," Julie said as Mrs. Bancroft, put the tray with a fresh pot of tea on the table, "You rang the police to report the gun stolen on Wednesday, why? Was that the day each week, say, you checked the guns, in the gun safe?" Julie asked.

"No, I needed the shot gun, crows have been ravaging the corn field and I wanted to scare them," he replied.

"So you do what, shoot them, or use the noise to scare them? Why not put a scarecrow up?" Julie asked.

"Birds are not as stupid as people think. If it doesn't move, they do not fear it and use it as a rest to perch on. I'm sure you have seen it on the telly, six crows resting on the arms. Even in airports they used bangs to scare the birds off, but they got used to it and it does not work now, well not as effectively, so they have hawks. A scarecrow may work for a season or two, but they get used to it; shoot a few of the buggers and they tend to stay away," he told her.

"Do I take it that you don't check on the guns at regular intervals, say monthly?" Julie asked.

"Inspector, we live in the country, I have six rabbits in the freezer and I go out shooting more or less every week. Last year a dog attacked my sheep and I shot it, as is my right. Six hundred pounds that dog cost me and no compensation."

"So, am I to assume that the gun was stolen the night before?" Julie asked.

"You can do, I opened the gun safe on Sunday, I did not check, but it all seemed to be in order. I do not count every gun in there, but when I opened it on Wednesday; I noticed it missing," he told her.

"What type of gun was it?" Julie asked.

"It was a Colt Shooting Master, point four, five calibre," he replied.

"And you saw it missing the day after Mr Tindal was shot, with a forty five?" Julie asked.

"I know what it looks like; reporting a car missing after it has been used in a robbery. I am not stupid, all I can tell you is on Sunday it was there, but on Wednesday, it was missing," he said.

"I accept that you can only report it when you see it, it just seems convenient. What about bullets?" Julie asked.

"I don't keep the bullets in the same safe, nor the shot gun cartridges. The guns are in the outhouse in the safe, which is bolted to the wall and it is brick built and the door is locked, to stop thieves. There is well over ten thousand pounds' worth of equipment in there and you lot are very ineffective at preventing thieves from stealing, my tools," he threw back at her.

"Unfortunately, we tend to be reactive, rather than proactive; it is the nature of the business. Now if you will show me the gun cabinet, oh before we do, van I have a list of the guns you hold in there? I understand this gun was not owned by you, so who did own it?" Julie asked.

"I have three shotguns, two over unders', and one side by side, one .22 rifle and one Webley revolver, my dad's from his time in the forces," he told her.

"I see, quite a collection, the .22 is for when you go hunting rabbits, is it?" Julie asked.

"It is that, or breaking your teeth on the pellets still in the rabbit," he replied.

"I presume you shine a light on them to get them to stand still while you shoot them, so you go with, a partner?" Julie asked.

"Yes, I take Bill my farm hand, his wages are not the best, farm workers are one of the worst paid jobs in the country. It is dirty, dangerous and poorly paid, so I give him half our catch," he told her.

"You must be a good shot then, to have six in your freezer and I presume six in his, twelve in total, in what, one night?" Julie asked.

"We do eat other things, not just rabbit stew every meal time. But in answer to the question, yes I am a good shot and we bagged fifteen that night," he said.

"So it went missing between Sunday and Wednesday, the two days you went to the cabinet?" Julie asked.

"Yes, what are you driving at? No, I did not shoot him, I was out hunting with Bill and we bagged just one rabbit, which I gave to him because I got the seven the night we bagged fifteen. They do not come out to play every night, you know," he said, now with an edge to his voice.

"I do know, very well, being a city girl; I could not go out the back door to hunt. My dad took me

127

on hunting trips to the highlands of Scotland, but we never used lamps, we considered it unsporting. Now the cabinet, if you please?" Julie asked.

He led Julie out to the cabinet and she was satisfied that it was secure.

"How did the thief get the gun? The door does not have a new lock so I presume they had a key, or did you forget to lock it?" Julie asked.

"Your forensic people decided that it had been picked, do you not read the reports?" he asked, challenging her.

Julie smiled at him, "Indeed I do, but the reports never cover my intuition and knowledge. So once inside then they are faced with the locked cabinet. Again from the reports, the lock was picked, and I am sure the officer who investigated the case suggested that the lock needs upgrading, not being substantial enough. Now if you will, open it, please?" Julie asked, not being fazed by his attack.

He unlocked the cabinet and opened it; Julie looked at the guns stood up at the back and the revolver on the top shelf.

"May I?" Julie asked, indicating her wish to touch the guns.

"Do I have a choice?" he asked.

"Yes you do, but I would then come back with a warrant," Julie told him and lifted out the first gun.

She broke it and peered down the barrel, "Hum, do you not clean your gun after use?" Julie asked him.

"Usually I do, but I was tired on Sunday, so left it and then I forgot till now, when you pointed it out; when you have finished, give it to me and I will clean it and then it does not get forgotten again," he said.

The next two were clean and then she picked up the .22.

"Again, not cleaned, here," she said, handing it to him, "So Sunday you used the shot gun in the fields to scare the crows and then on Tuesday, you used the .22 for rabbits? Were you tired on Tuesday as well?" Julie asked.

"Obviously, farm work is hard work and very tiring, I am currently working a fifteen hour day, come harvest time and it can be twenty hours a day. You have no idea how cushy your job is, set hours. What is it eight hours for a beat copper and for you just six?" he said raising his voice.

"Like any job, the more you put in, the more you get out. I average a twelve to fourteen hour day, so don't expect me to bleed, for you," Julie said calmly, and with a smile to emphasise her point.

She then picked up the revolver, "Do not shoot this gun, it is dangerous, the barrel needs a very good clean. If you do not intend to shoot it, have the firing pin removed, polished and mounted as a memento. Rust is eating away at the barrel," Julie told him.

"I have never touched it; I don't know why I keep it, except as being my father's, a keepsake," he said.

"It is a classic, not rare, but emotive, being the standard issue to the armed forces and to me, it is criminal to allow it to be destroyed by nature. This is a classic gun, used by our armed forces in both World Wars; in fact Webley guns were used as far back as the Boer war. If you wish to sell it, let me know, but before the barrel has completely corroded, away," Julie said.

"Do you have an interest in guns?" he asked.

"I have a collection of guns, their use or their purpose, is questionable to say the least, but as an engineering and craftsman product, you have to admire the skill of their manufacture. One millimetre out, and they are useless, there is beauty in the precision," Julie said.

"The next time I go shooting, would you like to join me?" he asked.

Julie smiled at him, "Not until this investigation is over and definitely not using lamps," Julie said.

"At least with lamps everyone is a kill shot and does not leave the animal injured to die a slow death," he said.

"That all depends on how good a shot you are; I have never left an animal to suffer," Julie said.

"Does that mean, not going with me hunting that I am a suspect?" he asked, shocked.

"For the killing no, I will check, but I am sure you will have a good alibi for that night," Julie said and left.

Chapter 12 - Moving In

Dan and Alex worked hard on Julie's house while she concentrated on the murders, this meant that the following Monday they did not begin the decorating as she had expected, but they helped her move in.

"Something is missing, Julie, I can't work out what it is," Dan said once her furniture was in place.

"My guns; until I have a secure place for them. The armoury at London is looking after them for me," Julie said.

"What, the police armoury?" Dan asked.

"Those Muppets, no way, the place Jones proved my theory," Julie said.

"This cottage is not really big enough, for you to display them," Dan said.

"No, you're correct, but when I get the extension which is planned for next year, it will be. I have always worked the same way, twenty five percent of my salary is my mortgage and based on my previous salary that is where I am now, with the increase with my promotion, I can afford a larger mortgage, so buying the house was based on my old salary, but now I can increase the mortgage by adding the two extensions, the conservatory for Alex and me to sip our pink gins whilst you mow the lawns and handle the side gallery," Julie said, laughing at him.

"I am not that sure you can even trust him to mow the lawns, Julie," Alex said, laughing.

"I agree, so Alex can mow whilst I drink the nectar from the local pub," Dan said.

"Dan ,you are beginning to sound like an alcoholic," Julie said.

"The criteria is the need, not the amount. I stop without any effects; I do not need to drink the nectar, I just enjoy it and so drink it whilst here. In Manchester, I do not drink anywhere near as much as here. Alex has now put a limit on my nightly intake, the B," Dan said.

"Be careful, Dan, I can reduce the amount," Alex said, joking with him, "I allow him two pints a night, any two, but not two from each barrel, just two," Alex added.

"I had heard you have doubled the landlord's beer turnover," Julie said, joining in.

"That is a lie, trebled more like," Dan bragged.

"Ha, ha, ha, that's the Dan I know. Big body and head; do not get caught drinking and driving on my patch," Julie said.

"He won't, I drive in the mornings, just to be sure," Alex said.

"Good, from now on move out of the hotel, stroke pub and into my spare room. Thank you both of you for what you have done for me. I mean with this case; I would still be decorating the first room had you not shown up," Julie said.

"I have enjoyed the time with Dan and I love decorating, so it was not work, I really enjoy it, thank you for having us. Do you know how long it is since I spent more than four hours with Dan?" Alex asked.

"That is my fault and I accept it, but that case needed our undivided attention, sorry, Alex," Julie said.

"I am not apportioning blame, Julie. Dan has always been committed and it is his fault, by and large, but that is the lot of a committed police officer and I accepted it when I married him," Alex said.

"Shall we go and book you out of the hotel, then we may as well have lunch there, my treat, and Dan; I will also allow you two pints," Julie said smiling at him.

"You are on," Dan said.

They left her cottage and went to the pub, Dan paid their bill and Julie ordered lunch for them, along with Dan's first pint.

"How is the case coming along?" Dan asked.

"I took on board your comment about it being a revenge attack brought on by the possible re-opening of the quarry. This opened up a new line of inquiry. Everet and Collins are good officers and work hard, but they are a far cry from the facilities and team we had in London. Then again, the crime does not have the same national and international focus that crime had," Julie said.

"You are not political and ruffle feathers; they had to recognise you for the arrest, but what the Super in London wanted was to get you dismissed, hence the promotion, but to a well-hidden corner, of England. For the rest of us, we did get a promotion, for closing a very complex and important case. What is your new Super like?" Dan asked.

133

"I have yet to meet her, apart from when I arrived and I know she is a stickler for the books. I asked for twelve officers to mount security on two possible victims and she allowed me six. With a name like Alex; it could have been either Alexander, or Alexandria. Let's hope I get on as well with this Alex as I do with your Alex shall we?" Julie asked, smiling at Dan.

"You have a DS and a DC, but no DI," Dan pointed out.

"Unusual, but they had to promote me and technically a Chief Inspector is not required in such a rural area, the top officer for these parts should be an Inspector. I got the promotion, but they buried me in rural England. Perhaps it is time for me to slow down; I have been running on high octane fuel for far too long," Julie said, smiling.

"Ha, you slow down? Never," Dan said, laughing.

"For a quiet country pub it does get busy, there was a queue for the ladies," Alex said when she returned.

"You missed nothing," Dan said.

"That means that you were talking about me, or the case and I suspect the latter," Alex said.

"In any crime there is means, motive and opportunity, of the three probably the most important to us is the motive at this moment in time. Once we have motive then we can delve to find the person, logically. The means tends to be rather obvious and the opportunity contrived, possibly, and as we investigate, then they become more obvious, but the motive is personal and indicates the person we need to find.

"Ever since the first crime, we have hunted for the motive and as yet have not found it, so the direction for the investigation is muddled. We have just opened up a new line of inquiry which I have to admit is Dan's fault and I hate him for adding confusion to our investigation with a new line to follow," Julie said.

"Why, am I not surprised to hear that? He can confuse the simplest of things," Alex said, laughing.

"She's right, you know; that is how I get confessions, I confuse them so much they sign," Dan said, laughing.

After lunch Dan and Alex went for a drive in the country and Julie went back to the station.

Collins was in the office and looking confused.

"Problems, Collins?" Julie asked.

"Not problems, just a list of names, twice the length of the people. One, Mrs Abigail Hunter, left one month after the last incident; her husband was the man that tried to save the child. She went away and changed her name to avoid the press and then remarried, so I have three names for her, plus four addresses. Obviously I made, rather tried to make, contact at her last known address, but she was not there and has disappeared. I have contacted social services to see if they can help and I am waiting for a reply. Ma'am, that is just one and there are more, similar to that one. I have a list of twelve people and thirty names and growing," Collins told her.

"How soon after the last accident did they leave?" Julie asked.

"I stopped at six months, people come and go all the time, but to be related to the incident I decided to stop at six months," Collins said.

"How many were related to the people who died?" Julie asked.

"Ma'am, this is a town, but come on, little bigger than a village. I would be hard pressed to find anyone not related to the victims. My wife's grandmother is the sister-in-law to the child's mother, so I am related to the child in some distant way," he told her.

"Not that distant, I would say the child was your cousin once removed, if I follow the link properly. Have you asked your mother-in-law if she knows where her auntie is?" Julie asked.

"There was a family rift and our side does not speak to that side, why, do not ask, I have no idea. Something to do with a conscientious objector during the last war, but that is not as clear as I would like," he said.

"Then. Collins. you have to ask and find her, This is a murder enquiry and goes beyond family squabbles," Julie told him. He accepted her comment.

The door opened and a larger than life woman stood there, her aura filled the room as did her smile.

"I am sorry I have had to wait a month to meet you personally, Chief Inspector. Holidays, sickness have prevented me from getting here, Superintendant Harris," she said. holding out her hand to Julie, "Now how are we with this murder?"

"Good afternoon, Ma'am, not that well, I am afraid, there does not seem to be a motive, rather we have several motives, which is opening up several lines of inquiry that have yet to be resolved. We have three deaths and each one could be by the partner apart from one. We have two deaths against the re-opening of the quarry and one for. We also have three deaths related to the original management team at the quarry, apart from one, yet she was," Julie told her.

"I see, but they are all linked in one way or another to the quarry, aren't they?" the Super asked.

"Yes, Ma'am, but even that is tenuous, the strongest link, but why? Was it because of them trying to re-open the quarry? If so, why kill a supporter, if they were trying to reduce the opposition?" Julie asked.

"So you have settled in then, good, I can see you are working on theories. Do you still need the extra officers? Patrols are thin on the ground elsewhere without these officers."

"Ma'am, that is the point, if it is because of the accident several years ago then, Sir Andrew's life is in danger. If it is because of re-opening the quarry, then I don't think it is. Without a motive we are groping in the dark, Ma'am. I must also say that with just three officers working the case, we are also stretched beyond, the limit. I also have two break-ins, one is part of my investigation and the other is being investigated by the Patrol officers, our constables. I am sure they are not related, but you think the other areas are stretched, not like here. I cannot mount a protection team with the normal resources, let alone now, with these murders," Julie said.

"I like an outspoken person who is not afraid to speak their mind, it keeps the air clear. You have the officers for one more week, is that clear enough, for you?" she said bluntly.

"Abundantly, I can see we are going to get on like a house on fire, unfortunately, everyone involved tends to get singed in the fire and I will not take the blame if Sir Andrew, is killed," Julie said, smiling back.

"Chief Inspector, your reputation precedes you, and I look forward to our little chats, but be careful it is only being singed and someone involved, does not get burned," the Super said, and turned to leave.

"Collins, you can come back in, now," Julie said smiling, she also liked a challenge.

"Nothing has changed, we have the extra officers till next week," Julie said and put her coat on.

She drove out to the manor house and asked to see Sir Andrew, She was shown into the sitting room and he joined her there.

"Sir Andrew, I have some disturbing news for you. I am afraid that I can only provide the security officers for one more week. After that I suggest you stay in the house until we have apprehended the killer," Julie told him.

"You do realise who I am and my prominent position as a government advisor. This is not acceptable and I insist that you provide protection, for me," he demanded.

"I have twenty officers, split over three shifts and with time off duty that means that on duty I have on average six officers, including me. They have to protect the public and investigate any crimes, keep law and order and now provide twenty four hour protection for one individual. I am sorry, but that will not be happening; perhaps you have some sway with the government, and can organise protection via them," Julie said, and got up to leave.

"I will be speaking to the Chief Constable about this, it is a disgrace," he said angrily.

"It is out of my hands, sir. I have limited resources and need to use them to the best advantage, which I am sure you will agree, is to catch whoever murdered, your wife and thereby making you safe," Julie said.

"Thank you for the information and warning, but I am not happy about it, you have a duty to protect, me," he said, still in the angry tone.

"That is not strictly correct, Sir, I have a duty to protect the public, not just you and to that end I will find the killer, hopefully before they strike again," Julie said.

"Who else is in danger?" he asked.

"We don't have names, just a theory, which is why the powers that be have decided that our concerns are not substantial enough to offer this degree of protection for one individual. There are several theories we are investigating and this is just one of them," Julie said, and made to leave.

"I see, so, I am not important enough, am I not? We will see about that, Chief Inspector," he said.

"I wish you well, sir, and keep away from the windows. Good bye," Julie said, holding out her hand.

He took her hand and shook it, asking the maid to show Julie out.

"Ma'am, I have been checking up on who was in the management at the quarry and Nigel Croft was the chief accountant then and is now the Purchasing Manager of the building firm. Do you think we need to protect him as well?" Everet asked, when she returned to the office.

"Ha, Sir Andrew only has protection till the weekend. What chance do you think we have of more officers for this guy? Go to him and suggest he stays indoors until we have the murderer. We need to fix the motive, then we will know who, if anybody, we need to protect. At the moment it is too fluid, it could be, or then again - we have three probable motives, therefore I cannot say with any certainty that either of them are in danger," Julie said, frustrated.

Everet left the office and Julie sat down to go through the reports again, in case she had missed something, but she hadn't, but she did decide that they were not killed by their respective partners, she did not have three murders with three perpetrators, there was just the one and they were linked to the quarry and the accident, of that she was now sure. She needed to find something to make her assumptions concrete. She was sure she was right, but to be able to close down any other line of enquiry, she needed something substantial.

Julie rang Bancroft and asked if Bill had a day off, he said that Bill did have a day off, Thursday; Julie smiled, that was the day after tomorrow and plenty of time for Bancroft to warn Bill.

Julie took her car and went to the farm, she called in at the farmhouse and asked where they were and then she set off to find Bancroft and Bill.

She found them as expected; she waited until the man she had not met came to the edge of the field and then stopped him and got on the tractor.

"Bill, I presume, I am Chief Inspector Ashton. I need to ask you some questions, please, carry on; I know how busy you are. Where were you last Wednesday night between say ten o'clock and two o'clock in the morning?" Julie asked.

"We left at ten o'clock to go hunting and returned about one thirty in the morning," he told her.

"Yes, Mr. Bancroft said that, and that you had a good night. Personally I don't agree with lamping, it isn't sporting to me but a necessity, because of the low wages. How many did you bag that night?" Julie asked.

"It was a poor night, I am sure he would have said so; we only got three, he gave me two and kept one for his freezer," Bill told her.

"I see; what about before ten o'clock?" Julie asked.

"I finished about seven o'clock, we needed the top field seeded with rye, and then I went home, had my dinner and a shower and watched the telly with my parents till it was time to leave about quarter to ten," he said.

141

"Where did you go shooting?" Julie asked.

"Shadow Woods, for a change, we usually go to Six Acre Woods, but Alan suggested we change site because we had shot a lot the weekend before. We bagged fifteen that night and killing so many makes them nervous, so we decided to leave that area for a week or two," he told her.

"Let me see now, Six Acre Woods is north of the town, isn't it?" Julie asked.

"Yes and Shadow Woods is east of the town," he told her.

"Yes interesting, Shadow Woods is about two miles outside of the town, but Six Acre Woods is what, a field away from the town?" Julie asked.

"Yes, it is one of our fields and we call it Town Field because it backs onto the town, well the outskirts," he told her.

"Logically, what about the guns, do you have dealings with them?" Julie asked.

"Alan shoots the rabbits, so I clean the gun, a .22 rifle with telescopic sights," he said.

"After Wednesday's shoot, when did you clean the rifle?" Julie asked.

"I didn't, we only shot for an hour and Alan said that he was tired, so to leave it till Thursday," he said.

"I see, but you have just told me that you were out from ten o'clock till one thirty; two and a half hours not one, now which is it?" Julie asked.

"We were out for that period, but only shooting for about an hour, we had to walk to the place and then wait for a rabbit to pop its head up to shoot it.

Like I said, only three in an hour, we spent most of our time chatting, lying on the grass," he said.

"When I went hunting we were told to keep quiet, do you think your chatting may be why the rabbits stayed, in their burrows?" Julie asked.

"I suppose it could be, Alan positioned us closer than usual to the site of their burrows," he told her.

"How far away would you say you were?" Julie asked.

"I don't know, about one hundred yards, may be less, from here say to the hedge," he said.

"Here to the hedge, well a little back, that is more like twenty yards, if that," Julie corrected him.

"It was dark and distances can be deceptive in the dark," he said.

"I am not surprised you didn't bag a lot, I bet those were early on as well, your scent would carry that far, let alone the noise of you talking. For a supposedly experienced hunter that is abysmal, he did not want to bag anything," Julie said. "So you have six rabbits in the freezer and you go out shooting again so soon, why not wait until you eat some of your frozen rabbits? Do you usually go when you have so many in the freezer?"

"Not usually, we go when one or other of us has just three in the freezer, in case they are being coy," he said.

"Did you clean the gun on Thursday, as you said?" Julie asked.

"No I over slept and Alan said that he had and that I needed to get out seeding, or we would miss

143

the dry spell before the rain, which had been forecast," he said.

"Do you know what guns were kept in the gun safe?" Julie asked.

"I saw them, but didn't handle them, apart from cleaning them, he has two over-unders, one side by side, a .22 rifle, his dad's old army pistol and another handgun," he said.

"Do you know what the other handgun is?" Julie asked.

"No, all I know is that he is keeping it safe for a friend, sorry, was keeping it safe, it was stolen," he told her.

"How did he seem when he discovered it missing?" Julie asked.

"I don't know, I mean he found it missing when he got up and he had called the police and they were there by the time I arrived," he told her.

"Great, thank you, and I am impressed at the straight furrows, sorry I don't know what you call them, you are seeding, not ploughing," Julie admitted.

"Drills, that is what we call the lines we are seeding," he said.

Julie smiled at him and made her way back to her car and the station, where she met up with, Collins.

"Ma'am, I am glad to see you, I actually have some good news for a change. Of the twelve females who left the village, two are in a nursing home to be near their children, not together you understand, two different ones, but can be crossed off my list. Two others are also elderly and living with, or close by, their children. A lot of the youth of the town leave to find work and some come back, but most do not so the elderly people leave now to be with their children, well, looked after, by their children," Collins told her.

"Very good, Collins so we can cross four off our list, can we?" Julie asked him.

"Yes, but only four names, they did not remarry, or change their name, so my list of names does not seem to have shrunk," he said dejectedly.

"What do you know about Alan Bancroft?" Julie asked him.

"He was a councillor up until his dad died and then he had the farm to run so stood down. He has never been in any trouble, a good solid bloke. He was about to get married, but she left, it was mysterious at the time, there didn't seem to be any reason why she would run off. I was in my teens then, and not on the force so I know very little of the investigation. Would you like me to get the file from the archives?" Collins offered.

"Yes, later, what about the missing gun, a Colt M1911, forty five automatic, so I believe? They went out shooting and when they came back, Bill put the gun away, according to Bancroft, un-cleaned, and he took it out to clean it the next morning, which was when he discovered the Colt, missing. I am not happy with his story; I think he knows more than he is telling us. Who owned the gun in the first place?" Julie asked.

"He is well liked in the town; he did work hard on the council and now works just as hard on the farm. He mechanised it, his dad was a miser really;

he still used horses and employed three men to work the farm. Alan brought in machinery and luckily for him, one of the workers retired and the other died out hunting, he accidentally shot himself. It is his, or was his gun that was stolen," Collins said.

"I am sorry; did you say he accidentally shot himself out hunting? With what, a rifle?" Julie asked, shocked.

"Again I was just a youngster at the time, I will get that file at the same time, I seem to remember that it was his handgun, but I will get the file, Ma'am," Collins said.

"Nothing is impossible, but it is not easy to shoot yourself with a rifle, especially accidentally, to be shot accidentally would be more to the point," Julie said.

"Do you suspect Alan Bancroft, Ma'am?" Collins asked.

"Not of the shooting, but there are some things that make my hairs stand. Can you pick a lock?" Julie asked him.

"No, Ma'am, I have never been trained to," he replied.

"See, with these two fine items, I will pick the lock on the door, now watch," Julie said.

She locked the door and then picked it while Collins watched her, it seemed so simple, then she gave him the implements and instructed him. Again he managed it, not as easily, but he managed it.

"Now look at the lock and tell me what you see?" Julie asked him and returned to her desk.

"Nothing, what should I have seem?" he asked.

"Exactly that, I am experienced, so would not leave a trace, but you a novice, look at all the scratches around the lock," Julie told him.

"There are none, Ma'am, what scratches?" Collins asked.

"Yet, at the farm there were scratches around the lock, why, a decent lock picker would not leave a mark and even an inexperienced picker would not, as you have just proven. Why assume the lock was picked because of the scratches? No finger prints is easy, they wore gloves, but then again the report does not say that there were none, does it?" Julie asked.

"No, Ma'am, it just said that the lock was probably picked, because of all of the scratches," he agreed.

"How well known is he to the forensic team?" Julie asked.

"He was the councillor who campaigned for law and order and he was on the police panel," Collins told her.

"By what you say he is well known to the forensic team. Who did the forensic tests on the lock, local officers?" Julie asked.

"Yes, as is usual, the call just went out as per normal procedure," Collins told her.

"I do not wish to cast aspersions against the team, but wasn't it a conflict of interests if they knew the victim?" Julie asked.

"I believe they should have backed down, in the interests of being seen to be impartial," Collins said.

"And I agree," Julie said, picking up her phone, "Simon, long time no speak, as it were, how are

147

you? Yes, I will not lie; I need a favour, how would you like to spend a day in the beautiful English country side, real ale, proper pub lunch and my company?

What do you mean, three out of four, isn't bad?" Julie was saying, laughing with them, "Yes, Saturday would be fine and then again you could come on Friday night after work and spend the weekend enjoying the country side. I have a spare bedroom, there would be no impropriety, in fact; I will even invite your girlfriend to make sure you do not get any ideas about my sublime body," Julie said, and laughed.

Collins could only hear one side of the conversation but it was obvious that they were good friends and work colleagues.

"I presume he is an old work colleague, from London?" Collins asked.

"She is and in my opinion the best forensic scientist in the Met, her name is Simone, but she is the male part of a lesbian relationship and to wind her up, I called her Simon and it has stuck, but beware, I, call her Simon, don't you try. She is one tough cookie and I have yet to work out whose fuse is the shortest hers, or mine,' Julie said in a light hearted way.

Rural England may be allegedly quiet, but that does not mean there is no crime. Over the balance of the week Julie and her officers investigated several incidents. There were three dog attacks on sheep, one burglary, two road accidents, two disturbances, (family arguments that got out of control). There were six shop lifting offences by visitors to the area. Added to this were several drunken offences leading to a brawl and driving whilst under the influence.

It was school holidays and the influx of visitors was welcome, but it inevitably brought in problems for Julie and her officers.

As usual Julie had her lunch in the pub, just a sandwich, which the Landlord gave her. He then made it known that a senior police officer was in the pub, which helped Julie by making people aware and to behave. So the sandwich was not free, as such, Julie and the Landlord, benefitted from it.

Her apparent free sandwich, was paid for on the Thursday, Julie was sat at her usual table, one where she could watch the pub and stood at the bar was a tipsy male. Another male joined him and then things began to change. Julie watched as it began; they seemed to be arguing about who was to be served next. Jim, the Landlord, did have it under control, or so he thought and then the one slightly more tipsy than the other pushed the other male and he began to move.

Julie was up in a flash and stood between them, her arms out, holding them apart.

"It is such a nice day, too nice to spend it in a police cell, don't you think? Chief Inspector Ashton at your service. Now shake hands, or I will arrest you under the public disturbance laws. The arrest is perhaps not the point, although upsetting, but to spend a day in my cells is not nice, when the sun has made an appearance," she said, smiling broadly.

"I was next and he pushed in," the one first at the bar said.

"If you wish to have another drink, you will do as I say," she told him.

"I am not buying a drink, I am here to pay my bill and I was speaking to the lady, not the man serving him," the other said.

"Jim, I will allow you to serve him with one more drink and then I suggest you suggest that he has had enough and ask him to leave. Any more trouble, call me and I will ensure he does not disturb your guests again by locking him up, in my cells. You will definitely not get a tan, in there," Julie said and went back to her table and her half eaten sandwich.

She watched as the men were served and the one paying his bill left quietly. The other man didn't seem to calm down, so Julie watched more closely.

He had not committed an offence as such and she felt she had warned him off, but it would not take much for her to arrest him. He drank his half pint quickly, which alerted Julie to problems, he was not finished yet. The way he made his wife and child leave was another sign she did not like, so she got up, thanked Jim and, still chewing her last bite of sandwich, she followed him out.

Her idea was that he would have the last drink, allowing the other man to get well away, but she had not allowed for his inflamed nature and his desire to seek revenge for the man, as he put it, pushing in. Quite a minor upset, usually dealt with by telling the person to join the queue, but he had been drinking and although Julie had felt it unnecessary to act before, as an officer, except to calm the situation. She now felt there was about to

150

be trouble and followed the man out into the car park.

"You fucking pushed in, you cunt, and spilled my beer," he shouted.

"Look, it's a nice day, let's forget it. I thought you were being served so I did not push in and I did not spill your beer. If I did, then I'll buy you another pint and apologise, but I never touched you. I would also appreciate it if you would control your language in front of my children," the other man said, stood by his car, his keys in the lock.

Julie moved quickly, seeing that there was about to be a fight, or punches thrown by the tipsy male.

She arrived just as the tipsy man threw a punch that was blocked by the other man. Before he could retaliate, Julie had the arm of the tipsy man up his back and face down on the boot of the car.

"I am arresting you for assault. You do not have to say anything that you later rely on in a court of law, anything you do say will be taken down and use in evidence," Julie said, as she put the handcuffs on him.

Julie pulled out her phone and rang the station.

"Chief Inspector Ashton, I require a patrol vehicle to the Market Hotel, to place in custody a man I have arrested for assault," Julie said.

"Hey, bitch, you can't do that! How the fuck are we to get home? I, cannot drive," the woman said.

"Madam, I warned your husband at the bar and he chose to ignore it. I am now proving my point, I do not make threats; I make promises. I suggest you

151

ask your husband how you are going to get home, because he is going to my cells, charged, with assault. The pub does have rooms and they are reasonably priced, there is a bus service to Bristol and a train service from there to London and various other places. Be thankful that he didn't take a punch at me, if he had, he would by now be on his way to hospital. This is a quiet town and I intend to keep it that way, hooligans, louts, and the vicious come here at their peril," Julie said.

She pulled him upright, away from the boot of the car as the patrol car entered the car park.

"D-do I have to make a complaint?" the other man said.

"A statement yes, but not a complaint as such, I saw the attack. So if you will be so good as to follow me to the station, I would appreciate it," Julie noticed he seemed unsure.

"Look, he tried to assault you and because his arm touched yours then it is assault, either way he is going to the cells for today. With a statement I can prosecute him, without one, it boils down to his word against mine. In that case, in the morning he will be released without charge. It is up to you if you wish to have him charged, or not," Julie asked the other man.

"I would rather enjoy the rest of our day here, Chief Inspector," he said.

"I understand and agree with your decision. Have you seen the parish church? It was one of the very few Catholic Churches spared by Henry VIII, perhaps he didn't find it, or according to popular belief, the villagers protected it from being destroyed when he fell out with Catholicism, erm, Rome, and the ceiling is a work of art, painted by the villagers, to celebrate it being spared. It is well worth a look," Julie told him.

The patrol car took the man away, and she got into her car, leaving his family stranded in the car park, there was nothing she could do for them. They were just other victims of his crime, as the perpetrator's families usually are.

The man demanded to see Julie and she decided to go to him.

"Look what about my family?"

"The cells do have a sobering effect on people. As for your family; I suggest you think about them before you act next time. With men like you, there is always a next time, you drink to excess and then start a brawl. I am sure your family do not wish to watch this manly display of bravado and fear you drinking to excess, because they know what will happen. It is too late to think about them now, the time for that was after me speaking to you at the bar. You will be held here until the morning, so I suggest you make a decision as to what you can do for them.

"As I see it you can stump up the cost of a family room at the pub, or the bus fare to Bristol and then the train fare home, depending on how far away you live. Then the room in the pub may be the cheapest option and by morning you will not be arrested for driving under the influence. See how much I have saved you, by arresting you, my other option," Julie told him.

"How much is the room at the pub?" he asked, now contrite.

"I can ask, a normal room is fifty pounds per night for bed and breakfast, the family room is obviously more expensive and there would be their evening meal, all in all say one hundred pounds for them to stay the night," Julie told him.

"My daughter sleeps with my wife sometimes, so they could share a normal room, couldn't they?" he asked.

"When is that, when you come home drunk and violent?" Julie asked.

"That has nothing to do with you," he replied.

"It has. You see, that is a crime, domestic violence is a crime, be careful, you are now on our radar, so what is it to be, the pub or the train?" Julie asked him.

"She will need to come here to collect my bank card to get the money for the pub," he said.

"No she won't, I will book her in and tomorrow I will take you to the pub to pay the bill with your card; that way I do not need to know your PIN, do I?" Julie asked him.

"Will he not want paying in advance, they usually do?" he asked.

"No, I will make sure he is paid. You will not be out of my sight until, it is paid and he will know that is what will happen, because he knows me. You do not and do not want to get to know me like that. All I need to know is; do you have one hundred pounds in your bank account?" Julie asked him.

"I do not have to tell you that," he said, trying to be bolshie.

154

"Then they can sleep on the streets and I will make sure the social services know what you are like," Julie said and got up.

"OK, OK, yes, I do," he told her sullenly.

"Good, I will make the arrangements then, I will need your wife's mobile number," Julie said.

Once she had it, she rang his wife and told her to meet Julie at the pub, where Julie acted for them, booking the last room. They were lucky, it had twin beds She booked them in for dinner, bed and breakfast and then gave his wife twenty pounds from her purse.

"Jim, add twenty pounds to the bill for me, please, I can't see them wandering about without any money," Julie said.

"Then allow me, I can do it as a cash back and saves you being involved," he told her, handing over the cash.

"You have the balance of the one hundred pounds if you need it, Jim will help you and he knows I will make sure the bill is paid, but no more than one hundred pounds," Julie told his wife and went back to the office.

"Ma'am, I heard you were a tough nut, broken bones, and the like?" Collins asked her.

"I do, but only when necessary, be careful, Collins," Julie replied, smiling at him, accepting the joke.

Chapter 13 - New Forensic Reports

Friday night and the desk sergeant rang Julie to say that she had a visitor.

"Simone, lovely to see you again and Madge, I am looking forward to a female weekend. I'm surrounded by males in here, can you believe it, three female, and that is all?" Julie said.

"No comment," the desk sergeant said in a disgruntled tone.

"I see they know you already," Simone said, laughing.

"No comment," the desk Sergeant said.

"I thought we could begin by quenching your parched throats at the local pub. Dan comes for the beer, Alex makes him work decorating my cottage, but he comes really for the beer and not to see me," Julie said, joking.

"Well, if it has his stamp of quality, then let's go," Simone said.

They left the station and went to the pub. Julie sat at her usual table after ordering two pints for Simone and Madge and a glass of white wine for herself.

"Julie, talk to me, why was it necessary although a pleasant one, to invite me down?" Simone asked.

"You are right; I need you as I said on the phone, to process a crime scene for me, mainly the padlocks. It is by now contaminated but I went this morning on a pretext to make sure the locks had not been changed. I would also like you to process the scene as best you can, knowing it has been contaminated. To say more would give you perhaps a direction and I do not want to do that.

Treat it as a crime scene and give me your report. As usual, I will tell you that a gun has been stolen from the property, hence the need for forensic evaluation," Julie told her.

"I can do that, but obviously the gun was not stolen last night, just how contaminated is the scene?" Simone asked.

"A couple of weeks," Julie admitted.

"A couple of weeks! Julie, there will not be anything left for me to examine," Simone told Julie.

"Erm, yes, there will, trust me. I do know most will be lost, but there is one element that will not be and that is where I need your expertise. As I said, to say more, to indicate where and why, would invalidate asking you to come, apart from looking forward to a very pleasant weekend together."

"Hum, so a morning working; followed by a weekend in the country, walking and sun bathing, I can live with that. You did pick the right weekend, Julie, wall to wall sun all weekend," Simone said.

"The hottest this year apparently," Madge joined in.

They had dinner and then Julie showed them to her cottage, which they loved, it was so picturesque and charming they fell in love with it immediately.

Saturday morning and after breakfast Julie took them to the farm and Simone suited up. She swabbed the locks and then looked intently at them

157

and decided that she needed to take one with her, the padlock on the gun safe. Julie, wise to her requirements had already bought a padlock, with which she could replace the one on the gun safe. Simone took one or two other samples and then they left.

Bancroft was not happy, telling them that the local forensic team had already been.

"Yes, they have, but they should not have, knowing someone involved they should have backed out to allow an independent team to investigate. Any evidence they found would be thrown out of court as biased. You do want to see the culprits caught and prosecuted, don't you?" Julie asked.

At that point Bancroft backed down, knowing that to say more would only make matters worse.

"Julie, this is what you want me to look at, isn't it?" Simone asked her.

"Why ask that?" Julie asked her.

"Picked, I do not think so, and I will soon have the proof. To make it appear picked, they were overzealous. Scratches appear on the inside which I will now check, but not usually on the outside, unless the person is clumsy and then there are scratches, not gouges. You knew, didn't you, but being new to the station, needed support, let Simone be mummy for you," Simone said, laughing.

"What are you now, a blue belt?" Julie asked.

"Yes, but I take my brown belt next week, then I will give you a match," Simone said, setting up her microscope.

"I would wait another three years before even trying, apart from the fact that I would lose in a contest. I do not follow the rules, I am army trained, so I win, to lose in battle means you lose your life, so I just win by any means. A kick to the groin and two fingers in the eyes is not allowed in a contest but in a street fight, anything goes," Julie said light-heartedly.

"I see now why they did not like you, in London, the powers that be, that is. The officers all liked you; they felt safe, especially after the incident with Dan. What was it, six to you, two to Dan, and you?" Simone asked.

"Something like that, don't tell me they still talk about it," Julie said.

"Some memories are long, as they should be, when you saved an officer's life. The rank and file still think you were treated badly. You and Dan could have cleaned up London single handed," Simone said proudly.

"I don't think so, but thank you. Actually, as you said wow at my home and the town I work in, it is beautiful and after the disappointment of being moved out of the action, I am getting to like it here. Tomorrow night William Smith will occupy a cell, he won't appear in court. He will just sleep it off and then be returned to his hut on the edge of the woods, where he lives.

"He is a very clever man, a professor in some science or other and quit the rat race. He can find magic mushrooms when there are none to be seen and has a skin full on Sunday, why, I do not know, but every Sunday he tries to drink the bar dry.

"Then there is Andy Pierce, he would like to possess the things other people have, he is not violent, he just likes to acquire nice things without paying for them.

"John Atherton, now he also like a drink, but does get violent and spends Friday night in the cells, as a rule, with a fine being imposed on the Monday. He does not hit out, he just threatens and breaks windows as a rule, public nuisance, crimes.

"Sally Nugent, she has had more men that all of us three have had dinners, hot or cold, the local prostitute. We tend to pick her up for soliciting once a week, she deserves a day off," Julie said, being glib, yet showing some of the characters of the town.

"So if there is a break in, you just go around to Andy's place, do you?" Madge asked.

"Yes at first, but he is not the only villain. What I am saying is that I wanted London or Manchester for the excitement, but now I have been here for a month or so, it would seem even this place is just as hectic in some ways and I need to use my brains, tact and skills more so. It has its own challenges which I never knew and I am enjoying them," Julie said.

"So do I take it that if you were offered a place in London, you would turn it down?" Simone asked.

"At this moment in time, I suppose I would. In London I led a team of officers, in isolation here I lead the community, not as the mayor or anything like that, but as part of the community if anything, I lead them in law and order and they know they can

160

rely on me. It gives me a warm feeling of belonging which I never felt in London," Julie said.

"Apart from the beautiful home you have," Madge said.

"And historic, archaeologists were called to the site oh fifteen… twenty years ago, so I believe and there was a mud hut on the site, obviously there was nothing left of it apart from different coloured rings in the soil where the posts had stood. Ladies, you are standing on ground that prehistoric man stood on and lived on," Julie said.

"This site has been a family home since Stonehenge, or before and is the size of a family hut and land. Big enough to keep an animal for milk and grow crops, vegetables for the table; the perimeter has not changed in all that time. This house was built, so I am told, around the time of Cromwell," Julie told them.

"But this padlock was not, these scratches are nothing to do with it being picked, as we agreed. Inside there are the marks say, left by the key, but under the microscope, there are no marks from it being picked. Chief Inspector, this lock was not picked," Simone told her.

"Did you find anything else?" Julie asked.

"Everyone holds a padlock in the same way, like so, to open it, meaning that any finger prints would have been over printed by subsequent users. In short no, nothing I could go to court with," Simone said.

"We are not in court." Julie said.

"My answer remains the same, sorry, Julie. Anything of use has been destroyed. I did dust the guns, and found a second set of fingerprints on the .22, but I could not find a match," Simone told her.

"That is interesting, was everyone printed for the purpose of elimination?" Julie asked.

"How the; would I know?" Simone said, gesturing openness with her hands.

"Because I told Collins to give you the list, for comparison," Julie said.

"He did give me a list, Alan Bancroft, his mother Helen Bancroft and that was it," Simone told her.

"What about Bill, the farm worker, erm, Bill, Bill,... Julie said trying to remember his last name.

"He was not on the list," Simone said.

"Then we need to print him as well. He works on the farm and has access to the gun cabinet. He cleans the guns after use, so he handles them and then puts them away. I will ask why such a prominent person was not fingerprinted, but for now we need to find him and print him," Julie said.

They went to his home and his mother told them that he was on the farm; Julie drove them to the farm and went to the field he was working in. There they took his finger prints then returned home.

"His fingerprints do not match the ones I found," Simone told Julie.

"How good was the print? I mean was the print smudged at all?" Julie asked.

"There were two and they were on the barrel after putting it away say, after cleaning, they were perfect prints," Simone said, with her hands showing how she thought they had been left on the barrel.

"We have been told that the gun was put away dirty and I suggested that he clean it, therefore they were put there after my interview with him, Bancroft. You did compare them to mine, didn't you?" Julie asked.

I do not normally because you wear gloves at the scene, but in this case, seeing as it was a few days later, I did and they were not yours, nor Collins, but I did find yours on the revolver," Simone said.

"Yes, I did handle that gun, a Webley shooting Master, a classic gun, in use by the British army since the Boar war," Julie said, smiling.

"You are the only person I know who can enthuse about a gun, nasty dirty, smelly objects," Simone said.

"I agree, Simone, but you have to admire the skill of the Gunsmith, one millimetre out and the explosion inside the barrel will not propel the bullet properly, allowing most of the gasses to escape. I also accept that a gun cannot kill, it is inanimate, only the person holding the gun can kill," Julie said.

"You have a point, I also accept that a gun, per se cannot kill, it is the shooter that is the killer," Simone said.

They tidied up and then went to the pub for dinner and a couple of drinks, Julie did not drink, but Simone and Madge did, enjoying the cask beers on offer.

"Excuse me, I hope you don't mind the interruption, but Colin Everet told me that you were looking for someone to help with the garden. I'm Granville from Meadow Lea Farm and I own the field behind you. We are planting a late crop of potatoes in it this year and when my son ploughs it ready for planting if you like, he will plough your plot and plant spuds. The crop will pay for us ploughing it and it will then be ready for you to seed it next spring, and there'll be a couple of bags of potatoes for you," he said.

"I don't know what to say! T That is very generous of you, Please, go ahead, I am not a gardener, so if you know anybody, please let me know," Julie said.

"I do, but now is not the time. It was just that my son will be ploughing that field tomorrow, so I needed to see you today rather than calling on you tomorrow. Potatoes are tubers and help break up the ground, preparing it for a nice lawn for you for next summer" he said.

"Great, feel free," Julie said, smiling at him.

"So he gets an extra acre of ground for his potatoes and you get your garden ploughed up. Get a rotovator, and in a weekend you can have it chopped up and then the next weekend seeded and a lawn by summer this year," Madge said.

"True, but that means that I have to work, this way they do the graft and I can relax," Julie said.

"Simone and I would do that for you," Madge said.

"Keep me out of it, Madge, I will be with Julie sipping a Martini by the side, watching you sweat," Simone said.

"See what I mean? Who in London would even offer to do that. I accept that he increases his crop and perhaps gets paid more than it would cost me, but it means more to me that I am accepted," Julie said.

They spent the Sunday walking in the woods, across the field Granville's son was ploughing carrying a picnic for lunch and then Simone and Madge set off for London around six o'clock that evening.

Monday opened with showers and Julie cursed that she had to walk to the road to collect her car. She would have a drive and garage built, but now it was too late, her land was full of straight ridges.

"Collins, bring Bancroft in and put him in the interview room. Ask him to assist us, but insist it is now that we need the help, not later," Julie told him as she entered the office.

Julie went to her desk, picked up her phone and rang the Superintendent.

"Ma'am, I have some very disturbing news and it calls into question the validity of the forensic reports. A principal person was not fingerprinted. The padlocks were not picked as in the report, and it is now too late to get any viable forensic evidence, to support any prosecution, because every crime scene will have been contaminated," Julie told her, Julie as usual did not hold back on her anger at the incompetence.

"Really, Chief Inspector, Monday morning and already angry. As I said I like frank and open people, but I do expect respect. What validity is there that these reports are genuine?" The Super asked.

"They were carried out by forensic scientists, not cowboys. I have three murders and not one scrap of forensic evidence that I can take to court. I am requesting that I use the scientists that can do the job in future. I do not want these cowboys anywhere near my crime scene," Julie said in a demanding tone.

"As I said, respect is a requirement when speaking to me. Your request, sorry demands, are denied, try again when you have calmed down," she said and hung up.

Julie walked up and down the office thinking and trying to calm down as Collins arrived with Bancroft and led him into the interview room, putting an officer on the door.

"Ma'am, Bancroft is in the interview room, he is not happy, he is busy seeding the fields and does not have the time to sit here," Collins told her.

Julie stood still, took half a dozen deep breaths and then led Collins into the interview room.

"Mr. Bancroft, thank you for coming in with DS Collins, we have one or two questions we need answers to," Julie said as she sat down and put the tape on, "Present are DCI Ashton, DS Collins and Mr Bancroft for the interview this is being recorded, but you are not under caution," she paused,, and then added, "Yet."

"Look, I am a very busy farmer especially at this time of year; we have a limited period to get the seeds in the ground. Will this take long?".

Julie smiled, "That all depends, Mr. Bancroft, on how honest, you are. You see, over the weekend I had a forensic scientist check the reports and she found that the scratches on the outside of the padlock have nothing to do with it being picked. Now scratches on the levers do indicate the lock having been picked, but they were absent, so the lock was not picked, Mr. Bancroft, who else, has the key?" Julie asked him.

"Who is to say that your so called forensic scientists are correct and the local ones are not?" He asked.

Julie smiled again, intimidating him, "I do. You see, when I first saw the padlock and the door lock with the scratches; I knew they were nothing to do with picking a lock. I have been trained in picking locks and how to check if a lock has been picked or not, but I do not have the qualifications, so I brought in someone who has and she confirmed my knowledge. Now we began in a friendly attitude, I am very happy to change that and arrest you for withholding information in a serious crime and then who would plant the seeds; with you in my cells, hey?" Julie asked him, leaning into him threateningly.

"I-I, OK, the gun belongs to Reginald Green as I told you, but I didn't tell you that I gave him a key so that he could get the gun whenever he wanted it," he said.

"Now on the .22, there are fresh fingerprints and they do not belong to you, your mother, or Bill the farm hand; so to whom do they belong?" Julie asked him.

167

"You have the padlock, anyone could have come in," he said.

"I see the promise has yet to sink in. I do not threaten, I promise, book him for perverting the course of justice; that is more serious than withholding information, far more, a prison sentence more," Julie said, and got up.

"Wait, wait, m-my girlfriend, she handled the gun," he said, ashamed.

"Why hide that? Most males do have girlfriends before they marry? Your mother told me that you were married," Julie asked.

"My mother is old fashioned and not happy with me living with my girlfriend so she tells everyone I am married. I do not want to upset her, she needs me and if I marry she will think I am moving away to a house in the town and that I will not be looking after her. At the moment I spend three nights a week with her," he said.

"I have seen your mother and she has a physical and mental illness, I presume some sort of weakness in her muscles and she is or feels, insecure. Why not suggest to her that with another female in the house, she would be better looked after?" Julie asked.

"Because I want a wife, not a nurse," he said.

"So, we now have a new face in the frame, don't we? Where can I find, Reginald Green?" Julie asked.

"Six feet under," he replied, being glib.

"I see and his wife?" Julie asked.

He looked at her, being glib had not fazed Julie, as he hoped.

"Under him, as in life," he said.

168

"Are you talking sexually or figuratively, you see, being glib does not help and it will take a lot longer to get the answers I want, delaying the seeding by far more than necessary. So answer the questions correctly and stop being funny, it only delays you from leaving the interview. D S Collins, caution, Mr. Bancroft, will you? We may as well get it formally on tape, seeing as he finds informally, funny," Julie said and left the interview room while Collins cautioned him and suspended the interview, for the tape.

Julie went to her office, something he had said sparked her imagination and she needed to check it. She picked up the list of the women who had left the town after the last accident and put it down again deep in thought.

"Ma'am, what is troubling you, can I help?" Everet asked, having seen her look at the list and then put it down, her brow furrowed.

"Reginald Green, what do we have on him?" Julie asked.

"I will have to get the file, Ma'am, I don't know the name," she replied.

Julie picked up her phone and rang the desk, "Sergeant Wilson, you have been here the longest, have you heard of a Reginald Green?" Julie asked him.

"Yes, Ma'am, he was the face foreman at the quarry, a nice bloke from what I can remember, he was never in trouble with us, a quiet man. He had two girls, what were their names now? It's on the tip of my tongue," he said.

"Sergeant, I appreciate your local knowledge, but I don't have time, so get me the file please, births, deaths and marriages, and anything we have on him, thank you," Julie said and hung up.

"Ma'am you still have furrows deep enough to plant potatoes on your brow, is there anything I can help you with?" Everet asked.

"No, no, it occurs to me that Collins is chasing females that left the village using their names as a starting point, but what if a female left and then married or married and then left?

"Is it possible for say a Miss Ashton to go abroad to marry and return as Mrs. Everet, but in a different town. This would mean that she would be lost in records, easy to track normally, but not when the crime was say, ten years old?" Julie asked.

"She would have to leave and enter on her passport, so could we trace her that way?" Everet asked.

"We could do, but not the way Collins has been tracking the females. He needs to contact the passport office for any females who have had a new passport with change of name in the last six years say," Julie said.

"Ma'am, what if she was a daughter, and married and moved away before the tragedy?" Everet asked.

"Then all the work Collins has done is probably a waste of time," Julie said, in a disappointed tone, "More to the point is, a female who is related, but left as perhaps as a young bride, twenty years prior to the incident, an auntie say, someone Collins is not even looking for," Julie said.

It was with her hand to her chin thinking about the age of the woman at Sir Andrew's house, who touched the wine glass, showing the waitresses where the glasses go.

It also crossed her mind that for some reason Lady Sophie, was the intended victim, but why, what purpose did it serve to upset Sir Andrew at the loss of someone, he loved?

Collins entered the office, beaming, "What has made you so happy?" Julie asked.

"My wife told me over the weekend that she is pregnant," he boasted.

"Congratulations. I'm so sorry to dampen your elation, well done, but I need you to increase the list of females to include any female leaving the town over say the last, thirty years," Julie said.

"Ma'am, that could make our killer say fifty years old, or older," he said, shocked at the increase.

"Putting poison in food or around a glass does not require strength; firing a handgun with practice, again does not require strength, a weak person aims for the lower body, allowing the recoil to bring the barrel up. The woman at Sir Andrew's house was mid-fifties, still not young, or as young as you have been looking at, but quite able to fire a handgun," Julie said.

"Yes, Ma'am," Collins said in a dejected tone, knowing the increase in the amount of work in the task, he had been set.

"Everet, I want you to stop looking into the angle that the partner was involved, it is a dead end. Instead help Collins track down these females, concentrate on women that left the village aged

171

eighteen to twenty; twenty to thirty years ago. Everet start making the list, Collins we have a silly man to question," Julie said.

They went back to the interview room; Julie slammed the file on the table and leaned on it threateningly.

"Right, you have two options, co-operate, or we have a nice cell waiting just for you, then how will your mother cope? I try very hard to be a nice person, but when faced with a person who protects murderers, I find it extremely hard, to impossible.

"I now know that you kept the gun for one Reginald Green, who is deceased, as is his wife, Mrs. Green, so who took the pistol. They had the key, didn't they?" Julie asked forcefully.

"I-I don't know, y-yes, they must have had the key, I saw it when I put the .22 back, but it wasn't there when I opened the case the next morning to clean the .22.

"Reginald asked my dad to keep it safe, because he wanted to use it on the management. My dad gave him the key to the gun safe, but not the door into the room, that way he could have access to his gun. He had to ask my dad for the key to the room, allowing my dad to make sure he was not about to kill someone, a safeguard, if you like. Then his wife died about a month after the second accident, which inflamed him, I mean he was ranting and raving at my dad about people being murdered for profit, basic safeguards were not in place. There were six holes in the perimeter fence, not one. Harnesses were not available; they hung from a rope when working on the face. Hard hats only arrived after the third death and, having lost his wife, Reginald was quite happy to die in prison. He argued with my dad, even threatened him, but my dad was a big man and easily kept Reginald at bay.

"It was felt, can I say; that he died of a broken heart for his wife and fellow workers who had for profit.

"I'm a farmer and know the value of profit and the necessity for it, but the owners were just greedy. They were happy for the workers to die so that they could increase their profits by not supplying basic, safety equipment.

"Seeing Reginald crying on my dad's shoulder had a marked effect on me, he was not soft, he was tough, a quarry face worker, like miners they are tough, it is hard graft," he told them.

"A good and moving story, but that does not answer my question, who has the key now? What about children, did they have any?" Julie asked, taking a different tack.

"Yes, a son and daughter," he replied.

"You were born in nineteen sixty two, making you forty three and as yet not married, why is that?" Julie asked.

"I have never met the right woman I suppose, my dad died when I was twenty four. I had girlfriends, but then when he died, being an only child and with a sick mother, I never got the chance to find a suitable partner, say, until six months ago." He had sadness in his voice.

"Could the key be with his daughter, and if so, how old will she be?" Julie asked.

173

"It could be, or it could have been lost and found by a stranger, who knows? She was born. let me see now, she went to the same school, junior as me and was in the year below me, so forty one or two," he said.

"If it was lost and found by a stranger, how would he, or she, know what it belonged to?" Julie asked.

"It wasn't a secret; everyone knew his gun was in my dad's gun safe, just like they knew when Granville bought a shot gun, he kept it in my dad's gun safe until he had one fitted. Chief Inspector, this is a small community and ten years ago it was a lot smaller, everyone knew everyone else's business. You have been here what, six weeks, and I know you are single, ex-army, ex-London where you caught a serial killer. You have had a Detective Sergeant Dan and his wife Alex to stay and recently a forensic scientist Simone, with her lesbian partner, to stay. There is as yet no gossip, well none to speak of, but give the town time, there will be, true or false," he said.

"The woman at Sir Andrew's house the day Lady Sophie was murdered, could she be Reginald's daughter? That is not widely known, but allowing for the jungle telegraph and your comment, I presume it is?" Julie asked.

"Yes, we know about the mysterious female and her description could fit Reginald's daughter, erm, Samantha, it is years since I last even thought about her. The son, now he was younger by what, six years, so as a child I did not really mix with him,

Gordon, that was his name. Now please, can I make sure my mother is alright?" He asked.

"PC Everet has arranged for a neighbour to stay with her, she is in no danger and Bill is there, but out in the fields. Thank you, Mr Bancroft, you have been very helpful, you may go home. Collins; arrange a car for Mr Bancroft, will you?" Julie asked and got up.

"Everet, begin a search for one Samantha Green, age forty one or two and so could be using a different name, being married." Julie told her.

"Ma'am, what about pressing charges against Bancroft?" Collins asked.

Julie smiled at him. "I am, or can be a bitch, but not that big a one, it would kill his mother, she is frail enough, so let him off with a police warning," Julie said.

"Ma'am, how did the person get into the room where the gun safe was,= if that was locked?" Everet asked.

"Everet, we try to be as human and considerate, as possible, whilst dealing with the scum of humanity. Bancroft's mother is very frail and he has been away for several hours, Think about her, not him, we know where he is and he is not about to run off. He is tied here because of his mother. We can always ask him tomorrow, he will still be here," Julie said.

Chapter 14 - Sir Andrew

The shrill tone of her phone woke Julie in the middle of the night.

"Ma'am, sorry to disturb you, but there has been another murder, Sir Andrew, shot," the desk sergeant told her.

"Who is at the scene?" Julie asked.

"PC Johnson, he decided to," the desk Sergeant began.

"Never mind that, I will speak to him later. Tell him to tape off the grounds and house, ring Everet and tell her to meet me at the house and I will ring Collins, Do not call forensics," Julie said.

She hung up, and rang the Super, "Ma'am, Sir Andrew has been shot. I want my forensic team to carry out the investigation and support to seal off the house and grounds," Julie told her.

"I have told you that I do not work well being dictated to by a junior officer," she said angrily, "First of all, how is, Sir Andrew?" she asked.

"The desk sergeant did not say that he had been taken to the hospital, or that an ambulance had been called, so I must conclude dead and hope he isn't. I did suggest that we keep the extra officers, Ma'am, with respect the forensic team involved in the break-in at the Bancroft farm was a debacle and totally incompetent, so I request Dr. Simone be seconded, Ma'am," Julie said, tight lipped, her anger at the failure being suppressed for now.

"I will authorise it and extra officers, but the ice under your feet is very thin, Chief Inspector, be careful," she told Julie, who then rang Simone.

"Simone, sorry to wake you, but I have another murder and want a forensic team, not a bunch of amateurs. My Super has authorised me to second you. I will seal off the area so you have an uncontaminated scene to deal with. Get here as fast as you can, please?" Julie asked her.

"Don't you need my boss's permission before you get me?" Simone asked.

"A formality, we do not have time for, my Super will deal with that problem, it is the least she can do. Now pack, come on, I need you here, now," Julie told her.

Simone knew Julie well from her time in London and she accepted that Julie could be aggressive and forceful even with friends so accepted the request made to sound like an order and woke Madge who helped her pack.

Julie knew it would take Simone three to four hours to get there, so she needed to make sure the scene was preserved. She drove to the house to see an officer stood at the front door.

"Good evening Ma'am," he said, saluting her.

"Evening, is anyone inside, Johnson?" Julie asked.

"Yes Ma'am, the live-in maid, Ma'am," he replied.

"He now has a live-in maid does he? Where is she?" Julie asked.

"I told her to stay in her room, Ma'am, to preserve the scene," he told her.

"Well done, Johnson. How come you were here so soon?" she asked him.

"I was on patrol, Ma'am, and decided that seeing as the extra officers had been withdrawn, I should swing around to just check on the estate. I have been doing this ever since the extra officers were withdrawn. I drive past twice each night," he told her.

"Good. Tell me what you saw, and heard quickly, be brief, I will read your report later," Julie said.

"I was driving past and heard a gunshot, or thought I had, so I drove up the drive, stopped, and got out to check the perimeter of the building. I saw a hole in the downstairs window and upon further investigation I saw Sir Andrew lying on the floor.

"I broke the window and opened the door, which sounded the alarm and I checked the prone figure of Sir Andrew and he was dead. I radioed in that he was and then his erm, live-in maid appeared at the door, she screamed and I escorted her to her bedroom, suggesting she stay there." he said.

Satisfied, Julie turned to go inside as Everet pulled up with another officer in a patrol car.

"Everet, you are with me, Simons, you are on the gate putting up the tape and stopping sightseers, Johnson help Simons and I want a patrol of the outer perimeter, as soon as more officers arrive," Julie told them.

Johnson gave Julie directions to the live-in maid's bedroom and she made her way to the actual scene.

Julie stood at the door and looked into the room. It was the library and between the door and the central table lay Sir Andrew, Julie surveyed the room, saw the open door Johnson had used and grimaced.

"I see the logic of breaking a broken window, but not in this case, that was evidence," Julie said to no-one in particular.

"Why, Ma'am?" Everet asked.

"The position of the hole and Sir Andrew's injury, the bullet hole, would be a guide as to where the shot came from. You need two points to create a probable line of fire. He is what, five feet nine inches tall and was shot in the heart, judging by the redness of his shirt and the tearing. The broken pane is at a slightly lower point, so the bullet was fired at an upward angle and from outside, or so it would seem," Julie said, still surveying the scene for possible clues without entering the room for the moment.

"Why do they shoot people in the middle of the night? I need my sleep," a short, stout man said. He was standing next to Julie.

"Why indeed, Doctor, could it be that the darkness hides their actions?" Julie asked.

"Possibly, but that does not help my sleep patterns. I presume I can view the body?" he asked.

"Yes, we are just trying to preserve as much evidence as possible, so if you would be so kind as to limit your actions to what is required at this point, I would appreciate it," Julie said.

He went with Julie to the body and began his examination of Sir Andrew.

179

"I would say, but please do not quote me; that it is a very lucky shot, or a skilful marksperson, the bullet entering the heart and shot from a distance. He is dead, officially, now. I will sign the death certificate as at one twenty seven, in the morning," he said, and got up.

"I hope you manage to get some sleep tonight," Julie said smiling at him.

"The Higgins baby last night, it was a problematic birth that kept me up half the night. I really must get a locum," he said wearily.

"I hope you do, I am not allowed one," Julie said laughing, as he left the room with a wave of his hand.

"Everet, I want you stood," Julie said looking around, "just there, so that you can watch the door and the French windows. No-one in or out," Julie told her.

Collins arrived just as Julie was exiting the room.

"Collins, so glad you could join us, what was it football, or practicing for baby number two?" Julie asked.

"Sorry, Ma'am, I went to pick Everet up, knowing she didn't have a car," he said sullenly.

"Everet is female; she very wisely rang the station to get picked up by a car, assuming that because of the seriousness of the crime that you would have the brains to get here as quickly as possible. But alas she forgot, you are male, didn't she, so even females are not perfect, just less imperfect, than males.

"My; that was sexist, wasn't it? I am angry, very angry, I warned the Super, I asked for extra help and this is the result of not getting it, so my underlings will feel my anger because I can't vent my feelings on my superiors," Julie said, fuming inside.

"Ma'am with respect, your superior is female," Collins said.

"No, she is just an accountant balancing the books, a sexless individual. In business they serve a purpose and are important, but in the emergency services, they hinder our work, a hospital ward closes, why, because they cannot fund it, not because there is no call for it. Not because it is no-longer needed, but because there are insufficient funds. To hell with the sick, we cannot afford to treat them, to hell with preventing crime and catching criminals, the damage they do, costs less than catching them so why fund catching criminals or preventing crime?" Julie said in temper.

Her emotions were running high, she knew he was to be a victim, but she did not have the funds or resources to do her job properly and that grated. Once again she was at odds with the powers that be and that was a fight she was determined, to win.

Julie and Collins went up to the live-in maid's bedroom, knocked, when she answered, they entered.

"Hello, I am Chief Inspector Ashton and this is Detective Sergeant Collins. We need to ask you some questions if you are up to it? It must have been quite a shock."

181

"Yes, it was, I mean he was just lying there, with that man kneeling down beside him," she said.

"You mean the police officer was kneeling down beside him?" Julie asked.

"Oh, was he a police officer? I didn't notice, I was, well am, in shock," she said.

"The man kneeling beside Sir Andrew, was he the man who escorted you to your bedroom?" Julie asked.

"Y-Yes, I think so, I have never seen a dead man before, or woman, I mean, I am in shock," she said.

"So you said, it is very convenient, this loss of memory because of the shock. What woke you?" Julie asked.

"Oh, I was not asleep; I was erm, well, getting ready for bed. Sir Andrew always checked the security before retiring. He made sure all the doors and windows were closed and locked," she told them.

"This is your room, is it?" Julie asked.

"Yes," she replied.

"Rather grand for a maid, don't you think?" Julie asked.

"In that context I suppose so, but there were only the two of us in this house so..," she said, leaving the sentenced unfinished.

"Madam, I am investigating several murders; I am not in the least bit interested in your love life, unless it leads me to the killer. Your reaction to the death of Sir Andrew does make me suspect that you are a live-in maid with extras. How emotionally involved were you with Sir Andrew?" Julie asked.

"I-I, what are you suggesting, I am shocked," she said.

"Look, this is a murder investigation and as far as I am concerned you are withholding information that could lead us to the perpetrator of this crime and for that I can offer you a compact room, Nuevo Riche, in the minimalist style. Do not mess with me. Were you having sex with him, and how long had that been going on?" Julie said angrily.

"We-we met in Cannes, six years ago, I was a waitress and we, well you know, and every month sometimes more often, when he could get away we spent the night together," she admitted, embarrassed at being found out.

"Thank you, so you had sex with him, yes or no?" Julie demanded.

"Yes," she admitted.

"And now; you look after his needs, is it just sexually, or do you clean for him, as well?" Julie asked.

"Erm, well, I do cook sometimes and help out a bit," she said uneasily.

"So when I ask the daily who comes in what you do, she will tell me that you cook a bit and clean a bit, will she?" Julie pushed her.

"Yes, Sir Andrew said that it would be more plausible if I did act like a maid when someone was in the house," she said.

"Then you failed, the whole town knows what goes on here," Collins said.

"Sir Andrew was about to divorce his wife, was it in favour of you?" Julie asked.

"I don't know what you mean."

"Was he getting rid of his wife so that he could marry you?" Julie asked bluntly.

"He hadn't said so, but he did love me so he could have been," she replied.

"Are you a natural blonde?" Julie asked, being glib, but the woman did not notice

"Yes," she replied.

"Collins, get the details, please, name, address, etcetera?" Julie asked him and left the room.

Julie was being glib about her hair colour; the roots were beginning to show through. She left the room, went outside and marked out an area where she suspected the bullet came from. She then began a search with her torch, hoping that the shiny metal of the casing would reflect in the darkness, making it easier to find than in daylight. Her knowledge of being a markswoman helped give her the angle and an approximate position for the person to be. She knew that to be stood they would have to be a dwarf to achieve the angle of the bullet and a lot closer than probable, being stood in the middle of the lawn. She decided that the tree line would have been her choice and prone. That was where she began to shine her torch and quite quickly spotted a probable target. Not wishing to disturb the scene she just noted where it was and went back to having a general look around. She noted points of interest, such as damaged wall areas for ease of access, flattened grass where a prone figure could have lain, assessing the potential of the point for the shot. Again from her experience she would have checked several positions before deciding on the one that gave her the best shot.

184

The library windows offered the clearest shot from a safe position. The bedroom windows were half obscured by the curtains and a shot from a tree is probably the worst position: leaves can shake obscuring the shot; branches can bend in the wind, no self-respecting marks person would ever use, a tree.

A level surface was the best position and the only place suitable was where she had found the casing, Sir Andrew was having extensive garden re shaping done and churned up ground seemed to be everywhere, in readiness for the new features.

Ironically it was a feature his wife had commissioned that he was destroying which made Julie question his wife's death, the motive. She began to wonder if his wife was the intended victim, but not by the murderer of the other victims, by Sir Andrew? If it was him then they did have two killers, but how to separate them, especially now he was dead?

Julie reasoned that she was the odd one out, the others were management of the quarry, she was the owner's daughter, so possible, but not totally probable.

He had access to the wine, the glass, the seating arrangement and most of all, who was to take the first sip.

The poison in the HP sauce was an anomaly, how could the killer be sure David Morris would eat the poisoned sauce? It was far too ambiguous and uncertain as to the accuracy, unlike a bullet, which was deadly accurate.

The extra officers had arrived and the scene was now secured, so Julie went home, back to bed to wait until Simone arrived, Julie had used the Super's embarrassment to get the people she wanted, because of the Super's order to withdraw the officers sent to protect him.

By nine o'clock in the morning she was back on site, greeting Simone and Madge, who doubled as Simone's assistant.

"Simone, thank you for coming so quickly, please follow me. We have two sites of particular interest, obviously the place he died and here. I spotted a glint in the torch light last night, which I presumed was the shell casing just over there. I also noted that the grass had been pressed down, indicating a prone position, which matched the angle of the shot, and trajectory, but it is my assessment, not fact," Julie told them.

"If we assume a six inch ejaculation," Simone said.

"Ejection is the word, you are looking for," Julie suggested.

"Madge, what is the word I am looking for?" Simone asked.

"Simone, you said that he was cute and you know my inclinations," Madge said, aggrieved.

"Sorry, Madge, Simone, you accepted her diverse sexual appetite when you got together," Julie said, trying to pour oil on troubled waters.

"Julie, the whole point is that she has to make up to me, and I can milk this one for a whole week," Simone said quietly, winking at Julie.

186

"Madge, the ejaculate should be one foot in front of you and two feet to your right," Julie said, now laughing at them.

"Do I need a ruler, or is it a guess?" Madge asked.

"I was stood here and it was fractionally to my right and from here, in line with the tree, does that help?" Julie asked.

"Not bad, you were out by six inches, I hope your aim is better," Madge said.

"It was dark and by the light of my torch. Madge, I didn't get up close, so as not to mess up your scene so that you could tramp, all over it," Julie said, joking with them.

"As you know, Julie, there isn't a lot we can get from here," Simone said, as Madge crawled around the site from Julie back to them to facing them and putting her hands up as if firing a rifle.

"I have a clear shot from here, although six feet back from the actual firing position. And as I suspected, here we have the stand indentations, the shooter was in the prone position and they had been here for a while," Madge said, moving forward to the actual firing position.

"I have to ask stupid questions; sometimes it is the only way I can get answers, any chance of DNA, or fibres?" Julie asked.

Simone joined Madge lowering their heads, and looking at Julie as if in shock.

"Julie, I mean there are stupid questions and then questions like that, even if the shooter didn't leave to go to the toilet and peed where they lay, which I am sure you accept as a sniper. The shower last night, the dew this morning and the fact that we would have to dig a two feet long by six inch wide trench to hopefully get a small sample for analysis," Simone was saying.

"OK, OK, I get the point," Julie said, realising just how ridiculous her question was and she turned to Everet, "I want four officers two feet apart to do a hands and knees search from here to the perimeter fence. I do realise I am clutching at non-existent straws, but do it. The shooter must have gained entry at some point, look for trampled grass, broken twigs, any signs of the ground, or plants being disturbed," Julie told her.

Chapter 15 - Some Clarity

"Collins," Julie called, "I want you to walk the external perimeter. It's not unreasonable for a sniper to walk the two miles from the village to here, but carrying a rifle, I doubt it. Walk this road; it is the only one that runs beside the perimeter fence. Look for tyre tracks or disturbed ground, somewhere a car could be parked. Take another officer with you."

"You rang, Ma'am," Dan said, bright eyed, and beaming at Julie.

"Dan, what the, - are you doing here?" Julie asked.

"I am your knight in shining armour, Ma'am. Having been asked to help this division, because they are short-handed, the Super asked me to bring a dozen officers to assist with your enquiries, Ma'am," Dan said, being overly correct.

"And you can stop that right now, or I will kick you all the way back to that great city in the north," Julie said, laughing with him, "It is great to have you here, Dan. How is Manchester?" Julie asked.

"The same, we had a recruiting drive and it was very successful, so much so that we had an excess of officers and seeing as this particular division was under staffed, they asked for volunteers to help out. I was perhaps the first in line. Alex can't join us, the girls are back now from their various trips and excursions to far flung places," Dan said.

"I would not call Southport a far flung place from Manchester," Julie said, laughing.

"She was there for three weeks before she came home on her days off and then had a suitcase, according to Alex, of dirty knickers and bras to be washed. Apparently the hotel she is doing her work experience in, washes the staff's uniforms for the live–in staff," Dan said, as if shocked.

"Dan, were you never seventeen? Why wash knickers when you can dance the night away instead?" Julie asked, smiling broadly.

"As long as it is only dancing, I remember well being seventeen and the things, I got up to," Dan said.

"Your girls are bright and know all about males and females and how to avoid complications," Julie said, now laughing at his anxieties.

"Well, enough of my dilemmas, what is going on here?" Dan asked.

"I am convinced that it is quarry related; Sir Andrew was the general manager when the accidents happened. All of the victims were middle to senior management, apart from the owner's daughter, she was just a secretary. But, she was the owner's daughter and the owner died a couple of years after the accident that closed the quarry, so obviously the killer could not kill him," Julie said.

"Apart from the question mark over her death being quarry related, wasn't Sir Andrew about to get divorced, dumping her? Her death would ease the financial burden on him, wouldn't it?" Dan asked.

"Yes, and as you imply, may not be related to the other deaths, but there is a link as well, so I am concentrating on the others as being all linked to the quarry, in one way or another. Once we solve those, then we can look at her death in more detail if it was not linked to the quarry, which we will find out once we solve the other deaths," Julie said.

"What I find interesting is the method; we have two killed by poison, one by a pistol and one by a rifle. Who changes the MO for every death?" Dan asked.

"A killer with a mission. They are using the most effective method available. Sir Andrew was told that his life was in danger and to avoid going out. So the killer could not get the poison into the house, and a close range shot was also out. Every person entering the estate was being checked, so it had to be a long range shot from the grounds," Julie suggested.

"You are the sniper, the ballistics expert, so why use poison for the other two?" Dan asked.

"Like I said; I am not including Lady Sophie fully, she is a probable, not a definite. David Morris, his death is so bizarre. I mean, she bought the HP sauce that morning especially for his sandwiches. How did the killer know she was going to make corned beef sandwiches for him and that she would need a new bottle that particular morning?" Julie asked.

"The answer lies in the question, they suggested it; David Morris and his wife did not decide to go to the quarry, they went because someone had said that they should. From the report they went to the pub the night before. Who sat with them, did anyone sit with them, or join them?" Dan asked.

"That's it, you can go back up north now; you have just solved my case," Julie said brightly.

"Do you mind if I sleep here tonight, before the long arduous trek back to the barren waste lands of the north," Dan asked.

"I will allow that, dinner in the pub tonight?" Julie asked.

"A great idea," Dan replied, "What do you want me to do?" he asked.

"The killer has to have come here by some means and carrying a rifle. Take some of the lads and do a house to house to see if someone saw a hunter coming this way. They will know by the rifle slung over his shoulder, or a car that is not known. Dan, this is such a small township that they know the colour of my knickers without asking, so I am damn sure they will know if a car not belonging to anyone has passed through the town," Julie said, laughing.

Simone came towards her in her usual professional walk, determined and direct.

"I have finished here, where is my lab?" she asked.

"I've set a room aside in the station and borrowed the equipment you will need, like a microscope," Julie said.

"Great, is it a micron, or gas powered microscope?" Simone asked.

"Simone, we may be in the country, but we are not in the dark ages. It is a normal one in the station, but a micron microscope at the central offices. The one in the station is electronic and linked to a computer. I already know it was a .22 bullet from the entry wound and there was no exit wound so how long before I have the bullet and the rifle?" Julie asked.

"Have the search team found the bullet casing?" Simone asked.

"Not yet," Julie replied.

"Then I cannot tell you the gun without the firing pin contact point on the casing and even then it is not a definite. And the bullet will be in my hands later today," Simone told her.

"Dan, you are with me, Everet, any place worth me sending Simone to check for evidence?" Julie asked, as she was walking towards them.

"Yes, Ma'am, about quarter of a mile in that direction there is a section of damaged wall and tyre marks in the dirt, I left PC Gordon standing by the spot to protect it," Everet told her.

Simone didn't need telling, she collected Madge who had just joined them and they set out for the spot.

Simone took a plaster cast of the tyre tracks and measured the distance between the tracks. The site was facing downhill and even though the driver had created a wheel spin to destroy the tyre tread pattern, they had rolled about a foot before the wheel spin, allowing Simone enough of the tread to make the plaster casts after brushing the debris carefully from the tracks. They also found flattened grass leading to the wall from the tracks created by walking on the grass and some blood on the wall, from probably a scratch.

Only the detailed and precise examination of the wall would have detected such a small amount of blood, Simone was, if nothing else, a precise, and exacting examiner.

They say that a person could get where water can't, well Simone was the type of person who could find that tiny hole.

Dan and Julie had arrived at the Bancroft farm and were being shown the gun cabinet.

"Mr. Bancroft, when was the .22, last fired?" Julie asked him.

"Oh, almost a week ago now," he replied, opening the cabinet.

Julie took the rifle out and sniffed at the barrel.

"Who else owns a .22 rifle in the town?" she asked, now looking down the barrel.

"Most of the farmers have a gun, Chief Inspector, in fact I think they all do, of one sort or another," he replied.

"Mr Bancroft, I asked specifically about a .22 rifle and I did not specify farmers. I asked; who else had a .22 rifle?" Julie asked with some force.

"It is a country town, and," he began. Julie jumped in.

"Mr Bancroft, you know me, or should do by now, shall we retire to the station, or will you answer my question?" Julie asked.

He relented and gave her a list of names which Julie took to the station and handed to the desk Sergeant.

"Cross check that list against licences, please, he was flustered and may have added a name without a licence, not thinking," Julie said.

They went to the office and sat at his desk was Collins.

"Well, Collins, do you have any news for me?" Julie asked.

"After the officers the Inspector sent to the houses leading out of the town; I sent them to the ones from the next town and they came back empty. No-one had seen anyone carrying a rifle or an unusual car, sorry, Ma'am.

"The pub has changed the list of guests twice since the murders started and no-one has returned; it was just an idea that they may not live in the town, or be staying in the town. So I widened the search area and I am currently ringing all the hotels, guest houses and pubs with accommodation, looking for a booking that stayed for the duration of the murders, or kept returning. And I am using a logarithm in the computer to check if a name comes up more than once," Collins said.

"How far afield are you checking?" Julie asked.

"I decided on a ten mile radius, assuming they have a car, Ma'am," he replied.

"And that is what, two hundred to three hundred possible locations?" Julie asked.

"Five hundred and counting, Ma'am," he replied disgruntled.

"Have you thought about being more focused? The killer has a connection to this town for the murders to be connected to the quarry. How many of the people who have left the town live within that radius?" Julie asked.

"I did think of that and Everet is looking into that aspect, Ma'am," he said, Julie smiled.

"See, Dan? Country folk we may be, but bumpkins, we are not. Like I said, I have a good team, but there is no doubt in my mind, it has improved, tremendously. Have you unpacked?" Julie asked.

"No. I wanted to get caught up on the case, but my suitcase is in my room and I am booked in," Dan said.

"What did you make of Bancroft?" Julie asked.

"I didn't get the feeling he was the murderer, or associated with the murderer; he is a fool perhaps, allowing a key to his gun safe to float around unchecked, but the safe itself is secure. I think he knows more than he is saying, he is protecting a friend, or someone he has feelings for, more of empathy than friendship," Dan said.

"I got the same feeling, I don't think he helped them take the gun, but I do think he knows, or suspects, who has taken the gun and they are a relative of someone who died at the quarry, so as you say, he empathises with them and is protecting them," Julie said.

"Brian Tindall, he also knew them, or knew of them, a son or daughter, or close relative of someone, who died in the accidents and as you have already begun, does not live in the town.

"Taking the radius Collins is using, how many ex citizens of the town, live within that radius and who are related to someone who died, at the quarry?" Dan asked.

"None that we have found. That was our first step, which is why Collins is now looking at the hotels, etcetera. Poison is predominantly a female choice of weapon, as you know, but we did not rule out a male killer. Unlike a male who dies with the name he is born with, as a rule, a female usually changes her name when married, which has made our search for a viable killer more difficult. The first two were by poison and led us to believe it was a female killer," Julie said.

"But now that the weapon of choice has changed; you are not as confident. It also begs the question, is it a serial killer, or a revenge killing, which from reading the reports you always assumed it was revenge and for what it's worth; I agree. I believe it is linked to the quarry and in particular, the death of the child, a distraught older sister, auntie or even mother," Dan said.

"I agree, but why use a gun? It is most unusual for a female killer to use a gun; a knife in a fit of rage has been known, or poison as you said, but a gun?" Julie asked.

"Says the sniper, why not?" Dan argued.

"Point taken, so they are army trained, perhaps?" Julie asked.

"Julie, we are in the country, guns are common place to control vermin. I accept it is usually the male who uses the gun, but a female can also use one," Dan argued.

"Ma'am, there has been a shooting, Colin Musgrave, the finance director, the gunman missed. He was wounded, though, and has been taken to the local hospital," The desk Sergeant said, entering in an excited manner.

"See, gunman, I rest my case," Julie said as she put her coat on.

They left the station and made for the local hospital. They asked at the desk and the nurse said that he was in surgery.

"I need to know what the prognosis is. Is the emergency doctor available, whoever saw him when he was brought in?" Julie asked her

"She is with a patient at the moment, I will ask her to see you when she is finished," the nurse said.

"Do you know where he was shot?" Julie asked, trying to get as much information as possible as quickly as possible.

"Not exactly, but in the side, lower abdomen," she said.

Julie creased her brow, questioning the aim of the shooter.

"Dan, why take such a low shot? Say he ducked, then a shoulder wound would be what I would expect, for it to be lower abdomen, they were aiming for his leg, why?" Julie asked.

"Julie, let's speak to the doctor. What if he was jumping up, then it would have been a chest shot, wouldn't it?" Dan suggested.

"No, there was a friendly match this weekend between two local town teams and he was one of the players. Six of my officers were on the team and they asked for the afternoon off and I saw the team list, I am sure his name was on it as the goal keeper. Collins was to be the Captain, then again, I haven't seen him for a few hours now. I did sanction the time off for them so we have an officer, on site," Julie said, somewhat excited at the prospect of getting a clear statement from a serving officer.

"So why are they not here?" Dan asked.

"What? This is the match of the year, Over Hampton has won for the last four years, it is the equivalent to Man City winning for four years against Man United, or Liverpool winning for four consecutive years against Everton and there would be a blood bath if it was cancelled.

"Officers at the ground will have given chase; he is not dead; so they will have treated it as an injury. But my officers will take statements from any witnesses and by the game continuing, the crowd will stay put, while the statements are being taken. Come on, Dan, Man united about to win against Man City after four lean years, the game must go on," Julie said boldly.

"Well, if it were Chelsea against Arsenal, the game would be abandoned," Dan said.

"But not if it was England versus the West Indies at the Oval, get to know your Chief Super," Julie said and laughed.

"I have to agree, especially if there was any chance of England winning, I do know my old Chief Super," Dan said, laughing with her.

They moved to the side to wait for the doctor to get a more detailed report and chatted about the case generally as they waited until they heard the clump, clump of boots, on the tiled floor.

"Ma'am, how is he?" Collins asked.

"Never mind that, this is a hospital, a clean environment, go and get showered. Look, you have left a trail of mud all the way to the door. Follow it out and come back clean, by then we may be able to answer the question," Julie told him and added, "Well?"

"We won 2-1, his save was magnificent and stopped it being a draw, their forward was twenty meters out and slammed the ball at the goal; it was on target, Musgrave took a dive and caught it right by the post and six inches off the line. It was beautiful, saved our bacon, Ma'am," Collins told her.

"Was that when, he was shot?" Julie asked.

"Yes Ma'am, he is a hero," Collins said, and turned to leave.

"Back here in ten minutes. To save time, don't bother with the make-up, Collins," Julie joked.

"Ma'am," he replied ,smiling at her.

"Make-up, Julie?" Dam queried.

"Females shower, dress and put make-up on, half an hour. Men shower and dress, ten minutes, a private joke, one Jones would understand, as well," Julie said ,smiling at Dan.

"Jones, as in, undercover, Jones?" Dan asked.

"As in bait, I read his file, as we do, and three years ago there was a spate of females being attacked, sexually, so they used him as bait and when he was attacked, they caught the swine. He is now serving twenty years for multiple assaults on women and two murders of women. Like Jones, he was the only officer that was close enough to fit, the profile," Julie informed him.

As Collins reappeared, the doctor was approaching them.

"How is the patient?" Julie asked, after introducing herself, and Dan.

"He will be fine, more of a flesh wound, another two inches and they would have missed.

The bullet entered here between the pelvis and the rib cage, in the fleshy part and from the back. It just missed the descending colon, clean through and through. We will keep him in for a couple of days just to be sure, but he will be up and about in a week or so, once the stitches are out," the doctor told them.

"I am glad to hear it, the bullet, sorry, a through and through, you said?" Julie asked.

"I hear he saved the match; what was it, ten minutes from time?" the doctor asked Collins.

"Yes, it was beautiful," Collins said smiling.

"Collins, nice to see you scrubbed up, now go back and find me that bullet, please," Julie asked him.

"Ma'am; can I spend two minutes clean, before going delving into the mud again?" he asked.

"Hum, it will have to be a fingertip search to find the bullet, so seal the ground off and let's look at the statements to see if we can localise the search for you," Julie said, laughing at him.

"The country suits you. In London it would have been, are you still here? Or why are you not on your hands and knees in the mud?" Dan asked.

"Dan, you really must start ear-wigging, they have just brought in a football player with a badly bruised ankle and I want to look at his shin pads. It occurs to me that a .22 bullet has spent most of it energy going through a waist and then falls down hitting a shin, not penetrating because of all the spent energy going through the waist, but still enough energy to cause bruising especially when

201

the shin is protected by a pad," Julie said, giving him a cheeky smile.

They moved to the area where the injured football player was and asked to see his socks and shin pads.

The nurse gave them the items and Julie began examining them.

"That has saved Collins a mucky job hasn't it, Dan? See the bullet," Julie said holding it up, "It was lodged in between the sock and pad," Julie picked up the bullet from the floor with tweezers and dropping it into an evidence bag.

"I have noticed, as I am sure you have that in every case, there is a second motive. Lady Sophie, was it revenge or to save divorce costs? Brian Tindall, revenge or, well not everyone, David Morris, revenge or a jealous wife, did she know he had had an affair? Sir Andrew, revenge for the quarry, or his late wife's lover's revenge. Now we have Colin Musgrave, is it revenge, or is it to win a football match, especially if it is such a grudge match? They are all weak, I admit, but it does beg questions," Dan said.

"It does, as does the weapon, male or female? The only consistent motive is the connection with the quarry, which is why I am concentrating my efforts in that direction," Julie said, "The shot was fired at his leg, I am convinced, but because he dived to save the ball from scoring the goal. He dropped lower, bringing his waist now in the line of fire. A bullet travels at one thousand seven hundred miles per hour, on average. Now to dodge a bullet once you hear the bang, if fired from five hundred meters away, even an Olympic sprinter would not be fast enough to dodge the bullet. Working on that basis, the bullet was fired as he made his move to save the goal and the shooter was at least five hundred yards away.

"Think about it, stood, it would have hit him high up in his thigh, he was preparing to move, crouched down ready to save the goal, now it would hit him say in the lower back, pelvic region and as he dived they fired, now moving him stretched out and at an angle, so the contact point changed again, to his waist and the opposite side. No matter how you look at it, it was not a kill shot, why?" Julie asked.

"I was with the group you trained in fire arms, as you know, and you said to aim for the body, a head shot is too difficult to be sure you find your target. Now the leg is thinner than the head, so again why shoot for the leg? There is too great a chance of missing. If you hit the femoral artery then you have what, three minutes to get it seen to? As you said in the tutorial, aim for the body mass, yet another anomaly?" Dan queried.

"That is a good point, not that I had missed it and it is very relevant. How did they know the poison would kill the intended victim? In both cases there was a strong element of chance," Julie said.

"It is my turn to buy dinner at the pub tonight?" Dan asked.

"It will be packed, I was going to invite you to mine, for dinner," Julie said.

"That was why I suggested it; the whole village will be there for us to ask questions. Did the

Tindalls mention their trip to the quarry and that they were taking sandwiches and needed to buy HP sauce? Loose lips, sink ships," Dam said.

"Walls have ears, not that I remember those days, unlike you, Dan," Julie said laughing, and moving away.

Chapter 16 - A Night in the Pub

The match was an annual event, it was played well after the football season was over, which seemed very odd, but as with most traditions the reason had been lost in the past. It was said that after a battle between Cromwell's army and the local royalist army, the winners, the royalists in this case, kicked the severed head of the losing general up and down the high street. It was a match between the farming community and the town's residents, but it was folklore, not fact, or was it?

Dan and Julie went to the town fish and chip shop and got fish and chips, which they ate in the car before entering the pub. It was as Julie had been told; standing room only and that applied to the beer garden as well. There were two more pubs in the town, but this one seemed to host this event, perhaps because it was the only one that could accommodate the town's folk and several of the neighbouring team at one time.

Julie and Dan began their move, circulating and congratulating the winning team and commiserating with the losers. From that evening they managed to find out who was in the bar the night before the Tindalls went on their trip and who was closest to them. Dan also found out that one of the crowd at the match; had seen a flash, a sharp flash of light from the tree line, behind the goal.

This was repeated twice more to Julie and Dan as they circulated, they all said that it was as, or just after, he threw himself at the ball, but it was at that point, in time.

By eleven o'clock, they felt they had heard as much as they could and left the party still in full swing. Dan went to his room and Julie drove home, it had been a tiring day from early morning till late at night, and Julie and Dan had been on the move the whole time.

Julie was showing the effects of a very long day the next morning as she arrived in the station to see a bleary eyed Dan sat at her desk.

"Well, I don't have one, yet," he said, smiling at her.

"Dan, I am getting too old for twenty four hour sessions. Eight hours sleep and a lukewarm shower and still not sure I am awake," Julie said.

"I know the feeling well and from the looks of things, we are not the only ones. Good morning, Collins and Everet, good night?" Dan asked.

"Too bloody good, we actually drank the pub dry; then again there were almost the residents of two towns drinking, some celebrating the others drowning their sorrows. The match is just the precursor to a bloody good drinking session, more the excuse, I think," Collins said.

"And what about you, Everet, sober enough to face the challenges of the day? Whilst you two were drinking the pub dry, we were busy working. We have here a list of twelve people who heard the Tindall's talking the night before they went on their trip to the quarry. We are interested in what they mentioned about their trip and who was sat close enough to have also overheard their conversation.

You two are not fit to drive so, Everet, you go with Dan and Collins, you are with me," Julie said, putting on a smile and energetic voice she had to summon from the depths of her being.

"Ma'am, both towns are closed today to recover, can't we take advantage of the break?" Collins asked.

"We are police officers and spring into action whenever it is needed and it is needed, now," Julie said.

"Julie, we are human also and I couldn't spring if my life depended, on it," Dan said.

"Ma'am, I saw Andrews adding a whisky to the Inspector's drink, how many I have no idea, but I saw him adding at least two. It was meant for the Captain of our team, but I noticed the Inspector picking up the beer the Captain had ordered, by mistake, two beers ordered side by side," Everet said.

"No wonder I feel so rough. I do not drink shorts," Dan said.

"So, no-one apart from me; they didn't add anything to my drink, did they?" Julie asked.

"No Ma'am, you were the only one drinking orange juice, I am sure it was an accident that the Inspector got the spiked drink. They were so busy, they pulled pints and put them on the bar without checking that the right person got the right drink," Everet said.

"But you noticed, and said nothing," Julie said.

"Not really, I did not hear what was ordered and presumed they got the drink they ordered, only now when the Inspector looks ill has it registered, that it was a possibility," Everet said.

"Then this morning is cancelled. Back here at one o'clock this afternoon to begin interviewing the people on the list," Julie said, formally, but inside she was glad of the chance to catch up on sleep.

Julie left the station and looked up and down the high street. It was deserted, just as Everet and Collins had said, it was a ghost town, even the mini supermarket was closed and that opened Christmas Day, three hundred and sixty five days a year it opened, but not today.

Julie went home and back to bed, setting her alarm clock for twelve o'clock.

She got up, showered, got dressed and left for the station. She was the first to arrive and sat at her desk. On it was the report from the autopsy. It read that Sir Andrew had been shot from a distance with a .22 rifle, the bullet had caused a sharp forced entry to his off left chest cavity, penetrating his heart and was the cause of death, which was instantaneous.

The forensic report for Sir Andrew's death was not yet in, but Julie already knew where the shot came from and that the casing found at the scene was a .22 bullet casing.

As she expected, the ground gave up no other clues because of the rain and dew that had fallen, washing away any evidence. It didn't dishearten her, because it was as she had expected, but it was a disappointment that they seemed to be no further forward. She also noted that the bullet removed from the goal keeper's side was again a .22 bullet, she guessed fired from the same gun. Ballistics would confirm that later. She mulled over that it seemed a bit extreme to shoot the goal keeper to win the match. Then again these inter-town matches were more intense even than inter-club matches from the same town. Inter-club matches were played with players from far afield, these inter-town matches were played by local residents and the pride of the town was in their hands so, far more intense, yet called friendly.

Julie began to wonder about the shot, where exactly it was fired from, was there some obstruction that prevented the gunperson from making it a kill shot? If so, why take the shot? Julie was professional and would never have taken a shot that was not a kill shot; it was pointless to her to waste a bullet. If the objective was to kill all the management team from that point in time; then why not take a kill shot? This bugged Julie; she could see no rhyme or reason for the action taken.

"Afternoon, Ma'am, thank you for the morning off; I feel a lot better and ready for action," Collins said as he entered the office.

"Afternoon, Collins, here, take this list and put numbers down the side and then photocopy it, give one to Everet and you take the odd numbers. I will ask Everet to take the even numbers. Oh, and ensure you are fit to drive, if not, take a driver with you, you will need a PC to accompany you anyway," Julie said.

"Are you not joining us, Ma'am?" Collins asked.

"No I am going to try and find the position of the shooter with Dan, starting at the football ground," Julie said.

"I see, by the way it will be the cricket ground by this evening, Ma'am ready for the match against Over Hampton on Saturday," Collins said.

"Will it be another grudge match?" Julie asked.

"Oh no, Ma'am, it is the local league match. You do know why yesterday was a grudge match, don't you?" Collins asked.

"No, I do not, something about kicking a head up and down the high street," Julie said.

"That's correct, Ma'am. You see, back in the times of the civil war, Little Hampton was royalist but Over Hampton was for Cromwell and the two towns had a battle. Obviously Little Hampton won, like yesterday," Collins said proudly.

"One win in five years, not a lot to brag about, is it?" Julie asked.

"Well, when we won the battle we chopped the head off the general on their side and played football with it. I think it was for like four years the town celebrated the win, kicking an imitation head up and down the high street. Now it is a football match. By the way, we have won six times over the last ten years, so we still are the best side, Ma'am," Collins said.

Julie smiled at him, accepting his pride in his town, "Six times, and how many goal keepers have been shot over the last ten years?" Julie asked.

"This is the first, but it is not unusual for the battle to begin in the changing rooms, several bloody noses have been seen entering the field and black eyes, Ma'am," Collins told her.

"I am so glad to hear it is a civilised affair," Julie said ,being glib, and added, "Will it be necessary for me to put extra officers in attendance for the cricket match?" Julie asked.

"No Ma'am, as I said, that is a league match, as the football matches are in the season, it is only this one match when the whole town goes mad. Next year it is away for us," Collins told her.

"Basically, it is an excuse to get paralytic drunk and start fights," Julie said.

"I suppose so, but in the reverse, we fight, then play and then get paralytic. It is like the actual event, they fought the battle and then played with the head and then after the war, they became friends again, so it is a re-enactment, if you like," Collins said.

"I do not cancel the fights and enjoy the match and the drinking. It is your liver you are injuring," Julie said.

Julie gave Everet a list and they both set out, as Julie and Dan set out for the football field now converted into a cricket field.

Julie and Dan entered the field and made for the goal area, Julie stood approximately where the goalkeeper had been shot and looked out at the open field to the tree line. She asked Dan to stand where she had stood and made her way to the tree line, then looked back. Satisfied she was in the right area; she called Dan over and then began the painstaking work of looking for signs of where the shot had been fired from.

Dan found what he felt was a potential place, because of the flattened grass. Julie joined him and smiled.

"Well done, Dan, see here the bark has been scraped? The shooter stood here and with the recoil, they scraped the barrel against the tree," Julie said, smiling at their luck, "Now, from here I can see the whole of the field, but that branch keeps blocking my view. As a professional I would remove it, it would make little difference to anyone finding my position, the grass is flattened where they stood for quite a long time. There is the scrape on the bark and probably a bullet casing, so chopping off the branch would mean little or nothing, but to the sniper, it was a problem.

"It was such a big problem that when the branch blocks the view you automatically bend down to see below it, happening as I presume it did, at a critical point, and you miss," Julie said, eyeing up the position.

"I can see your point, but you are hidden and with a camouflage suit on; that branch creates the perfect cover," Dan said.

"I agree, so you have to make the decision, cover or ability, I would choose a different spot, one that meant that I could, or would be successful, rather than cover. Come here and now look, success, and not as much cover, but adequate, just six feet away, so why choose that spot?" Julie asked.

"I have no idea, but I am sure they had a reason, like where to rest the gun over there, there is the branch to rest the gun on, steadying it," Dan said.

"I am glad to see you are awake, now what does that tell us?" Julie asked.

"That the killer is not a good shot?" Dan asked.

"Perhaps more so that the killer is not used to holding a rifle. They hit Sir Andrew perfectly but they were in the prone position and with a stand, here the prone position is not available being on a slope and with that mound of dirt in the way, so they needed to be elevated, hence the branch as a prop," Julie said.

They both got down on their hands and knees and began to search through the grass for the casing, moving carefully and slowly towards the position.

"Julie, is that what we are looking for," Dan asked, indicating a spot.

Julie used her pen to lift it up. "No, this is a forty five casing and it is weathered. It has been here for a few months by the look of it, but that there is what we want," she said, pointing to a casing almost touching where the last casing had come from.

"Glad I could be of help, Ma'am," Dan said, joking.

"Ha, you help, a degraded old casing you pointed to, not the nice shiny new casing half an inch away," Julie said ,joking.

"It goes with the territory, allowing the boss to find the casing, I just gave them the location by indicating an old, casing," Dan said.

Julie sat down and looked at the casing; Dan put rubber gloves on and lifted it off the pen.

"Hum, it appears to me to be the same gun, the indentation from the firing pin is in the same place, just off centre," Dan said, using his expert voice.

"Is it just below, or above the centre line?" Julie asked glibly.

"That all depends on which way you hold the casing, Ma'am," Dan said, laughing.

"As you said, it is not the position of the indentation, because not all the bullets are loaded positioned the same way, but there are minute differences to every firing pin and ballistics will be able to tell if the same gun was used," Julie said, smiling at Dan; it was good to be working with him again.

Dan dropped the casing into an evidence bag and put it in his pocket. They got up and made their way back to the field.

"Dan, where was the witness who saw the barrel flash?" Julie asked.

"About where you are," he replied.

"Then how come no-one else saw it? This side was quite full of spectators, so why was she the only person to mention it?" Julie asked.

"All the action was in the goal mouth, so it follows that the crowd were looking in that direction, so why didn't they see, the flash?" Dan asked, reinforcing Julie's question.

They left the field and caught up with Everet as she was about to knock on a door.

"Have you spoken to Mary Hawthorn yet?" Julie asked.

"No Ma'am, I am working logically down the streets, rather than following the list, to save me going back and forth," Everet replied.

"Good, sensible, Dan and I will have a chat with her; you can cross her off your list. I want to know if anyone saw a muzzle flash, if they do not mention it, then ask the question directly. It seems strange that the whole of the crowd were looking in that direction, yet only she mentioned it, odd, don't you think?" Julie asked her.

"Ma'am, not really, she was on the force and is perhaps more observant. I was at the match. I didn't see it, but a fight broke out, well, not a physical fight but an argument and it was intense, that made me look away from the action, to ensure it didn't end up in, fisticuffs. A player said that our man was offside and the linesman said he wasn't.

"Our goalkeeper saved the ball and then kicked it right down the field, Andy, our forward, headed the ball to Greg who then scored and the player argued with the ref that Greg was off side. They went back to the middle and restarted, but the player was still in an argumentative mood and went to the linesman to continue the argument, having failed to win with the ref. The player grabbed the linesman by his shirt and that was when the shot rang out, just as I was about to go and take control, so I didn't see the flash either," Everet said.

"I see, so you think the crowd's attention was taken off the game by the altercation?" Julie asked.

"It is an explanation as to why, but a lot of them would still be watching the match. These rifts are quite common; it is as if they will do anything, to avoid defeat. This year's match was quite civilised by comparison, last year there were broken bones, erm, one arm, one leg and two noses, I think," Everet informed her.

"Next you will be telling me that was just at night in the pubs?" Julie asked.

"No, Ma'am that was on the pitch, as you saw, at night it is party time, all friends again, the battle ground is the match, Ma'am," Everet said.

They left Everet to her job and went to Mary Hawthorn, they knocked and she answered the door, inviting them in.

"Please, have a seat, Bill, put the kettle on. I have been expecting you," she said.

"Yes, I have just been told that you were in the force and the point you indicated was perfect, perhaps as I should have expected from a former officer. Were you based at Little Hampton?" Julie asked after introducing Dan and her.

"At first as a junior officer and then when I had cut my teeth, as they say, I moved to the Met up in London and stayed there until I retired as a Sergeant. I was the first female officer to be trained in weapons. I think it was more being politically correct than anything, they needed a female to be trained in firearms to balance the books, as it were," she told them.

"I see, so you would notice the muzzle flash, because of your training?" Julie asked.

"Being trained as a police officer taught me to be observant. I see, as I am sure you do, things other people wonder if they saw it, or not. Ah, the tea, thank you Bill, Bill is my husband," she said, introducing her husband to them.

"Were you at the match, Mr Hawthorn?" Julie asked.

"I think it would be easier to ask who was not at the match. Grundy, he has a cow in labour and called the vet out, she was having a hard time with it and Harris, he is late planting and had to carry on seeding, or miss the crop. Apart from those two everyone in the town was there; oh, and you, four murders in a small town like this must be keeping you very busy," he said.

"Did you see the muzzle flash?" Julie asked.

"Yes, but my wife told you about it, so there was no need for me to mention it," he told them.

"There is, if only to corroborate Mrs Hawthorn's statement. I don't seem to have your statement, yet my officers interviewed everyone at the match, at the ground. Why don't I have your statement?" Julie asked.

"I am ex British Army Medical Corp and I was in the ambulance with the patient, I am not a doctor, but rendered first aid. I was the idiot who ran onto the battle field unarmed and rendered first aid to the wounded, to try and save their lives," he said.

"I see, so you were not on the field when the officers were taking the statements. Dan, will you do the honours, please?" Julie asked.

Dan got up and took Mr Hawthorn to the next room to take his statement.

"Sergeant Mary Hawthorn, yes the mists of time are clearing; I saw your photo in a magazine as the first female officer to be qualified as a firearms

217

officer. They were promoting the force for female officers, equal rights and all that," Julie said, Mary smiled.

"I never did like that photo, it made me look fat," she said.

"Have you seen the current lot with all the body armour? A size six looks like a size ten," Julie laughed.

"There's not a lot I can add to my statement," she said.

"No I have read it, and it is pretty concise and precise. In relation to the pitch, where were you stood?" Julie asked.

"I was about ten feet nearer to the goal, from the centre line, our goal in that half and on the road side," she said.

"That would make it that the tree line was on your right and the barley field on your left, is that correct?" Julie asked.

"Correct," she replied.

"You had an unobstructed view of the goal mouth and the tree line. Did you see anything to help identify the gunperson?" Julie asked.

"I am sorry, perhaps when I was in the force; I may have spotted something, but at my age, the eyes are not as good as they used to be. That field is relatively small, by today's standards, long and narrow. Even so, the person must have been a good two hundred and fifty yards away and at that range I would be lucky to tell if it was male, or female, just a blur, an indistinguishable shape," she said, giving Julie a smile.

"Do you wear glasses?" Julie asked.

"Yes, just for reading," she replied.

"Was your husband on your right, or your left?" Julie asked.

"My left," she said.

"I find it quite odd that you were the only person to mention the flash, in the statements, can you offer any reason for this?" Julie asked.

"I would assume, that because the game was so intense at that point, all eyes would be on the goal mouth, it was my peripheral vision that saw the flash," she said.

"Not the altercation between the linesman and the player from the other side?" Julie asked.

"Again, that was not in full view and it happens all the time, to not so much cheat, but gain an advantage, so we tend to ignore it," she said.

"But you did, see it?" Julie pressed her.

"Yes, we all did, and ignored it, as I said," she said.

"What I don't understand, is with them pressuring your goal, why one of their players was not involved, but arguing over something that had happened two, three minutes earlier?" Julie asked.

"He was not involved, they had substituted him, but arguing with the linesman meant that he was not where he should have been. Like I said not cheating, just gaining an advantage," she said.

"Was that so that they could cheat, by taking his eyes off the game?" Julie asked.

"It was and always will be, tit for tat. I have seen thirteen players on the field for one, or both sides. It is not the game, it is a re-enactment of the battle, but without guns and swords and as they say, all is fair, in love and war," she said.

"Clarity at last, it is a free for all, using a football as an excuse," Julie said.

"With some rules, I mean they do not allow weapons onto the field of any description," she told Julie.

"But fired from the tree line is acceptable?" Julie asked.

"No, that was nothing to do with the football, they would not stoop so low," she said.

"It did only wound him and you did say, 'anything is fair in love and war,' didn't you? Had he not made the dive to save the ball from going into the goal, it was a leg shot and not intended to kill, so it could be as you said fair, being a war, couldn't it?" Julie asked.

"If you put it like that it is possible, but I do not believe it was. We do have morals bent perhaps for the battle, but not broken. Can I get back to you: I will make enquiries just to be sure?" Mary asked Julie.

"This is police investigation, I cannot allow you to investigate a crime," Julie told her.

"I understand, but I know people and a friendly chat will yield far more than a heavy handed police, investigation. Trust me; I do know what I am doing. I will have the culprit in your hands within twenty four hours, if it is because of the match," Mary asked Julie.

"Twenty four hours is all I can give you, but I will need names, and addresses so that I can verify your conclusions. I will also assure you that I will do any checks unless you feel I have been heavy handed?" Julie asked her.

"No, definitely not, I can live with that," Mary said, adding a smile for reassurance.

Dan and Bill re-joined them and Julie thanked them for their help and they left.

"I am not sure I have acted correctly, but I have accepted help from Mary, tell me I am not a fool, Dan," Julie said.

"You're not a fool, Julie, an idiot perhaps. Why on earth did you accept, her help?" Dan asked being glib.

"She is an ex-copper; she knows the locals and how to approach them. I got the feeling that she is the messenger for the jungle telegraph, if not, 'The jungle telegraph," Julie said, laughing.

"You know, Julie, it would not have taken much for it to have been a kill shot, or to have paralysed him," Dan said as they drove back to the station.

"Dan, from that position the gunman was lucky to have hit him; it was an amateur shot at best. He, or she, was more concerned with being hidden than being accurate," Julie said, as they parked the car and got out.

"Far be it from me to argue with an expert, but-" Dan said.

"Dan, how far is it from your thigh to your heart, two, three feet? A miss by an inch is unlucky perhaps, but two to three feet, is poor marksmanship," Julie said.

"I accept that but what if the shot was accurate and intended to injure, rather than kill?" Dan asked.

221

"Mary Hawthorn is going to find that out for me, hopefully. Did Mr Hawthorn, shed any light?" Julie asked.

"Not really he saw the dive and the save and then heard the bang and the goal keeper didn't get up. The players shouting alerted him to the incident and he ran over with his first aid bag and rendered first aid until the ambulance arrived, then he went with the patient to the hospital," Dan told her.

By the time they arrived back at the office it had started to rain, the clouds had been building up and it was expected, but not the cloud burst, thunder and lightning that greeted them as they ran to the station.

It was a relatively small station with the front desk and then behind a door at the back of the front desk was the main office where all the detectives worked, beyond that there were two interview rooms and down below were the cells, all four of them. Off to the left was the dining area and canteen, with the changing rooms behind that area.

Julie as the Chief Inspector had her own office on the floor above, but she preferred to be in the action and spent most of her time in the main office. Recent cuts in budgets had reduced the force by a quarter, making several desks available for her to use.

Dan also commandeered a desk in the area, although he also could have had his own office.

Julie felt that the powers that be had panicked when the death of Sir Andrew had been announced and drafted in a dozen officers to assist in the enquiry, but the culprit seemed to be a ghost.

Forensic evidence was at best, sketchy, there seemed to be no direct motive. In almost every case there was an alternative motive, which was thin, but could not be ignored.

It occurred to her that they were all linked by the deaths at the quarry, because they were all middle to high management at that point in time, but the killings did not portray the signs of a serial killer.

Usually a serial killer would select a particular type of victim, say, a female with blonde hair that reminded them of their lost love, Here there were female and male victims, their ages varied, their hair colour, the only commonality was that they were management at the quarry when the accidental deaths occurred. This said to Julie that it was revenge killings, rather than a serial killer.

Everet and Collins were in the office working on reducing the residents who had left the town since the deaths, trying to make the list as short as possible before beginning interviews with the suspects.

Chapter 17 - A Lead

"Ma'am, I have one here that looks interesting, one Miss Vivien Ashton, sister to the boy that was killed. She emigrated to America with her new husband one month after the boy's death.

"They left on her new passport, she changed her name when she got married to Collier, taking her husband's name and she came back to England last month, when the argument about the re-opening of the quarry was building up steam.

She slipped under our radar because they divorced and she re-married, so entered the UK, in her new husband's name, Ramashkin. It has taken us quite a bit to get the information, because the foreign office had to contact their American cousins, to find out the details of her change of name," Collins told them.

"I don't suppose you know their whereabouts at this moment in time, do you?" Julie asked.

"No, Ma'am, they are touring Europe and have visited France and Spain, so far. Again it is with thanks to immigration, we have that information. What flagged it to me was that they visited the UK, then went to France and then came back, before going to Spain, which is where the trail ends, so I suppose I do, somewhere in Spain," Collins said.

"Do we have dates as to when they were in the UK?" Julie asked.

"That I do have and they were here at the time of all of the deaths, hence the gap, England for the first three, Lady Sophie, David Morris and Brian Tindall, then in France and back for Sir Andrew and Nigel Croft, and now Spain," Collins said.

"That is very interesting; she most certainly has a good reason to want them dead, so we have motive, but what about means and opportunity?" Julie asked.

"Still to be investigated, they were in the pub when the Morris's were talking about their trip to the quarry and sat close enough to hear them, according to one of the witnesses I spoke to. They flagged up that it was her, which led me to investigate what had happened through the Foreign Office, they stayed at the pub, but under Ramashkin, as you would expect," Collins said.

"Ma'am, one of the people I spoke to mentioned her being there, as well. It was more out of sympathy for her losing her younger brother like that. She was twelve when he was born and she looked after him more so than his mother. She always did like her booze, according to my witness," Everet said.

"Why do I get the feeling there is more to this than you are saying?" Julie asked her.

"It is hearsay Ma'am, so not valid as such, but so it goes; she married and had Vivien, her husband was killed in Iraq and she took to drowning her sorrows. Twelve years later, sorry, eleven, say, again in a drunken stupor, she had sex with a man unknown and little Tommy was the result. Vivien was twelve and because her mother was, well, never seemed to be sober, she brought up, Tommy," Everet said.

"That raises a question, was Tommy going to go with them? She was more of a mother to him than his biological mother was. If not then it feels odd that she would desert him like that?" Julie asked,

"My source didn't say, but I will check," Everet said.

"Does this mean that we now have a viable suspect?" Dan asked, knowing that was what Julie, at least, was thinking.

"Call it maternal instincts, from what Everet has just told us, the mother never bonded with her child, it was an inconvenience because of a drunken, randy night, but her daughter did bond, because she was the one looking after it. I believe that it was her maternal instincts and that she was the one that felt the loss of her child. It doesn't sit well with me, but I can see the mother bringing the child home and dumping it on the daughter and picking up the bottle.

"At twelve she would in all probability be starting her periods, growing breasts and growing up rapidly. The maternal mother would abandon the baby, never really wanting it and because of the drink, not have any feelings for it, as such, being more interested in the booze," Julie said thinking allowed.

"I see what you are saying, Ma'am, but having gone through the birth, wouldn't she at least have some feelings for the child?" Dan asked, being correct, because he was in the station.

"In all probability, but repressed by the desire for alcohol. It is a very strong drug when you are an alcoholic, like a drug addict who steals from their parents. They do have feelings for their parents, but stronger feelings for their fix. Their family become just a bank to beg, borrow, or steal from, to get their fix," Julie said, pacing up and down the office as if in a daze, as she considered all the options.

"I accept that being from America they have easy access to fire arms and a few pops say, at a target and they feel good, but they would not be allowed to carry one on the plane. so how did they get the rifle?" Everet asked.

"Ask the Chief Inspector, a few hundred yards away from Heathrow, if you knew where to go, there was not just a dealer but an arsenal. It took Serious Crimes two years to get sufficient evidence for a search warrant, but when they did - boy, was it a bust, every firearm you can mention including two RPG's and ammunition," Dan told her.

"They had supplied most of London's underground and gangs; every weapon was allegedly, untraceable until they made one and now the leader is serving life, I know the group you mean, yes, they were on our radar when I was there. Weapons are not that hard to come by, if you know where to look. Everet, how would you like to kill me? Say, I can be a right bitch, can't I? Bossy and over bearing on a good day," Julie asked her.

"I-I wouldn't say that, Ma'am, you have helped me a lot, and I appreciate it," Everet said.

"Then you have yet to see the real Julie, in action. I mean you have passed your detectives exams, and you are still a PC. Why hasn't she moved you, is it because she is a right one, holding you back?" Dan asked Everet, but adding a smile.

"I see, well putting it like that, probably," Everet said, taking the inference.

"Oh yes, I can be, now tonight you would be advised to go to the Dog and Duck, obviously not in uniform, but very angry, about a slave driver of a boss. Who shall we say has just sacked you, because you needed to visit your seriously ill husband, in hospital? She also has just bought a new car, a Jaguar, and cut your wages by twenty five percent, money you rely upon.

"I would suggest that you ask at the bar for a slim line gin and tonic and when the bar man says, "Don't you mean a gin and slim line tonic," you smile and say, "I know what I want." You will then be contacted, and you will buy a forty five magnum with a clip. It is undercover, and you can refuse, but Dan and I will be in the pub having a drink and then arrest the person who gives you, the gun.

"Uniform have asked for our help with this and it fits nicely into our plans because the seller may be the person we are looking for, who supplied, the rifle. We know where the handgun came from, even if there is still a question mark over how they got it, but that we can deal with, later," Julie said.

"What time do you need me to be there?" Everet asked.

"Early evening, say seven o' clock," Julie said.

"I will see you there then, obviously I will not acknowledge you," Everet said.

"Draw five hundred pounds from petty cash and barter, stick to your guns, oh what a pun, sorry about that," Julie said, laughing.

"Is five hundred enough, Ma'am? I would have thought they cost a lot more," Everet said.

"In London, perhaps, I think he will start at say seven hundred, but we also believe he offers a return and disposal service, for a fee, obviously. That is when you offer the balance, another five hundred after the job, to dispose of it. He may ask for more and you agree, or to have the job done for you; do not agree, you must buy the gun for the prosecution to stick. I think he may have disposed of the rifle for the gunperson, which is why you walk out of there with the gun and hand it to me," Julie told her.

"Ma'am, I am willing to do it for you, but I am not fire arms trained, so is it legal?" Everet asked.

"Can we say we are bending the rules a little? You will have possession of the gun for less than ten minutes, just the time it takes for you to walk to us in the car park and hand it to me. I will be observing you the whole time and I am trained," Julie said.

"Then may I ask why don't you do it?" Everet asked.

"Point one, never ask if you can ask, because in future I will say no, you cannot ask, but this time I will answer the question. It is because my picture has been in the papers as a Chief Inspector, yours has not," Julie told her.

"Why not just ask for a hand gun for a lady, isn't a Magnum 45 a powerful gun?" Everet asked.

229

"Yes, very powerful, but it is also the gun that Bancroft lost and I would like to see: one, where he dumped it, two, if he dumped it, and three, if it was stolen, or handed to the killer. We know a third party had a key to the safe, but did they also have a key to the door, which was allegedly locked, and picked," Julie told them.

"I see, many birds with one stone," Everet said.

"Indeed, I will test fire it and then have a miniature tracking device fitted and you will return it, so that we can find out where or how he disposes of the guns. I suspect he does not, he resells them. Ballistics have several bullets from unsolved murders in the areas around here and they were all by a .45 the same gun," Julie told them.

"How come there are live people around here then?" Dan asked.

"This is a large patch, because the dwellings are sparse, there is about the same number of people in the area as in a district of London. The crime rate is lower here, but villains can travel from London to here to commit their crimes and we have local villains as well, so all in all we are not that far short of a similar crime rate to London," Julie told them.

"Being such a large area, how long would it take to attend a crime here?" Dan asked.

"If we take your fight, they would be long gone before I got to you. Taking the four and a half minutes it took me to arrive say, times it by six, so about twenty minutes, if I were on the far side of the patch. The forensic team work hard, but lack the equipment and can be bought, or persuaded not to look as deeply as Suzy and Madge will," Julie said.

"Has their report come through?" Dan asked.

"Yes, I was just reading it; they have a finger print from the shell casing, but no match on file," Julie told them.

"Makes sense if it was the sister, she left before she could commit a crime, or had committed one, perhaps, and his would not be on file, being American," Dan offered.

"Let's call it a day, Dan I will pick you up at half past six, it will only take fifteen minutes to drive there, it is in the next town and we will have a drink in front of us when Everet arrives," Julie said.

"Julie, isn't it dangerous using Everet? She could be recognised," Dan asked as she drove him to the hotel.

"No, she came in from a patch outside the area to increase the CID in the area but the old Inspector was sexist and delayed her move from uniform to CID. He retired and I was sent. When I arrived, I thought she was new to the police force, but I was wrong. I can be occasionally, very occasionally, she was new to CID, and has been here for four months now, as I found out when I read her file. I think he was asked to retire a few months before his time, a good officer, but as I said, sexist, which does not fit the profile of the modern police force," Julie said.

"Why does that remind me of someone I know? They tend to bend the rules; which again does not fit the profile, but are very good at their job," Dan asked.

"Ha, point taken, see you at six thirty," Julie said, laughing.

Chapter 18 - Undercover

Julie arrived to pick Dan up. He was waiting for her outside his room. The rooms were in a long, low two storey building, his was on the ground floor, and his door led outside.

It was a balmy night and he was enjoying the night air and the smell of the flowers that lined his door way. As he waited another guest walked past him and spoke, he was now engaged in conversation with them as Julie pulled up.

He made his excuses and made for her car.

"I can't take you anywhere, who was that?" Julie asked.

"Just another guest and his wife they're touring England for their holiday. They're from America, on their way to Hastings tomorrow to see the battlefield and castle and then on to London, before going home. Typical American, going anti-clockwise around the country, arse about face," Dan said, joking.

"Do you have a problem with Americans?" Julie asked.

"No, not in the least, apart from them being over-paid, over-sexed and over here, they are just fine, in America," he said.

"Didn't your grandmother marry one, an American airman in the war?" Julie asked.

"No, an American is my grandfather, but he didn't hang around long enough to see his daughter, or for that matter marry my grandmother," Dan told her.

"I see, so we avoid any conversation involving Americans, do we?" Julie asked, "Your mother and grandmother did a good job of raising an awkward sod like you," Julie added, laughing.

"The awkwardness is inherited from my Grandfather and I can prove it, look at my eldest, and then the youngest, the eldest inherited the awkward streak," Dan said, adding to the joke.

"That's just growing pains as she becomes a woman," Julie said, laughing.

"When we enter what are we, husband and wife, lovers?" Julie asked as she pulled up in a parking space.

"Boss and secretary, on a dirty weekend, mid-week," Dan suggested, being funny.

"Can you type?" Julie asked, inferring he was to be the secretary and laughing.

"Twice as good as you; I at least use two fingers," Dan replied.

"Just good friends on a night out is probably the best option," Julie said, Dan laughed and agreed.

They entered and looked around. It was a typical man's pub, dart board, pool table and tiled floor. The only thing it lacked was the acrid smoke floating around from all the pipes and cigarettes.

A portly barman looked at them as they entered, Julie smiled at him and sat at a table by the door while Dan did the gentleman thing and ordered their drinks, an orange juice for Julie being the driver and a pint for himself, which he brought back to the table and smiled at Julie as he placed her drink in front of her.

"What I do for the job," Dan said with irony.

"You complain; what about my dress, sat on these grubby seats?" Julie said and smiled.

"Ha, you can wash your dress; these trousers have to be dry-cleaned.

Julie took another look around the place. By the bar were two men drinking pints and over by the dart board was another man with a pint in front of him. She noticed that the barman was helping himself to a pint and then went to the two men stood at the bar and began to chat to them.

A few moments later Everet entered and looked around before going to the bar and ordering her drink.

Julie and Dan could not hear what was said but it seemed to go as planned. She ordered and he questioned it and she made the reply, then he got the drink for her and she went and sat at a table three down from Julie and Dan, as he had indicated and then he went to the phone.

Five minutes later a man entered and called out, "Taxi for Everet." She got up and left the bar.

"Not as we expected," Dan said quietly.

"No, so we wait until she returns," Julie said.

"What if she has been recognised?" Dan asked.

"I doubt that, had she been, then they would not have carried on with it. I need the ladies," Julie said, and got up.

She walked to the bar and followed it to the far end, she stopped and looked around as if lost and the barman went to her. It was obvious to Dan that she asked for the ladies and he told her where it was and she went, then came back to Dan.

"By the phone there is a card for a taxi firm, 'Alan's cabs,' I am sure he read the number when Everet made her enquiry. So I asked for the ladies, making my way to the point where I could read the card," Julie told him quietly.

"I noticed that as well, but how will they know when it is for a taxi and not guns?" Dan asked.

"Simple, a new number every week and they do not ring the firm, but a mobile number for a person, who has a disposable phone, once used, he will throw it away," Julie suggested.

"You have a good point, just one driver working for Alan's cabs and they are contacted by phone. It could be that Alan's cabs are the dealers and one or two of their drivers are the contact point," Dan said.

"I like that even better, the dealer is now remote and the deal is done over the radio by secret code, perhaps. This means that Everet will come back with nothing, apart from an expenses chit for a taxi ride," Julie said.

"And a gun and to get it she will hopefully meet the actual dealer," Dan offered.

"No, the driver will take her to a place and collect the gun while she is in the cab. The only person she will see is the driver, but she may know the location for a raid later," Julie mused.

"You'd better get another round in, she may be a while," Dan said.

"Oh you are so gallant aren't you, what is it?" Julie asked.

"Lager tops, to help disguise the taste," Dan said.

"They do have beer on tap," Julie told him.

"Yes, but judging by the state of the place and what the locals are drinking, I'd rather play safe. Real ale has to be looked after and from the state of the place, I mean if you can't keep the public area spotless, what chance have we got with the cellar? Real ale is alive and has a limited life, lager is sterile and sealed, so I would rather, play safe," Dan said.

"What is the top for?" Julie asked

"Taste," Dan replied begrudgingly.

"Hurry and drink up, Everet is back," Julie said peering out of the window.

Everet entered the pub and went through to the toilet and then walked out, Dan smirked and left his pint on the table.

"Don't you think that looked odd, us both leaving our drinks?" Julie asked.

"I am sure everyone but locals, would do the same. To say that place is the pits would raise it, in my estimation" Dan replied.

"I have seen worse places, but not that much worse," Julie said.

"How did it go?" Dan asked Everet.

"Very well, I have a .45 in my bag and two clips of ammunition. He took the five hundred and wants seven hundred to dispose of the gun. He wanted to know who it was for and if I had ever fired one before. I said that I was ex-army and had fired one before and it was for my cheating husband, to which, he said he needed my husband's name," Everet told them.

Julie smiled, "Got it, he will check the newspapers for the death being announced, as a safeguard. If we do not put the death in the papers, then he will suspect something and it will be dangerous for you to return it," Julie decided.

Whilst they were talking Everet handed the gun to Julie, with the clips and then got in her car. She left the car park, turning to the left and they left, turning to the right. Everet had taken the shortest way back and Julie the longest way back.

The exercise had gone well and Julie was now in possession of an illegal gun. After dropping Dan off she went home and put the gun in her safe and then went to bed, happy with the evening.

The next morning she got up and after breakfast took the gun to the ballistics laboratory, where she test fired it into the tank and retrieved the bullet. She handed it to the scientist and waited whilst he checked it for striation, and then against unsolved crimes.

He handed it back to her, smiling, Julie then drove to the station.

"A very good night, team, this gun was used in six crimes, two murders and four armed robberies, where the gun was obviously fired. By the day after tomorrow we will have the tracking device, which I am assured will look like a bullet and will sit in the clip. That is the gun, Everet, what about the person?" Julie asked.

"I don't know what you hoped for, but he took me to a deserted warehouse and told me to wait in the cab after I had given him the money. He then went inside and came out with the gun and handed it to me wrapped in a cloth. As told to, I slipped it in my handbag and he brought me back to the pub. I didn't get the impression that he was the dealer, more a courier and I doubt that the guns are stored at the warehouse, more of a collection point, making everything once removed," Everet said.

"This means that we have the little fish, but not the big one we wanted. We have yet to return the gun, and see what happens then. How is it to be returned?" Julie asked.

"Easier, I just ring the taxi number I was given and ask to be taken to the pub. I leave the gun in the cab and go into the pub for a drink and then I can book a taxi home if I wish, or walk, he told me with a smirk. I suppose that gives then time to get clear away and check if the murder has been reported," Everet said.

"I would think so and to make sure they are not being followed, hum," Julie said, a furrow appeared on her brow as she considered what she had been told.

"What is the range of the transmitter?" Dan asked.

"Only about a mile, it is powerful, but a mile at thirty miles an hour is only two minutes which is not long enough to avoid detection and an eye in the sky is just not warranted for this operation," Julie said, considering her options.

"Would, say, three minutes, help?" Dan asked.

"Obviously, but how to get three minutes? Even then to avoid detection we would have to be very careful," Julie said.

"My next door neighbour's son has a drone and he is good, what if I ask him if he will fly it for us? It isn't something you can just do, it takes practise," Dan offered.

"Do we not have a drone, Ma'am, and pilot?" Collins asked.

"We do, but I would have to apply for the use of it and that can take weeks. To be fair, this is not a high priority in the scheme of things, being a small time gun runner, when in London there are much bigger fish to fry. Dan, we would be taking a civilian on a raid, which is somewhat frowned upon, if not downright illegal and against any, and all regulations," Julie said, liking the idea of a drone, but not taking a civilian on the raid,

"Then we will have to do a full and thorough risk assessment of the raid," Dan said.

"It has legs, shall we say, but I am very nervous. Dan, you do the risk assessment and plan it for Friday, four days away. They will not expect you to hang onto the gun for too long, but they probably will accept that you have to bolster your courage, so not do it immediately, a week at the most, perhaps?" Julie asked rhetorically.

"I thought a drone had to be in sight to be able to see where it is going, apart from military ones which have cameras?" Julie asked.

"In the broad sense you are right, but his dad works in a factory where they make the larger drones for military and commercial use and an

239

operator of a small drone can operate a larger one. The controls apparently are basically the same, it is just the range that is farther," Dan said.

"The army use pilots to fly the drones, the controls are not the same, are they?" Julie asked.

"Let me make all the enquiries. Drones vary in size, for a combat mission I presume they need a pilot, but a larger yet small drone does not. I admit I am making an assumption, but let me ask the question?" Dan asked Julie.

"There is no harm in asking, I can always say no," Julie said and Dan picked up the phone.

"Ma'am, I did notice that he had the radio tuned in to the police channel and was listening to it," Everet said.

"We know that the pistol used to kill Tindall was a Colt 45, and that this pistol is not the same one. So we must presume they still have the gun and that the rifle used to wound Croft was a .22 which also has not surfaced, but could have been supplied by our mystery taxi driver, being the local gun dealer.

"I think it is time we had a more serious chat with Mr. Bancroft," Julie said and picked up her phone, "Sergeant, send a car around to the Bancroft farm and bring him in, wearing handcuffs, arrest him for withholding evidence and trying to pervert the course of justice, by withholding valuable evidence and put him in the interview room, then tell me where he is," Julie said and put the phone down.

"Ma'am, can you arrest him for perverting the course of justice? Isn't that more of a court room thing, withholding evidence yes, but not, perverting it?" Everet asked her.

"Blur the lines, but never prosecute when you do," Julie told her.

"Is it just to frighten him, then?" Everet asked.

"Use your judgment. Our last chat was just that, it was not under caution, but this time it will be. So it would be thin ice if I was to prosecute, but after this interview I will have a case for withholding evidence and lying under caution," Julie told her.

It took the officers sent to collect and arrest Bancroft half an hour. The desk sergeant told Julie he was in Interview Room 3.

"Mr. Bancroft, I must caution you than anything you say will be taken down and used in evidence against you in a court of law and that you do not say anything that you later rely on in a court of law.

"Present at the interview are Chief Inspector Ashton, Detective Constable Everet and Mr Bancroft.

"Mr Bancroft, you said that the door to the outside of the outhouse was locked and that the lock was picked, is that correct?" Julie asked him.

"Yes," he replied.

"You also told us that the lock to the gun safe was picked, do you wish to change that statement?" Julie asked him.

"No," he replied.

"So you are saying that both locks were picked by a person and or persons unknown to you, is that correct?" Julie asked.

"Yes," he said.

"Then I say you are a liar, forensic tests have shown that neither lock was picked. Who has the key to both the outer door and the gun safe?" Julie demanded forcefully.

"As I told you, Reginald Green asked my dad to hold his gun for him, keeping it safe and he has, or had, the keys, but he is dead and the keys were not recognisable as the keys to the locks. They were just in the bunch found on his person. What happened to them, I have no idea, after that," he said.

"So it is possible that the keys are still out there and in the hands of the murderer. Why then did you say that the locks were picked when you knew full well that the keys were not in your possession?" Julie demanded.

"I-I never thought about them until now, when you mentioned them," he replied.

"You told me earlier that Mr Green had been given the key to the gun safe, but not the outer door. Are you now saying that you lied and in fact he did have both keys?" Julie asked him.

"I-I forgot he had them, I remembered he had the safe key but I forgot he had both keys," he replied.

"Knowing that the security of the gun safe had been compromised with his death, why did you not change at least one of the locks?" Julie demanded.

"I-I never thought about it. My dad dying, Reginald died two weeks before my father and it hit me hard. I was in grief and had the farm to run. The guns were the last thing on my mind," he replied.

"So far removed that four days later you went out shooting with Bill. Mr Bancroft, I am this close to arresting you and unless you start telling me the truth, I will arrest you. What will happen to your mother then, do you care so little for her that you will protect a murderer, rather than your mother? I am disgusted with you," Julie said in a raised voice, "Chief Inspector Ashton and Detective Everet are leaving the room, the interview is suspended," Julie said. She switched the tape recorder off, and left the room.

Mr Bancroft dropped his head in his hands and sat there sullen and ashamed.

Julie and Everet went back to the office where Dan was busy working out his risk assessment and Collins was helping him.

"No work to do, Collins, how are we with the statements?" Julie asked.

"I have collated the statements and put a report on your desk, Ma'am. As you will see, there is little to add, several people saw the Morris's, who were overheard by a few people, including the Ramashkins. No-one noticed that the Ramashkins were taking more notice of the conversation, than anyone else," he told her.

Julie began to walk up and down the room, her hand to her chin and her head bowed as she mulled over everything they knew, which was not a lot.

"Ma'am, there was one interesting point that came to light, the shopkeeper did say that apart from Mrs, Morris, there was only one other person in the shop, a man. They didn't know him then, but his picture was in the paper. He was the goal keeper who was shot. They are new to the town, Ma'am," Collins added.

"I don't see the relevance, apart from coincidence, but make a note and keep it in the back of your minds. I do not believe in, coincidence," Julie said and continued to walk up and down, the office, deep in thought.

Chapter 19 - Arrested

"Ma'am, I have completed the risk assessment and. with Collins help I believe it will work, very well. First of all my next door neighbour is willing to allow his son the help us flying the drone. He also told me that they have a larger than average drone for competitions, one that has been fitted with a camera and can be flown over longer ranges. They race them, he told me, several hundred miles. This means that he can be in the pub and the drone a hundred miles away, London even, so he will be safe, well out of any action.

"The drone will pick up the signal from a mile away at one thousand feet, which at night will make it almost invisible to the naked eye and will relay the signal to us at the pub, with vision. I suggest we still follow the gun but at a safe distance to reduce the time between him arriving and us arriving with armed response," Dan told her.

"Right, Everet, you are to kill your husband on Thursday night. I will ensure it goes in the papers on Friday morning. When you will ring the taxi and arrange to be picked up, at let me see, we can't wait until dark it will be too late, but dusk should be fine, so say; nine o' clock. Collins, we need armed response; that is your job and Dan, the pilot is your job. We need him here straight after school and you'll need to organise petrol money for his trip. Leaving after school, he will be here for seven, seven thirty, time for dinner and to get set up, ready for nine o' clock when Everet is to be picked up," Julie said, thinking out loud.

"He usually goes to bed by nine," Dan said.

"How old is he?" Julie asked.

"Eight," Dan said.

"Eight," Julie said, shocked.

"Yes, like computer games, kids seem to be more adept at using them. He has won trophies for his flying. In fact he holds the record for the longest flight and the quickest. He had to fly his drone at one thousand feet with only a two percent tolerance in height, which meant that he had to land twice during the flight to refuel at agreed places. Like a rally, with check points, and within a corridor, go outside the corridor, or over, or below the height and it added penalty points. He won the first prize, beating adults and youngsters," Dan said with pride.

"So he is an ace, but still only eight years old," Julie said disapprovingly.

"J-, Ma'am," Dan said, almost forgetting himself, "I did say that it would be for about an hour and his dad accepted it. He needs to be outside to get a clear signal, but under the porch at the pub he will be, yet protected from the weather," Dan said.

"Dan, we can't do it at the pub, be sensible, I have a tent, we will do it in my back garden," Julie said, forgetting that her garden was furrowed with the potato plants, more concerned about the boy.

"I doubt the drone taking off with your furrows, Ma'am," Dan said.

"I thought drones had vertical take-off?" Julie questioned.

"Yes, they do, but it does need to be flat, Ma'am," Dam said smiling.

"Then you can flatten an area for the take-off. As I said, the boy is your problem," Julie said, smiling at Dan and joking with him, yet making the point.

"Sir, if you like, I will get my dad to do it, he can lend you some flags and lay them carefully, so as not to damage the plants and for the tent - how big is it?" Everet asked.

"That is what, I like a well-informed officer, on the team," Dan said smiling at her.

"It isn't small; all of us can stand up in it and with a table. I presume he will need a table to put his things on, like the screen for the camera," Julie said.

"It's radio controlled, but linked to a computer, he flies the drone, but all the data will be fed to a computer with a map of the area and the images from the camera, so at least six feet square," Dan said. guessing.

"It's much bigger than that, so we'll be comfortable and Dan. you can help me dismantle it on Saturday and lift the flags. I don't want the drone taking off in the town. Let's try and keep it as secretive as possible," Julie said.

"There is just one small item, the fuel tank, because of the weight it only holds a small amount, say quarter of an hour's flying time, it will take a couple of minutes to refuel it, but how long will it take to get to it?" Dan asked.

"If we are close on a mile behind the taxi, then it will not take that long and it can take off again before the taxi is out of range, hopefully?" Julie asked, querying her idea at the same time.

"If I might say. Ma'am, we do seem to have all the angles covered," Dan said and it was agreed that the raid went ahead.

By the time Julie arrived home on Friday night; she had organised the local paper to enter a story about the murder in the paper, not headlines, but on the front page and Everet's dad had organised the laying of the flags two separate areas about three feet apart, one large one for the tent and the other about three feet by four feet for the landing pad.

The four of them then began to erect the tent and by six o'clock everything was ready for the pilot's arrival.

"Everet," Julie said, shocked, "What about power? Will you ask your dad if he has an extension lead to reach from the house to the tent, we can borrow? You can take it home with you once we have finished," Julie asked her.

Everet left them and went home to get the cable. When she came back she asked Collins for help carrying the equipment in.

"What equipment?" Julie asked.

"He said that we will be working in the dark, something he had forgotten, so he gave me the cable with two dual sockets and some lights," Everet said.

"Come on, we will all help," Julie said.

They carried the equipment to the tent apart from the plug for the socket which Julie plugged in to a socket in her back room, fed the cable through the window; then carried it to the tent, feeding it as she went.

"Two lamps, two screens and a computer, so we need five sockets, I'll get an extension lead from the house," Julie said, trying to cover all bases.

It was seven fifteen when they heard a car pull up outside and Dan went to open the door for them. Dan did the honours, introducing, Mr Alan Greenwood and his son Brian, to Julie and the others.

"I just want to say thank you very much for your help, we have set up in a tent in the garden for you with a landing pad next to it. Now, Captain Greenwood, is there anything you require?" Julie asked him.

Brian Greenwood blushed at the compliment, "I-I am not a captain, Ma'am," he said, blushing.

"Let me see now, the person controlling and in charge of a plane is a captain, aren't they?" she asked him.

"Y-Yes, I suppose so," he replied.

"Correct me if I am wrong, but will you not be flying this aircraft and be in-charge, of it?" Julie asked him.

"Yes, that is what you want me to do, isn't it?" he asked shyly.

"Then, as the pilot and in charge of the craft, that makes you, the Captain. So Captain Brian, if you will follow me, I will show you what we have set up for you and then you can tell us if it is right, or if we need to change anything," Julie said and watched as he seemed to grow another two feet in height with pride.

They finished setting up the tent, connecting the computer and screens and he looked at the landing pad and agreed it was as he needed and then they went inside.

"I would offer you a drink, like the rest of us, but because you have to fly it is not allowed, but you can have a soft drink if you like. How about a glass of coke cola, with ice and lemon?" Julie asked him.

He smiled at her and accepted the offer, this was better than winning the trophy; she was calling him Captain.

"What is the flying time for your craft, Captain," Julie asked him.

"Quarter of an hour, erm, Ma'am," he said, unsure what to call her.

"Please call me Julie, I am a virtual passenger on your craft, as we watch the villains trying to escape, but you are going to make sure they don't by following them and instead of being sat on the craft. I will be looking down just the same, but via a camera; that is the idea, isn't it?" Julie asked.

"Yes, my dad told me that we needed to follow a car; how will I know which car to follow?" He asked.

"Inside the car there is a transmitter and we will follow that, I have the frequency right here, so all we need to do is set your receiver to the frequency," Julie told him.

"Cool," he said, excited at the adventure.

"Dan, I want you to assist the Captain, here. Collins, by the front door there is a can of petrol, put it in your car and follow the drone at a safe distance. keep in contact with Dan with your mobile. Do not use the police radio. Everet, time for you to go home and make the call," Julie said. organising them and picked up her mobile, "Sergeant, time to get ready, check weapons and load the van. No, radio contact whatsoever, use your mobile phones, from now on," Julie said and hung up.

Julie left them, going to her car, cocking her gun on the way and putting it in the waist band of her trousers. As she made a move, Dan led the Greenwoods out to the tent and they set up, checking that everything was in order and warmed up the engine of the drone ready for take-off.

Julie drove to the starting point at the head of the three vehicle convoy and waited for the off. They didn't have to wait long before Julie's phone rang and they were off. She pressed the brake pedal twice to alert the other vehicles and then drove off. At the end of the lane they had to wait whilst the taxi passed them and then followed, but more slowly, allowing it to speed ahead. Julie noted that he was breaking the speed limit, she was doing the thirty miles per hour permitted on this road and he was leaving them behind.

The vans were unmarked and they delayed their exit from the lane, allowing the taxi to get out of sight, before pulling out; Julie rang Dan.

"We are airborne and tracking the vehicle," he said and then said that it had stopped, Julie stopped as did the other vehicles behind her.

"The taxi is on the move again, I don't know why it stopped, they've not arrived at the pub yet," Dan told them.

Brian's father was in the car with Collins at the rear of the line of vehicles. He was there to refuel the drone from the petrol can in the boot.

They continued to follow Dan's directions over the phone as he watched Brian fly the drone following the taxi. Half a mile down the road Julie came across Everet stood by the side. Julie stopped, and waved the other vehicles on passed her.

"What did he say?" Julie asked Everet.

"To put the gun on the floor, and to wait here, for him to return," Everet told Julie.

"Are you OK?" Julie asked her.

"Yes Ma'am, a bit chilly, but I will survive," she replied cheerfully.

Julie set off, not wishing to change anything, in case it didn't go as planned, but felt uneasy about leaving Everet alone by the road side.

The officer with Julie rang the lead vehicle and told them to speed up and then pull over to allow Julie to pass them. It was only five minutes before they needed to pull over, so that Brian's dad could refuel the drone. Julie passed them at that point and the vans with the armed officers carried on with her. They knew that there were no turn offs for a good two miles and Brian had managed to land the drone close to the gate for the field. A minute later it was up in the air again and had re-established contact.

Because it was a country lane that twisted and turned, the taxi was still within range for the straight line of the radio signal. Collins now put his foot down to catch up with the other vehicles.

The phone rang in Julie's car and the officer answered it.

"It is the Inspector Ma'am, he says that the taxi has stopped. It appears to be a deserted farm, Ma'am," he told her.

"Ring the others and tell them to stop," Julie said.

"Ma'am, the drone is almost out of fuel," he told her.

"Then bring it as close as possible to our location and tell Collins, I need it up there as fast as possible," Julie said irritated.

There was a buzzing noise and then the drone landed right next to Julie's car. Brian's father rushed to re-fuel it. Again he was efficient and the drone took off again, just in time to see the taxi driver stood by a pond, throw the hand gun into the pond, then return to his taxi.

Julie got out of her car and went to the first van.

"Let's wait, block the road and be ready to arrest him," Julie said.

"Ma'am, he has turned left, away from our position," the officer told her.

"Forget it, we follow him. Michaels, where does this road lead?" Julie asked when they were back in the car.

"It does lead back to the town, Ma'am, but a long way around and not passed where he left the PC, Ma'am," the officer said with concern.

"Dose it lead anywhere else?" Julie asked.

"Yes Ma'am, the next town, Over Hampton," he said.

"Ring DI Dan Williams and warn him not to follow the taxi into the town unless he has to go up rather than allow it to be seen," Julie said.

"How far away is the town from here?" Julie asked.

"A good quarter of an hour, Ma'am," he told her.

"Can you find a landing place close to the town for us to refuel?" Julie asked.

"Ma'am, there is a field which is fallow, about quarter of a mile this side of the town," he told her.

"Ring Collins, tell him to speed up and wait there for the drone, I want them waiting with the petrol can open, ready and then ring Control and tell them if he turns that way, which I suspect he is going to," Julie said.

The officer did as told, it was organised and Collins passed them, speeding up, but avoided catching up with the taxi, getting just close enough to make re-fuelling quicker.

The taxi did turn left at the junction and Brian flew to the site, landing behind the hedge, before the taxi was anywhere near the landing area. It passed the site and Collins again seeded up and they arrived as the taxi entered the town in the distance.

The drone was refuelled and back in the sky as the taxi turned into the car park for a night club. Dan asked Brian to zoom in, to try and get a picture, for facial recognition. Smart manoeuvring by Brian got the shot Dan was hoping for, as the driver walked to the entrance someone must have shouted to him from a upper floor and he looked up, smiled and waved at the person, showing his full face.

"Ma'am, the driver has entered the night club," the officer told her.

"Good, we can now block him in," Julie said and led the convoy into the car park, indicating for them to stop and block the taxi in.

Julie got out of her car and organised the officers.

"I want two of you here by the taxi and two hidden, the others by the side of the club, split to face front and back. Collins, you are with me and Mr. Greenwood, please go across the road to that pub, well away from the action, I'll buy you a pint," Julie said, ensuring the only civilian was safe.

Julie linked arms with Collins and entered the club; the door man gave them an odd look, but didn't say anything. Once inside Julie realised why the odd look, as semi naked females wandered between the tables serving over priced drinks. She looked around, and guessed that there were less than six female customers and they were not with a man. Every other female in the club was in a bra and a G-string, or bare breasted. Two of them were cavorting on the poles in the corner stages.

Julie went up to the bar, somewhat brazenly, if you were to ask Collins, and smiled at the bar man.

"An orange juice and a Heineken," Julie said.

He served her and she paid and then she leaned in and asked him where her taxi driver went.

"I haven't seen a taxi driver, was he in a uniform, so that I would know if, I had seen him?" he asked.

Julie took out her phone and showed him the image Dan had sent her of the driver.

"Look love; just look around and tell me if you can see him, we are busy," he said and made to move away.

"Erm, Ma, erm," Collins stumbled.

"What?" Was all, Julie said.

"Over there, isn't that him?" Collins said, pointing to the far wall.

Julie smiled and agreed as they moved off towards him.

"Hello, sorry to trouble you, but I am rather annoyed. You see this taxi driver here left a female friend of mine stood way out in the country on a dark night, alone. I presume you did intend on completing the service she paid you for?" Julie asked the three men sat at the table.

"Piss off, lady, what is it to you?" he asked.

"It isn't very chivalrous to leave a lone female on a dark country lane at night, is it?" Julie asked, noting one of the men looking to the side and giving a rather large man a funny look.

The man came closer, Julie noted him and made a mental note as he approached them.

"I do not want any trouble, just for this man to do his job, properly and convey the female to the pub, as requested," Julie said with a smile.

The rather large man now put out his hand to grab her. As quick as a flash she turned, took his hand and bent it back, making him kneel before her and complaining about her damaging his hand.

"Shush, I know it hurts, but unless I do this, there will be no permanent damage, now be quiet. I must warn you my hands are licensed. What was that you were saying. that you were just about to leave?" Julie asked him.

"Madam, you are making a very big mistake coming in here and attacking us. I suggest you leave before you, get hurt," one of the men said, as three more blokes came over towards them.

"This is the easy way, but if you want it the hard way, then I will happily oblige," Julie said and hit the man who fell backwards unconscious. She drew her gun pointed it at the man who had spoken, "Armed police, Detective Sergeant Collins, close this place down," Julie said.

Collins got on his radio, and called the armed officers in to the club. They burst in and pushed the people inside back against the wall.

"I am arresting you for trading in illegal firearms; anything you say will be taken down and used in evidence against you. You do not have to say anything that may harm your defence which you later rely on in court. I presume you all heard that because it applies to you all," Julie said, as they were read their rights again by the officer putting the handcuffs on them and leading them out to the waiting van.

"You can't do this, your search is illegal and the arrest," a man said, coming up to them.

Julie gave him her condescending smile, "What is illegal? Come on, you tell me what part of this tonight, was illegal," Julie asked him.

"You do not have a search warrant," he said.

"I have not searched the place yet, Collins, get me a search warrant, will you, next?" Julie asked the man.

"You entered illegally," he said.

"How did you enter, by walking past the doorman and paying the entrance fee, if so then you also entered illegally, because that was how we entered. Next?" Julie asked him.

"I saw you assault that man," he said.

"Do you mean the man who assaulted me, the one I defended myself against?" Julie asked him.

"Y-You hit him once you had secured him, that is assault," he said now beginning to realise he was up against someone who was as well versed in the law as he was.

"I needed my hands free to defend myself against the four other men, now making their way towards me, at which point I informed them that my hands were licensed as lethal weapons. I also told them that I was an armed police officer, at which point I arrested them. Now, are you a solicitor?" Julie asked him.

"As a matter of fact, I am," he said proudly.

"Then I am going to need your name and address so that I can call on you, to make a statement. I have to book the criminals in, so I can't do it right now, how about tomorrow night say, seven o'clock?" Julie asked him, noting the wedding ring.

"Erm, no, erm, can we make it ten in the morning at my office?" he asked.

Julie twisted her head, and closed an eye, doubting his suggestion, "I am afraid I will be very busy all day tomorrow, three criminals to interview and arrest, a case to build and present for prosecution, I will not be free before seven

258

tomorrow night. I presume you are anxious because your wife will be at home then, but then again perhaps if you had thought about that earlier, then the problem would not exist, would it?" she asked him.

"Erm, look, erm, I may have made a slight mistake earlier; I am sure now your actions were perfectly legal and I must compliment you on such a daring and successful action," he said.

"So Tuesday morning at your office say, ten o'clock, will you be free?" Julie asked him.

"I am not sure, but I will make myself free for you, erm?" he asked.

"Oh, yes, Chief Inspector Julie Ashton, sorry, and this is Detective Sergeant Collins. You will also notice that the alcoholic drink I bought him has not been touched and that my drink, as the driver, was orange juice," Julie informed him.

It took the officers left at the scene another hour to get all the names and addresses of the customers and staff, by which time the van with the men in, had dropped them off at the station and returned for the officers. Julie did not wait, she left, taking Mr. Greenwood back to her house and Brian with the drone, having collected Everet up on the way.

Once the place was locked down, Collins organised the search warrant before they began the search.

Chapter 20 - Interviews

"Good morning Mr. Musgrave, I trust the en-suite accommodation was to your liking and the room service?" Julie asked him.

"What, are you mad? The food was crap and the bed hard so no, bitch," he said.

"I am sorry to hear that, we do try to make it as comfortable as possible, allowing for the circumstances and seeing as you will be enjoying the accommodation for several years; it would be a good idea to get used to it. Now shall we dance around the subject, or are you willing to save my time by telling me all about your gun running activities?" Julie asked him, after the introductions for the tape.

"I want my solicitor," he said bluntly.

"I am sure you have had the opportunity to inform your solicitor, so we can wait. Interview suspended at oh nine, twenty," Julie said and left him sat in the interview room, alone.

She returned quarter of an hour later with her half-drunk coffee and his solicitor.

"We do try to be accommodating, interview resumed at, nine thirty five," Julie said and named the people in the room.

"Mr. Musgrave, we put a tracking device in the clip of the gun the taxi driver sold our officer. We then followed the tracking device to a deserted farm, where the taxi driver threw the gun into a pond. We then followed him to your night club.

There we arrested you with two others. After obtaining a search warrant, we searched the premises and during the search we found the brown envelope containing the seven hundred pounds we gave the officer.

"We found it on the seat where you were sat, well away from where the taxi driver, was sat. Upon checking the serial numbers we found that they matched the ones given to our officer. Why was the envelope next to where you were sat and not in the possession of the taxi driver?" Julie asked him.

"He owed me one thousand pounds and that was the first payment," he said casually.

"I see, so he still owes you three hundred pounds, does he?" Julie asked.

"Obviously," he said and leaned forward on the table between them, badgering Julie.

"Where do you keep your licence?" Julie asked.

"In my wallet," he said.

"Then why did we not find a gun licence in your wallet, if that is where you keep it, for the guns in your office, which I have noted were not being kept in a safe and secure location, being on the desk and in the unlocked cupboard?" Julie asked him.

"That one at home, you should have said you meant my gun licence," he said.

Julie smiled at him, "Yes, perhaps I should have made myself clear about that. So to save my officers time, where will the officers, searching your home at this moment in time, find the licence?" Julie asked him.

"It will probably be in the top drawer of my desk, but there are private papers in that drawer, so

261

it is locked and if you damage it, I will claim compensation. You have nothing on me, bitch, there is no evidence linking me to his activities, because I am not linked," he said, trying to delay her.

"Interview suspended at nine fifty five. I am going to open that drawer. You will wait here until I return. Now give me the key, or I will open it by any means necessary. I have a valid search warrant, so I can chop it up if necessary and you do not get compensation," Julie said, turning the tables on him.

"It is an antique and I have lost the key. It is very valuable, I am waiting for a locksmith to open it," he told her.

"Then it is a pity because I will open it, good bye," Julie said and got up.

"W-wait, it might be this one," he said relenting.

Julie left them, and went to the house, she entered, went to the desk and opened the drawer with the key. She searched through the drawer, but couldn't find the licence. She scooped the papers up into an evidence bag, sealed it, then signed it with Dan and returned to the interview room as soon as his solicitor joined them.

"Mr Musgrave, I have here for the tape an evidence envelope with the contents of the alleged drawer, I am now showing Mr Musgrave's solicitor that the bag is sealed, and signed by two officers as being the entire contents of the said drawer. I will now open it in front of Mr Musgrave and his solicitor," Julie said and opened the envelope.

She tipped the contents on the table and asked Mr Musgrave to indicate the licence.

"Perhaps it is in the drawer at my night club," he offered.

"Had it been in there; then I would already have it. It wasn't, try again. While you are thinking, start to think about how you came to be in possession of at least one firearm used in a criminal activity. Not the one the taxi driver threw in the pond, one we seized from the night club. The others are being tested and I am sure there will be more," Julie said.

"I did not rob, or kill anybody," he shouted angrily.

"Perhaps not, but conspiracy to rob, and the supply of firearms is not a light sentence. Once I have the full list, then we can talk. At the moment, shall we say, twenty years is the least you can expect," Julie said. She closed the interview down and left him with his solicitor.

It took the ballistics team the rest of the morning to test the gun, and then Julie had him and his solicitor, brought back into the interview room.

She entered and slammed the folder she was holding down on the table, in front of him and sat down, she then introduced those present for the tape and then looked hard at him.

"Mr. Musgrave, in that folder is the list of the criminal activities where you supplied guns, for. I will not waste my time offering you any sort of reprieve for information. Six murders you supplied the guns for and twenty five armed robberies. I am charging you with six counts of aiding and abetting the murder of six citizens, to be named, and the supply of arms for twenty five robberies, by aiding and abetting the said robberies before and after the

263

fact, again to be listed. Collins; take him back to his cell, write up the charges and then charge him formally," Julie said, making his predicament perfectly clear to him and his solicitor, who shook his head in dismay.

"Ma'am, I watched you in the interview room and you were brilliant," Everet said.

"Flattery will get you nowhere, he became complacent and slipshod, that was all and I used it to my advantage. Had it not been as severe as it was, then I could have made a deal with him, but I didn't, why? That is because I have the taxi driver yet to interview and he was only the delivery man. I will throw the book at Musgrave, but the taxi driver I will make exceptions for as the delivery man and I have the second in command as well," Julie told her.

Julie left the station, going to the pub to meet up with Dan for lunch.

"I hear you nailed Musgrave," Dan said.

"We did, but I did not waste time following up with him. After lunch I will tackle the second in command. With the evidence you found at the night club, I do not need a confession. When I interview the second in command then it may be advisable," Julie said, in between bites of her sandwich.

The conversation continued as they ate lunch and drank their coffees. Dan never drank on duty, that was for later. Dan asked why she hadn't waited for all the searches to be completed and Julie told him that she had Musgrave. Because of the evidence in his office, he was complicit and could not argue the point. The other two were slightly more difficult, but she did have Everet's report against the taxi driver and he was to be next.

Dan went back to carrying out the searches with the teams and Julie returned to the office. She asked the desk sergeant to organise for the taxi driver to be put in the interview room, with his solicitor. Again Julie entered and listed the people present for the tape.

"I am so sorry that you have had to wait for so long before being interviewed, then again it has given you time to get used to your accommodation for the next twenty years. That is what you are looking at for aiding and abetting the murder of six people and of aiding and abetting the armed robbery of twenty five places.

"I have here the report from my officer who went undercover to get the evidence against you of supplying guns, so there is no question about you being charged with that crime, but what about all the others? Mr Musgrave was very helpful; I mean why did you ask him to hold the weapons for you?" Julie asked him.

"What do you mean? He was the boss, as you saw, I handed the money over to him, all I did was deliver the parcels for him and at the time I did not know what was in the parcel. He told me that he had smuggled gold into the country and the people had bought some of it," he said.

"So you did know if he told you it was gold, didn't you?" Julie asked him.

"Y-Yes, but I didn't know they were guns which is what you say they were," he said.

"You will have to help me here. If I had delivered a lump of gold to someone and they didn't want it. I would not throw it into a pond, yet we have you on camera doing just that. Why throw a lump of gold into a pond?" Julie asked him.

"He told me it was gold, but that woman said that it was lead just painted to look like gold, it was a scam he was pulling. I did not want to be involved so I threw it away and then went to him to get her money back," he said.

"I see, so why did you hand over the seven hundred she paid you, if you were going to get the money back?" Julie asked him.

"I-I, well, erm," he said, and shut up.

"You really should listen and take note, I did tell you that our undercover officer had bought the gun and returned it as you suggested. We have this on camera and the bank note serial numbers match the ones in the envelope we saw you give Musgrave. Was that his cut for holding the guns for you?" Julie asked him.

"No, no, I swear he was the dealer and in gold, as far as I was aware," he said.

"Look, I do not like to waste time, I have several murders to solve and if you help me; I will tell the judge that you did help with our enquiries. Then again we have the officer's statement that you sold her the gun and then that you took it off her, which to me makes you, the dealer. So you decide twenty years high security, or five years in a normal prison. Oh, and don't forget that if you are the dealer then Musgrave must not be and he will spend the five years, instead of you.

266

"One of you will spend twenty years in a high security prison, the other five in a normal prison. You decide which of you is to serve which sentence," Julie said and got up, stopping the tape and leaving the room.

She didn't hear what was said, but she did see through the two way mirror that the solicitor was painting a rather bleak picture, from his face, and gestures.

She returned after half an hour, sat down and started the tape.

"Mr. Smith, as I said before someone was the dealer in guns, the other person was a helper only. What I want to know is; which of you was the dealer and who was the helper? The difference is fifteen years in a maximum security prison," Julie asked.

"What I want is immunity from prosecution and a new identity," he said bluntly.

"What I want is a Ferrari, but like you, I am not going to get it," Julie said.

"I know names and places, remember I delivered the guns, so I know who bought them and what for," he said.

"Great, that just adds another five years to the sentence for withholding evidence. Or, if I like what I hear; I could argue your case with my superiors, but let me be perfectly clear, you are in no position to make demands. Now interest me, or I will have you charged," Julie told him.

"Andrew Bentley is the other driver who delivers the guns, I delivered the one for the mini market robbery, that was to George Harris. The one

267

for the murder of Wendy Parker was to Simon Thomas. Does that interest you enough to go and get my immunity?" he asked her.

"It does, as long as there are more. I have six murders and twenty five robberies, how many can you help with?" Julie asked him.

"I delivered the guns to people, I did not know what they were for at the time of delivery, but when they handed them back; I knew what crime had been committed and put two and two together. On that basis, I know who killed three people and committed ten armed robberies," he told her.

"That is not strictly true, is it? Because you asked my undercover officer what she wanted it for, didn't you? You knew prior to delivery what the gun was to be used for, so do not try and bluff, me," Julie said, allowing her anger to show.

"OK, I did know, and delivered the weapons, so you now know that I can put a gun in the hands of a person and crime, what is that worth?" he asked, leaning in to Julie.

"I will find out, but I am sure it will not be immunity, but a slap on the wrist is what I will try for, no prison time," Julie said.

"You might as well kill me if there is prison time," he said uneasily.

"If I had my way; I would shoot all three of you, do not tempt me," Julie said.

Julie stopped the tape and left them talking as she went to her office, picked up the phone and called her superintendent. It was not a comfortable conversation, but they did manage to agree that his information was worth a reduction in the charges against him.

Julie went back into the interview room and did not put the tape on.

"Fred, my offer, and it is the only offer I can make, is that you serve six months in an open prison. The crime you committed is far too serious to be granted immunity. You were complicit in three murders. We will ask for twelve months, which with good behaviour means you will serve just six months. Take it, or leave it," Julie said.

She saw him look at his solicitor, who nodded to him and he opened up, giving Julie the three murderers and all ten criminals who were guilty of armed robbery.

"Fred, thank you for your help. I will now have you formally charged with aiding an armed robbery, by delivering the firearms for, the robbery. This is a diluted charge, which will carry a twelve to twenty four month prison term. Because of your assistance in clearing several other crimes, we will ask the judge to take this into account and to reduce the time to a maximum of twelve months as a first offence," Julie told him.

"Sergeant, send someone to 15, The Avenue, please, and arrest one Andrew Bentley for the supply of firearms to a person, or persons unknown, contrary to the firearms laws. I'll get the section later, just fetch him in and show him to a cell, I'll interview him later, or I might just ask Dan to do it," Julie said, feeling pleased with herself.

"Not a bad day, Ma'am," Collins said as she entered the office.

"Not bad at all, Collins, several unsolved murders and armed robberies solved, but the one we are dealing with still eludes us. We have a suspect, a very good one, but they are not in the country and may not even return. Get onto the Spanish police and see if they can help locate the Ramashkins," Julie said.

Late in the afternoon Dan returned with a broad smile on his face and a carrier bag, which he dumped on the desk.

"The spoils of gun running, Ma'am," he told her, emptying the bag on her desk, "Twenty five thousand pounds, hidden under his bed, along with a .45 calibre pistol. I arrested him on a charge of having an unlicensed gun and brought him back. He is in Interview Room 2, Ma'am," Dan told her.

"Then I suggest you allow him to digest his current situation while you have a well-deserved coffee, and then you can interview him. Frederick Smith has confessed to his part and implicated Bentley in the gun running as a delivery man. We have charged the boss, Mr, Ted Musgrave, with running the business and you can have Jimmy Harris as well, after Mister Bentley," Julie said.

"Thank you. Ma'am, I will look forward to our little chat with Mister Bentley. Will you be joining us?" Dan asked, being glib.

"No. I suggest Collins, Everet, was with me," Julie said and left the office.

All in all it had been an excellent day, some thirty crimes solved all at once. All that was left was for her to organise the arrest of the individuals, which would not be as simple as it sounds. The criminals were by now spread all around the country and she decided that the arrests needed to be synchronised to avoid the criminals alerting the others involved, even so, it was a big feather in her cap.

Several more guns were found in the pond, searched by the underwater search team, and were being taken to the ballistics laboratory to be dried out, cleaned and then test fired. Only the barrel was needed for the striations, but it needed to be dry and clean before firing.

At times like this when Julie needed peace and quiet to plan how to organise the arrests, she went for a walk, or stood gazing out of a window. Her eyes saw nothing, as her brain ticked over all the anomalies and problems they could face. Half an hour later she found herself outside the grocers and went inside.

"Hello," she said, smiling broadly.

"Hello, Chief Inspector; how was your day?" the shop keeper asked her.

"Very well, thank you, I don't suppose you can remember anything else about that morning, can you? For you I suppose it was pretty eventless, just another day?" Julie asked him, perhaps hoping her good luck would continue.

"Yes, it was really just that Mrs Morris bought the HP sauce and I only remember that, because I have repeated it so many times to various police officers and the woman who. - Now, wait, no, sorry I am so, so sorry, I-I got it wrong. The woman was there next to her, but Mister Croft was also there and he, no. I can't visualise it, they were both there.

271

The big woman I described and Mister Croft, but he was lower down, I only just caught a glimpse of him, he was bending down and come to think of it, he also bought a bottle of HP sauce. I remembered her, because she didn't buy anything and my prices are not cheap, but I am cheaper than the other local shops, I can't compete with the supermarkets," he told her.

"Little things do come to mind later, when the dust has settled, as it were. So there were three of them, Mrs Morris, who bought the HP sauce we are interested in. Mister Croft who also bought a bottle and this mystery woman, who we think helped out at the big house the day Lady Sophie was killed, is that correct?" Julie asked the shopkeeper.

"Y-Yes, Yes, I remember it now. Please come behind the counter, now as you can see that aisle is not in view, you can't see down it, so I had a mirror put in, and now I can see down it. Now, the woman was stood up and selecting a bottle of Dijon mustard. Mir Morris was this side of her and bent down reaching for the HP. Now this side of Mrs. Morris and hidden by the woman was Mr. Croft, but I need three people to show you, all I saw was the people, but as Mrs Morris came to the counter, the woman made for the door and as she moved away, at that point I saw Mr Croft for a second before he moved out of range of the mirror and into my view at the counter," he told her.

"So in your statement you said you saw the woman, hand the HP to Mrs Morris, is that correct, or did Mr Croft hand it to her?" Julie asked.

"No, it was the woman who handed the HP to Mrs Morris," he confirmed.

"I need to be sure about this, who handed the HP sauce to Mrs Morris?" Julie asked him.

"I saw her hand it to Mrs Morris, the woman, she smiled and Mrs Morris thanked her, I am sure about that, it was just Mr Croft that slipped my memory sorry, does that help?" he asked.

"Not really, yet it does, it adds another person to the growing list," Julie said with a smile.

"How, wasn't he shot?" the shopkeeper asked.

"Yes he was, a very good point," Julie said and left the shop going back to the station.

Once again she closed her mind and allowed her thoughts to dominate the extra information.

Chapter 21 - New Evidence

Julie had always thought that there was something odd about the shooting of Croft and the more she analysed it, the more convinced she was that it was staged and that it went wrong. To get some clarity, she didn't go back to the station; instead she walked about as if in a daze, mulling over the events, before returning to the station and Dan's beaming face.

"I presume they confessed?" Julie asked him, seeing his face as she entered their office.

"Two signed and sealed confessions and now three confessions implicating Musgrave as the boss. Ma'am we have a slam dunk case water tight and, well it couldn't have been better if we had caught them in the act," Dan told her.

"Dan we did, remember, Everet, and the drone. What did the pond reveal?" Julie asked.

"That is the icing on the cake, six more guns, including a .22 have been found. Ballistics are working on them as we speak," Dan said.

"Sorry Dan, it is good work, but I have had a funny feeling about Mr Croft. You know me and ballistics, it just was not right. The wrong place, the angle was not good, the cover was, but that limited the sights and made it too easy to miss the target. They didn't select the best place; they selected perhaps the worst place, why?" Julie asked him.

"Could it be because they are not as good, as you?" Dan suggested.

"Flattery will not work, Dan; an amateurish amateur would not pick that as a place to take the shot. Uneven ground, branches blocking the view. No, Dan, even you said it was not a good place," Julie said considering the place the shot came from and registering her doubts.

"It was perhaps the worst attempt," Dan said.

"Dan, they missed. Every other shot or attempt was planned and the delivery was accurate. Had this been the first attempt, then I might have accepted it, but after four attempts and all successful, why miss because of bad planning, when all the others were planned to perfection? It does not, add up." Julie said.

"Over confidence," Dan offered.

"No, I would expect the shot to be taken from a much better vantage point and without the same risks. There were much better places on the right hand side of the pitch again in the trees and without the risk of the bullet being through and through and injuring someone else. How can you shoot the perpetrators of a crime, in your view, and take the risk of killing an innocent?

"The shot was fired into a crowd, come on, Dan, would you fire such a powerful gun into a crowd when you wanted to kill one person? It was bound to be a through and through, from that range, unless it hit bone," Julie argued.

"Not everyone has your knowledge about guns; I would not know that it would be as you said, I would expect the body mass to stop it," Dan argued back.

"I accept that, Dan, but would you, say you wanted me dead, would you shoot at me if I were stood in front of a crowd? What if you missed?" Julie asked him.

"No, I admit I would not, then again I would not shoot anyone, so the point is moot," Dan said.

"Look, Dan, from the side here, you can shoot and if you miss then the bullet will be lost, there is no-one stood in this area, but from here, twenty two men are, so why take the chance?" Julie asked.

"Sir Andrew, about the same distance and they took a heart shot; does that sound like someone who misses, they were confident that they could kill him," Dan said.

"But they didn't and would never have, at worst a leg shot, a broken femur, but it was not a kill shot, why?" Julie asked.

"I think you are reading too much into this, Julie, over thinking it, we need to find that woman. She was in the shop, at the big house and in the area at the time of every murder and she was the big sister to the boy that was killed: means, motive and opportunity," Dan reminded her.

"Maybe I am, but I do not want to ignore it, nor the fact that Croft was in the shop when Mrs. Morris was and next to her when the woman handed her the HP sauce, yet he failed to mention it," Julie said.

"Julie, when did you find that out? I didn't know he was in the shop." Dan asked her.

"An hour ago, I did my thing and wandered, ending up in the shop, so I asked him was there anything he had forgotten to tell us, now things had calmed down. He told me that Croft was in the shop next to the woman and Mrs. Morris. It may be nothing, but I want him put on the list of suspects, along with, Ramashkin," Julie said.

"Far be it from me to question you, but he was a victim," Dan said.

"Was he, or was the gunman supposed to miss? Now if I were the shooter, then it was an ideal place to miss, excellent cover and with the shot ringing in our ears, a great opportunity to escape. No need to take careful aim, just make sure it was high enough to miss everyone and from that point, very easy," Julie said.

"Aren't you forgetting something? They didn't miss, four inches to the right and he would have been paralysed for life and if shooting up into the air, how come they hit him at leg level?" Dan asked.

"Easy. It had rained, the ground was slippery and they slipped, lifting the barrel when they fired, or fired because they slipped, with the same result," Julie said.

"I will accept that, but how did he put the poison in the wine when he was not at the house?" Dan asked her.

"Dan, I am human, I do not have all the answers, just more than you. Your round tonight," Julie said, with a broad smile for him.

"It is a celebration, so the boss usually buys the first round," Dan retorted.

"Not when the boss cracked the case wide open and allowed their understudy to take some of the credit, being of a very generous nature," Julie said, laughing.

"Who, the understudy, being of a very generous nature, besides I bought the first round last night, come to think of it, I bought every round last night," Dan said, as if annoyed.

"Dan, the police bought every round last night, we were on expenses because we were working. I am sure you will not forget to put your claim in, will you?" Julie asked him, laughing with him.

"Heaven forbid that I might," Dan said.

Julie's phone rang, she answered it and was told that the Ramashkins had been stopped at Bristol airport entering the country. Julie smiled and, after telling Dan, they ordered their dinner, ate it and then went back to the police station to await the arrival of the Ramashkins.

They had enjoyed a leisurely dinner, there was no need to rush, it would take a couple of hours for them to arrive at the police station, which allowed Dan and Julie to review their notes ready to interview the Ramashkins.

Dan and Julie entered Interview Room 2, to see a police officer stood by the door and Mrs Ramashkin, sat at the table.

"Good evening, Mrs. Ramashkin, I am Chief Inspector Ashton and with me is Detective Inspector Williams. I am sure you have heard about the death of Sir Andrew Mac Adams. We have been interviewing everybody who worked in the house on the day of his death. Unfortunately you stood in for a member of staff who was taken ill and then left the country the day following his death and slipped through the net.

"This is why we have had to resort to the measures we have had to use.

"I am led to believe that you were standing in for a cleaner and had the dining room, entrance area and the reception rooms to clean. I am also led to believe that you showed the waiting on staff where the wine glasses needed to be placed. Is this correct?" Julie asked her.

"I am not happy about being taken at the airport and brought here in a police car; it looked as if I had been arrested. What will the neighbours think? It was shaming for me and my friends," she said.

"As I said, had we been able to interview you at the time, this action would not have been necessary, but you do seem to be slipping in and out of England regularly and we needed to speak to you. Now, was my information correct?" Julie pressed her.

"Yes, can I go now?" she asked.

"I do have a few more questions for you. Did you see anyone enter the dining room after you had shown the waiting on staff where to place, the glasses?" Julie asked.

"No, do I need a solicitor? All I did was show them the correct way to set the table, the Mac Adams were very particular about being correct, I should know I worked there long enough," she said.

"At this moment in time you are not under caution, so it is not necessary, but you can have one present, if you wish?" Julie advised her, "That is something we didn't know, so you were employed at the house, previously?" Julie asked her.

"Yes, it was common knowledge, I have nothing to hide, some five years I worked for that miser, before my first husband took me to America with him and I have never looked back," she said.

"Why did you come back? Was it just a holiday?" Julie asked.

"No, when we left I owned a house which I rented out for the income. Because we won the local lottery, a few million, I decided to sell and had papers to sign, which I could have done on line. Then my best friend at school decided to marry and I, erm, we, decided to make a holiday of it, signing the papers, touring Europe and being a bridesmaid at my friend's wedding," she replied.

"That helps explain why you seemed to be in and out of the country so much, perhaps you can give me your itinerary?" Julie asked.

"Sure, we arrived and spent two weeks visiting old friends and signing the papers, then two weeks in France and back for the wedding, then Spain and another two weeks here, clearing the house and visiting friends before a week in Italy, then a week in Germany, before flying home from there," she told them.

"Did you see anybody at the house?" Julie asked.

"Look, I do not know the names of the people there, they were students, he is too tight to employ professionals and they were in and out of the rooms. I hardly spoke to them, apart from the waiting on staff, obviously, Sir and Lady Mac Adams and Vera, the other cleaner. We spent a bit of time catching up on old times, Vera and I; that is. The

280

only thing I said to the students was where the glasses needed to be placed and then I left them. We had to work to a time, he said he would pay us a set amount, twenty pounds, there was four hours' work, but cash in hand, it equated to five pounds an hour once you deducted, Tax and National Insurance.

"Like I said, he was tighter than a duck's arse. My friend needed the money, it was not much, but every penny counted for her, so I did the work and gave her the money. I didn't need it, with a few million in the bank," she said.

"Why not just give her, some money?" Julie asked.

"He would have sacked her if the work was not done and, as I said, she needed the money, so I did the work for her, to make sure she kept her job," she told them.

"Would it be fair to say you hated him, despised him?" Julie asked her.

"Yes, he was the epitome of Scrooge; all he cared about was the money he got and if you died, because he failed to pay you your money, he would not shed a tear for you. I am glad he is dead, he was a Dinosaur from Victorian times and with their values," she told them.

"That is a very strong reaction, I have to ask, seeing as you have such deep rooted feelings about him, did you poison the wine?" Julie asked.

"I wish I had, but no, I did not, the wine was in the cellar and brought up after we had left. Ask Nigel Croft, he arrived as we were leaving. I bet Mac Adam, asked him to select the wine for dinner; he is quite a boffin about wines. I find it quite odd

281

that you would ask a person invited to dine with you, to come early on to select the wine. Mac Adams knew nothing about wine, Croft advised him about wines to put down to resell later at a good profit. The bottles have to be turned apparently every so often and Croft was detailed to go to the house and turn them and that old skinflint never even gave him a bottle of cheap wine from the supermarket. It wasn't said, but you knew your job was on the line if you didn't do as asked; like my friend and that was why I filled in for her," she told them.

"I understood that Croft was invited to the dinner, but couldn't make it because his wife was ill, do you know if that was correct?" Julie asked her.

"She could have been on her death bed, but he would have expected Croft to go and select the wine; he could miss the dinner, but not selecting the wine. One was obligatory, the other just required, there will be a black mark on Croft's record for missing the dinner, but the sack for not selecting the wine," she told them.

"What can you tell me about Lady Sophie's, glass?" Julie asked.

"The tray of glasses was on the side, I saw the staff looking at them and I felt sorry for them. All the glasses look the same, but they are not, etched on the base of the wine glass is a letter, Lady Sophie's glass has an 'S,' etched on it, with an 'A,' on his glass, all the others are plain, and," she was telling them.

"Wait, you said that her glass had an 'S,' etched on it, on the base?" Julie asked, shocked that they had not been told.

"Yes, she had a thing about bacteria and she only used the crockery with her initial on it; her plate had an 'S,' on it, every item had her initial etched, or printed on it, even her cutlery. It wasn't emblazoned on the glass for all to see, just a small mark if you like, to identify it and that was why I felt it my duty, can we say, to show the waiting on staff.

"Had she not got her glass, then all hell would have broken loose. I also told the kitchen staff to make sure her plate was the last one to be served to the females. I did it for them, showing them the 'S' and explaining the order of service, ladies first, then guests and finally the host," she told them.

"So, if I wanted to poison Lady Sophie; it would be quite a simple job to poison her glass, wouldn't it?" Julie asked.

"Yes, if you had the opportunity to," she said.

"Did you have the opportunity to poison her glass?" Julie asked.

"She was an angel, he was the devil Had he been poisoned then the question would be valid as a possibility, but not her. Lady Sophie asked the local grocer to put a hamper up for my friend and she paid for it, a week's groceries. No, I would never kill her, I owe her for my friend," she said.

"Do you own a gun?" Julie asked her.

"We live in America, everyone owns a gun. With our winnings we bought a ranch and have two shot guns, two rifles and two hand guns, one each," she said unashamedly.

"I presume you know how to handle one, then?" Julie asked.

"We used to go to the range, but now we have a range of our own on the ranch and I am not a bad shot," she said, bragging a little.

"Did you know Brian Tindall?" Julie asked.

"Now he was a creep, there was something about him that didn't sit well with me; I didn't dislike him; I just, didn't like him," she said.

"What was it that you didn't like about him?" Julie asked.

"It is hard to explain, he was smarmy, erm, and it felt as though he was undressing you when he looked at you, those piercing eyes stripped you," she said.

"What about David Morris?" Julie asked.

"He was different, a nice, sweet guy, a little soft if you like, but harmless enough, he doffed his hat to you, old fashioned, but quaint. I liked him," she said.

"How long will you be in England, in case we need to ask you any more questions?" Dan asked.

"We fly out a week tomorrow, but we are leaving this town the day before, to stay in the airport hotel; it is an early flight," she told them.

"Just one more thing, we were told that you handed a bottle of HP sauce to Mrs Morris, is that correct?" Julie asked.

"Let me think back, a lot has happened since then. Yes, I remember now Mr. Croft was taking one from the shelf and Mrs. Morris asked me to step away so she could get one. She was in a hurry and he gave it to me and I gave it to her," she said.

"He was picking one from the shelf and handed it to you, is that right?" Julie asked.

"I think so; he was about four inches from the shelf when he handed it to me. So I presumed he was going to buy one, but it was mid-way, so I suppose he could have decided not to buy one and be putting it back. Who knows?" she said, a little confused.

"Thank you very much, and again I am sorry about the way we brought you in for the interview. You have been very helpful, so it has turned out that it was very important that we speak to you. Officer, see that Mrs Ramashkin is taken to her friend's house for us, will you? I presume that is where you are staying, like the last time you were in England?" Julie asked her.

"Yes, it is, thank you," she said, being polite.

The officer escorted Mrs Ramashkin from the room and Julie looked at Dan.

"I believe her, what about you?" Julie asked Dan.

"I do and I suppose her statement is just a little bit more justification for your theory," Dan said.

"It is way past my bedtime, see you in the morning," Julie said smiling, but tired.

Chapter 22 - Evidence

Julie went home and flopped on the bed; she couldn't sleep, her mind kept running over and over the events of the day. She was confident she now had a valid suspect; all that remained was to get the evidence to convict him. Her eyes closed, she rested, thinking, her problem was how to get the evidence? The avenue of the gun runners was a blank; they had not supplied the weapons. She knew the pistol came from the Bancroft farm, but where had the rifle come from?

She also wondered if he was supposed to be shot, or was the gunman a bad shot and had hit him unintentionally.

Her alarm woke her, sleep had eventually come, she got up, showered and got dressed, then had her cereal and left for the office with her covered mug of coffee to sip on the way, as she continued to mull over what to do next.

"Morning, I have cracked the case with Dan's help and not forgetting your valuable contributions, even if only to close down avenues, to bring to the fore one single avenue for investigation and focussing our attentions.

"Mrs. Ramashkin is no longer a suspect, late last night she was brought to the station; Dan and I interviewed her. We discovered that she was not the only person in the shop when Mrs. Morris was buying the HP sauce, Mr Croft was as well and he handed her the sauce to give to Mrs. Morris rather conveniently.

"Although the gun runners supplied a lot if guns for criminals, none were used in the crimes we are investigating, but it did clear up several unsolved crimes, so well done, but of no use, to us.

"Collins, I need you to check every and all gun clubs in the area, to see if he is a member. Everet, I need you to check licences to see if he has one and Dan and I will pay him a visit to see how he is doing. He has been sent home, released from the hospital," Julie said, organising her troops.

"Ma'am, the Super has been in touch via e-mail, to say that she is back from her vacation and wants a report on your progress, can you give her a call? She has a new assistant and she is not up to speed yet, which is why it came to the main computer and not your own, Ma'am," the desk sergeant told her as they were leaving.

Julie gave Dan a sullen look and turned around heading back for her office, with Dan.

"Ma'am, I hope you had a good holiday?" Julie asked her.

"Never mind that, what about the overtime and extra officers, is there anybody left to protect in that town?" She asked in a blunt tone.

"As Mrs. Ramashkin entered the UK last night, Border Control brought her to the station, and we interviewed her. Dan, and I are satisfied that she is not the person we believe was the killer, but it did open up another angle, which we are about to check.

"The extra officers were just for the one evening, Ma'am, and as a result of that action we

287

have closed and are about to close over twenty open cases, it was a very valuable exercise, Ma'am.

"We have sent ballistic reports to the relevant stations, with the name of the person hiring the weapon and obviously the weapon. All, 'T,'s, are crossed, and 'I,'s dotted, we can put the weapon in the hands of the suspect at the time of the crime. Unfortunately it did not help with our current case, or any past cases, but several other districts will benefit from the exercise so they have no need to complain about, overtime. They are the beneficiaries, not us, Ma'am," Julie said bluntly, eager to get on her way.

"I have heard about your blunt approach, you sneaked in behind my back, asking for the extra officers while I was away and, I presume flashed your eyes at my aide to get his help. I told you that there was to be no more extra officers. We have to work to a budget and you have spent your budget for the next two months. Do not ask for any more officers, they will not be forthcoming," she said in a blunt tone.

"That is not only unfair, but unwarranted; with the help of those officers we solved several crimes. The stations that have benefitted from the exercise should be made to pay for the officers. not the only station that did not get any benefit. At this moment in time I am too busy to be bothered with you. I have a killer to catch, but later I will go over your head about this. Now, rather than doing accounts, allow me to be a police woman and do my job, even if you can't," Julie said and slammed the phone down.

"Julie, that was not very diplomatic," Dan said.

"If she thinks I joined the police force to sit and crunch numbers, she has another think coming. I will do my best to not over spend, but it is more important that we catch criminals. Isn't that our job?" Julie asked, in an angry tone.

"I totally agree with you, it is our job, but there are limited funds and we must do our best to stay within those limitations. Now take a dozen deep breaths and calm down. Croft has just come out of hospital and we don't want him to have to go back in, do we?" Dan asked, smiling at her.

"What am I going to do when you go back to Manchester? Everet and Collins just don't have what it takes to control my temper like you do. Well, shall we go, while I still have a job?" Julie asked Dan, smiling at him.

"Why not, as long as you are back in control, Ma'am?" Dan asked.

They left the office and went to the Croft house; his wife answered the door and smiled at them.

"I presume you are here to find out who wanted my husband dead, he was very lucky," she said, greeting them.

"Yes, he was and we do have a few questions for him to help with our enquiries," Julie said after the introductions.

They were shown through to the lounge where he was sat on the settee, dozing.

"It took a lot out of him coming home in the ambulance," his wife told them.

"It does, how are you feeling, Mr Croft?" Julie asked politely.

"Tired, but not in as much pain, thank you. How can I help you?"

"It would appear that every member of the management team at the time of the accidents are being targeted. You had a middle management role at that time, as the store's manager, yet up to now it has been the senior management that have been targeted. Can you suggest any reason as to why they targeted you?" Julie asked.

"They seem to be targeting every member of the management team that gained from the accident, as it were. I am now the purchasing director for the building firm," he said.

"So you believe it isn't a vendetta against the management of the time, but against those who were promoted. Is that correct?" Julie asked him.

"Yes, what they do not realise is that we all worked very hard to gain the promotions, they were not just handed to us on a plate. Ten years I worked in the stores from a lackey to the manager, I earned the promotion," he said proudly.

"I have no doubt that you did, it takes a long time when working in dead men's shoes, having to wait for someone to leave to get the promotion you deserve. As you know I am new in this area, but I have heard that there was a cover up and perhaps the discussions about re-opening the quarry is the reason because of the cover up. Do you think that could be the reason and if so, by whom?" Julie asked.

"There was no cover up, it was thoroughly investigated and the verdict was an unfortunate accident, misadventure; that was the coroner's verdict. The fence was checked two days before the blasting as we always did and it was perfect," he said agitated by the question.

"I am sure you are correct, but it means that the fence was cut in those two days, by whom? Do the local kids have wire cutters and do they carry them around with them, in case they need them?" Julie asked.

"It was decided that the inspection was flawed and he missed the damaged section. He paid the price, he was sacked," Mr Croft told them.

"Did he admit his error?" Julie asked.

"Eventually, but not at first, as you do, he tried to bluff it," he said.

"That accident seems to be the reason for the murders, so it would help me if I knew who the inspector was and his address," Julie said.

"B-Brian, no, I am sure it began with a 'B,' erm," he stumbled.

"How long did you work together?" Julie asked.

"I think about six years, my memory is not good with names, but I'd know him if I saw him," he said.

"I presume a responsible job like that, would be given to a foreman, at least," Julie said.

"Erm, yes, it was, we had ten foremen at that time, various areas, so I didn't know all of them, more a passing smile and hello," he said.

"Thank you very much, Mr Croft; and I hope you are soon back on your feet again," Julie said, getting up ready to leave.

They made for the door and Dan turned back, "One more thing if you don't mind, the gap in the fence where was it?" Dan asked.

"On the left hand side, about half way down behind the foreman's shed. We were very busy and had several foremen covering the three shifts. During daylight hours, we would blast not every day obviously, but the stone could be moved and dressed during the night, ready for next day delivery," he told them.

"I see so it was a twenty four hour operation, impressive. When was the fence checked?" Dan asked.

"That was the other element in why he was sacked; at dawn, they said that he missed it because of poor light, it should have been checked in daylight," he said.

"So it was a night time foreman who checked the fence then?" Dan asked.

"Yes, his last job before going off shift at six o'clock in the morning. They also suggested that in his hurry to go home he was not as careful as he should have been. After that, it was handed over to the day foreman, as his first job, but the quarry never re-opened," he told them.

Dan and Julie went to the office at the building firm, as one might expect, it felt in disarray with all or most of the senior management dead or injured. They went to reception and asked for Human

Resources, the receptionist rang a number and they were shown to an office.

Julie introduced them and they were told that the person they were dealing with was a Gillian Granger. Julie looked at her, and smiled, as is perhaps normal, but it was more of a recognition smile as she shook hands with the ginger haired, and freckled faced female, a memory of a long lost friend in Afghanistan.

"Thank you for seeing us, when we are sure you are very busy selecting people to replace the lost management. It must be a very traumatic time for you and the company.

"We are investigating the murders of your senior management and it has come to light that a night foreman was dismissed as a result of the accident when a child was killed. We need that foreman's name, and address. Do you have the records of employees at that time?" Julie asked.

"Not to hand, but I can get them. Do you think he killed the management?" she asked.

"It is too early to tell, we have several suspects we are investigating and this is just another avenue to be, investigated," Julie told her.

"It will take me till tomorrow to find the name and address. The file is not in this office, but because the firms are connected, we do have those files in storage," she told them.

"From what you have said, I suspect the files are not on these premises. If that is the case, I will send an officer to go with you, can we say one o'clock this afternoon. That way, I can have the file by tonight, it is very important," Julie said, smiling her 'don't try anything, I have your number' smile.

"Y-yes, fine," she said, realising Julie was not to be cheated, or ignored.

"Sergeant, send an officer to Mrs. Granger's office at the builders, she is the head of human resources and escort her to find the old personnel files from the quarry. I want them to bring the file for the foreman who was sacked, as a result of the death of the child. We do not have a name, so they will have to find the relevant file and I doubt Mrs. Granger is being as helpful as she could be," Julie said.

"I got the same impression, she was hiding something," Dan said as they walked to their office.

"What about Croft, what impression did you get about him?" Julie asked as they hung their coats up.

"The same, he is hiding something, and he is not as innocent as he pretends to be, but is he the killer; that remains to be seen," Dan said.

"I don't know if he was fired at to hide the fact that he is the killer, or to get police protection and they missed, hitting him by mistake," Julie said.

"Hum, I have to agree, Ma'am," Dan said as Everet entered the office.

"Most of the town's folk have a licence, more often than not it is for a shot gun and they go clay pigeon shooting, but there are several rifles licensed as well. Mr. Croft has a licence as does Mr Bancroft, as you know, Sir Andrew, Mr Morris and Mr Tindall, they all have a shot gun licence and a rifle licence, Mr Tindall, Bancroft and Sir Andrew also have pistol licences," Everet informed them.

"Do you know if they have the guns they are licensed for?" Julie asked.

"In every case they are alleged to have the guns. We know that Bancroft has lost a gun, but the others are accounted for. Sir Andrew, again we have seen the guns and they are all accounted for. Mr. Morris, again all his guns are accounted for. This afternoon I am going to check up on the other two and I have advised the widows that they are not licensed and need to have the guns removed to a licensed property, or person, Ma'am. I did wonder, if Bancroft would hold them in the interim?" Everet asked.

"That is the obvious solution, but not the best. I have joined the local gun club and I believe that is the best place, ownership does not change hands, but the guns are secure until sold on," Julie suggested.

"Ma'am, I was surprised to find out that Mrs Croft, was licensed, that is the only household where the guns can stay with a licensed person," Everet said.

"Really, she is licensed? Now that is interesting and explains the shoe prints in the mud at the scene. Heeled shoes are not good footwear when firing a gun, that is perhaps why we saw the slip marks and the depressed heel at the end of the slide," Julie said.

"Could she have put them on because the branch was too high and needed that little lift?" Dan asked.

"Very possible, two inch heels would make her the right height," Julie said, thinking about the scene and Mrs. Croft's height.

"I would like to speak to Mrs. Croft if you don't mind and you go to Tindal's house. I also want you to arrange for a firearms officer to collect the guns and move them to the gun club. I will speak to the club," Julie said.

They ate lunch and then Julie spoke to the club, making the arrangements and then she left with Dan for the Croft residence.

As before Mrs. Croft answered the door and Julie smiled and apologised for having to return. They were shown into the lounge where Mr. Croft was once again on the settee, and covered with a blanket, but awake.

"As I told your wife I am sorry that I need to come back with more questions, but this time they are for your wife. You see I have found out that you own a .22 rifle and I need to see it," Julie said.

"Why, it has never left the gun cabinet and why would I poison Sir Andrew? He was good to me and I respected him. You do not seriously suspect me of the murders, do you?" Croft asked, shocked at the implication.

"We suspect everyone until we have a suspect, supported with evidence," Dan said.

"Where were you the afternoon your husband was shot?" Julie asked Mrs. Croft.

"I don't like football, so I was at home," she said and laughed. "I love my husband. I would do anything for him; he is the kindest, gentlest man you could ever wish to meet, it is ridiculous to even think that I could try to kill him. You are barking up the wrong tree," she said, in an angry tone.

"Then you won't mind if we take the.22 for forensic examination. I can get a court order if you object, but that would only make me very suspicious about what you are hiding. Several murders perhaps, which would entail a protracted visit to the station, rather than the nice warm settee you currently occupy," Julie said, smiling at them both, in turn.

"W-Why do you need to take the rifle?" Mrs. Croft asked.

"I want to see if the bullet removed from your husband, is the same as one test fired from that rifle. You see; I do not believe you are the multiple murderers. I believe you had a warped thought that you would be next and to be fired upon would elicit police protection, but it went wrong and instead of hearing the shot it hit you.

"Mrs Croft, when firing a rifle, or any gun for that matter, do not use poor footwear like heels, or stand on slippery ground on a slope. I am surprised that you chose that particular place for the shot, but it was not intended to be fatal, or to wound, just to be heard, but a bad choice of footwear and position led to your husband's injury," Julie said.

Julie hoped that by being obvious, they would break down and tell her the truth.

"Get the gun, Caroline, we can delay the inevitable by a couple of days, but we cannot avoid it. You don't have any evidence without the gun, but why spend two days in the cells while you get

297

the court order to get the evidence," Mr. Croft said in a dejected tone.

"A confession would also be nice," Julie said.

"I was in fear for my life; I am the last of the old management left, so it was my turn next. That was the only position that gave her a clear shot at me, being in goal, but it was as you suggest, meant to hit the ground, but she slipped. What is going to happen, to us?" he asked.

"You will both be charged, you with conspiring to wound and your wife with discharging a firearm in a public place. Those are the least severe crimes I can offer you. I believe there was no intent to injure, let alone murder, but you are not going to get away with it. That was a very dangerous thing to do. What if it had missed you and hit one of the other players and killed them? Your licences will also be revoked for both of you," Julie said.

Julie got up and followed Mrs. Croft into the office where the gun cabinet was. She opened it and Julie removed all the guns, asking Dan to stay with the car while she carried them out and placed them in the boot.

Julie then turned to Mrs, Croft and read her the caution and formally arrested her and Dan arrested Mr. Croft. They were put in the back of the car and taken to the police station, where they were put in an interview room to write their confessions.

"Dan, we seem to be skirting around the edges, multiple arrests for unsolved crimes, after the arms bust and now a misadventure situation, but no nearer to solving the crime before us," Julie said. dejected.

"I don't know, Miss Pessimistic, credit where credit is due. We did solve several old cases and one that was linked to our crime, but not part of it, clearing that from the books and we have a new suspect to investigate, so all is not, lost," Dan said.

Chapter 23 - Good Bye Dan

Julie was just about to leave the office with Dan when her phone rang.

"I have decided to withdraw all the extra officers, the case is dead. Mark it up to experience and get on with arresting the local thieves and running the station. This is the one that got away and if you ever speak to me again like you did the other day. I will have you thrown off the force. The multiple arrests you enabled has saved you this time, but do not rely on it to save you in the future. Inspector Dan Williams will report for duty at eight o'clock on Thursday morning, the day after tomorrow. Do not say anything, just do as told," the Super said and hung up.

"I was expecting that, the backlash. I did push it, didn't I?" Julie asked Dan.

"I did say that at the time, but you will never change. When do I report to Manchester?" Dan asked.

"Thursday, like leave tomorrow, drive back and then report the next day at eight o'clock," Julie said, her head bowed, peeking up at him, asking the unasked question.

"No Julie, I still value my job," Dan said.

"Then we have tonight to solve this crime," Julie said.

"Why are you staring at me like that? You know I do not like to leave a job unfinished. Twenty four hours is the time we have left; I will need to get some sleep, it is a long drive back," Dan said.

"Ma'am, the file you asked for," an officer said, entering her office.

Julie took the file and opened it. "Walter Harrison, that is a name I recall, but where, somewhere in this lot is that name," Julie said and began to sift through the papers on her desk and open the files.

Dan joined her, "I felt I knew it as well, Julie, but it is in the mists of time, we have had so many names, thrown at us," Dan said.

"It isn't a relevant name but a throw away one," Julie said, throwing discarded papers on the floor.

"Julie, an epiphany, Ramashkin, wasn't that the name of her first husband, Harrison? The one that took her to America?" Dan asked.

"Now I know why I like you, yes it was, but what connection does this Harrison have with her? Was he her first husband? If so, when did he return, or is there some other connection?" Julie asked.

"I'll begin now by sending an e-mail to the border authorities, asking when one Walter Harrison entered the UK, probably from America. We should have a reply by morning," Dan said.

"Mark it urgent, very urgent. There is nothing we can do now until the morning, six o'clock start and then we can make contact with the local hotels to see if he is registered in any of them. A photo would be nice," Julie said, organising them.

"Passport office. I'll e-mail them as well, he must have a passport to have left the country and

301

the American Embassy, in case he now has American citizenship," Dan said, and began typing.

They stayed another half hour sending out e-mails to try and save as much time as possible. To close the case in the time available, they would need to hit the ground running.

Julie dropped Dan off at the hotel and then went home. She again lay on the bed, eyes closed, as she mulled over the case. Every suspect so far seemed to have an alibi of some sort or other, or reason not to have killed the victims. Yet it still bugged Julie that they were the main suspects, ones with the motive, opportunity and means. Were they all in it together?

Ramashkin was not in the country when Sir Andrew was killed, but Croft was a good enough shot to have taken the body shot. Ramashkin handed the poisoned bottle of HP sauce to Mrs. Morris but she implicated Croft. Ramashkin was at the big house when Lady Sophie was killed and so was Croft. Both of them were available when Tindall was shot and he would in all probability open the door to them.

None of her suspects were available for all the murders, so was she hunting a conspiracy, two or three people who between them killed the victims, creating an alibi, for each other?

Now she had a new suspect, this Walter Harrison. Was he the murderer alone, or were the others involved in some way?

Her alarm woke Julie; she got up, dressed and headed for the office with her flask of coffee to sip on the way as she mulled over the same questions as the night before.

"Morning, Dan, Oh, Everet, couldn't you sleep?" Julie asked brightly.

"I had a vision, well a thought really and no, I couldn't sleep as it kept me awake. We have been chasing a single perpetrator. What if it was not one person, but two or more of the suspects so that they created an alibi for each other? It couldn't be Ramashkin, because she was in France when Tindall was killed and so on?" Everet asked.

"I like the way you are thinking and now if you add to that the fact that one Walter Harrison was the foreman who was sacked for failing to see the breach in the fence when the little boy was killed. He was also married to the sister who raised the little boy. The fuzzy edges become a little less fuzzy but he was the one who took Ramashkin to America, so it all falls apart, if he is still in America," Julie said.

"He could now have an American passport. You have to be resident for five years before applying for citizenship and they moved there six years ago," Everet told them.

"We did know that and that is why we asked the American Embassy if that was the case at the same time, but I am glad to hear that you are on the ball. We will need it; Dan goes back at six o'clock tonight, so we have just under twelve hours now to find the killer," Julie said.

"I'll be sorry to see you leave, Sir, we make a good team, but I am sure the Chief Inspector and I will solve this in time," Everet said.

"Not the point, Everet, I do not leave a case half finished, it grates and irritates me like an unstoppable itch. We will close the case before I leave, even if I have to disregard an order," Dan said.

"Everet, get on the phone and ring around the local hotels, say a ten mile radius and ask for anyone who was registered say one day prior to Lady Sophie's death. Dan, get in touch with the American Embassy and chase them for his passport details and I'll begin with the border control," Julie said.

They rang everybody and nagged, berated and cagouled the person on the other end of the line. Julie had a short fuse and she was on the point of exploding.

"Look, I have now spoken to four imbeciles who are incapable of connecting me to the right person, are you going to make it five? I am a serving police officer and have the authority to arrest people who interfere in a police investigation by withholding evidence. Now connect me with the right person, or if it is not the person who can help me, pack a bag, because I will have you arrested and a night in a police cell is not the best means of an evening's entertainment.

"I need to know if one Walter Harrison has elected to become an American citizen and if he has entered the country in the last three months.

"This is a high profile case and, as far as I am concerned, you are withholding vital evidence by wasting police time, so wake up and get me the information I need before I lose my temper," Julie said aggressively.

"He does have an American passport now, having got citizenship and they told me it was last used at Kennedy ten weeks ago" Dan told her.

"Did you hear that? He is now an American citizen and left Kennedy Airport ten weeks ago. What a pleasure it is to have an efficient government official, but a pity it has to be an American while the British waste my time, shuffling me about," Julie said, getting more and more annoyed; switching the phone to speaker and putting the hand set down.

"Madam, you are through to the right person. I deal with Americans visiting the UK, along with my colleagues. Ten weeks ago you say, let me see," she said and the line went quiet.

"It is Chief Inspector, I am a right Madam when roused, but my title is Chief Inspector," Julie said, putting the record straight.

"We do not have a Walter Harrison entering the country from America ten weeks ago nor nine weeks ago, we do not have a Walter Harrison entering the country, Chief Inspector," she told Julie who hung up.

"Dan, get on to Heathrow, I want CCTV footage for the two weeks ten weeks ago, use the face recognition program. We need to know if he has entered the country and is still here. Ah, Collins, good morning, you are on CCTV footage with Dan. Everet, any luck?" Julie asked.

"I think so; there is a man who registered as a Paul Simons at the Grand in Higher-Sands- by-the-

Sea, it is a coastal town about twenty minutes away. The reason I say I think so, is because it is the wrong name, but he arrived at the right time and is still there," Everet said.

"Good enough for me, well worth a ride out there to speak to him. Da you are with me. Everet, use your sharp eyes and wit to help Collins, we need him entering the country," Julie said, putting her coat on.

"Dan, with luck, we will catch him eating breakfast," Julie said.

"You could have taken Everet with you, she did find him," Dan said.

"I know that, but the way I drive when in a hurry, blues and twos might frighten her, you are used to it," Julie said.

"That does not mean I accept it and it does not frighten me, believe me, it does," Dan said.

"We need to get there before he leaves, we will be there in fifteen instead of twenty," Julie said, ignoring Dan's comments.

"I would just like to get there in one piece," Dan said.

"I took the Army's advanced driving test as part of my training for security work protecting foreign dignitaries and then the police one, because they did not recognise the Army test, so trust me I can drive fast safely. You didn't think John Wayne drove the Capri that jumped Tower Bridge, did you?" Julie asked.

"No, a stunt driver did, but that wasn't, was it?" he asked clinging on for dear life as she did a hand brake turn.

"No, I only did the test jump," Julie said casually.

"You do not plan on jumping this car, do you?" Dan asked.

"Dan, they are stripped down to essentials to be light enough to almost fly and without a passenger, especially one your size. We would be lucky to make a four foot jump with both of us aboard and a full tank of fuel, plus the risk of explosion on landing. A ruptured tank and sparks are not a good mix," Julie said.

"Public toilets, pull over while I change my underpants," Dan said.

"It wasn't that bad. I kept the speed down for you, see sixteen minutes, I would have been here in fourteen had I not thought about you," Julie said.

"I appreciate the consideration," Dan said, being glib, "There," he added pointing to the hotel, more of a guest house.

Julie pulled up in front of it and they got out. Dan followed her to the front door, Julie rang the bell.

An obese woman answered the door; Julie introduced them and asked to speak to Mr Simons.

"He is eating breakfast, please, follow me," the owner said, showing them into the dining room.

"Mr Simons, or is it Mr. Harrison? I am Chief Inspector Ashton and with me is Detective Inspector Williams. We need to ask you a few questions," Julie said, introducing them.

"How can I help you?" he asked.

"Firstly we need to identify you, do you have any photographic proof of identity?" Julie asked him.

"Not on me, my passport is in my room," he said.

"OK, we can wait. Please finish your breakfast, Inspector, can you arrange a coffee for us please, while we wait," Julie said.

"Is your visit pleasure, or business?" Julie asked.

"A bit if both really, I am the overseas sales manager for a pharmaceutical company and I am here to set up a new branch in the UK. I decided that it would be a good time to visit the country, so I included a holiday with work, to do some sightseeing," he replied.

"I see, have you ever visited the UK, before?" Julie asked.

"No, never, which was why I decided it was an ideal opportunity," he replied.

"Please, excuse me, we had a near miss on the way here and my stomach is unsettled, I need a bit of fresh air," Dan said and got up. Julie knew it was an excuse to contact the American Embassy again.

Dan was gone a few minutes and when he returned he smiled at Julie.

"Mr Simons, as a foreign visitor you are required to carry photographic proof of identity at all times and seeing as you have not got it with you, we will be escorting you to your room, so if you will, please?" Julie asked, indicating he lead the way, when he had finished his breakfast, indicating he stand and lead them to his room.

They entered his room and he opened a drawer and handed them his passport.

Julie looked at it and then smiled at him, "Now Mr. Simons, I will ask you to accompany us to the local police station. Failure to comply will mean that I will arrest you and use any reasonable force to detain you, so please, object," Julie said giving him a broad smile, with meaning.

He did as asked and they took him to the local police station and had him put in an interview room.

"Right, identity, you are, or were one, Walter Harrison. We have your date of birth and address. My Inspector rang the American Embassy whilst you ate breakfast and they confirmed that you changed your name when you applied for citizenship last year.

"I need the name of the pharmaceutical company you work for and the reason for the visit, because I do not believe you," Julie said.

"Pfizer, and I am the overseas manager," he said.

"Pfizer, we can soon check," Julie said, not believing him.

"When you do, ask for Mr Adam Schultz, he will vouch for me," he said easily to Julie a little too easily.

"OK, wait here, won't you," Julie said and they left the room.

Julie made the call to America and asked for the human resources manager, explaining that she was a chief Inspector with the British police force.

"Hello, Cynthia Hutchinson speaking," an American voice said.

Julie said hello and introduced herself, "I am interested in a Mr. Paul Simons and a Mr. Adam Schultz. Do you know either of these men, are they employed at Pfizer?" Julie asked her.

"Can I ring you back? I need to access the files," she said.

"I can wait, it is urgent and very important," Julie replied. She had the woman and didn't want to let her go.

"Adam Schultz, you said, let me see, yes, we do have an Adam Schultz, he works in the factory on the lines. Now a Paul Simons, 'P,' 'P,' where are they, ah, yes, here we are, now, 'A,' 'A,' no, I cannot find a Paul Simons. We do have a Peter Symonds, but not a Paul Simons," she said.

"Thank you very much I appreciate your time, can you now put me through to Adam Schultz, if that is possible?" Julie asked.

"No, that is impossible; there is a line in the staff room, which is monitored, but not on the factory floor," she replied.

"Then why did he suggest that I speak to Adam Schultz, if it is not possible. The Adam Schultz I was told to speak to is in management, possibly a director. Paul Simons is reputed to be the overseas sales manager, so the person I want must be the person he would report to," Julie explained.

"No we have just the one person named Adam Schultz and he works on the factory floor, he is hourly paid and not a manager of any description, not even a foreman, in fact he joined us just three months ago," she said.

"The phone in the canteen, staff room, I presume it would be quite noisy?" Julie asked.

"No, it is in an ante-room, but only receives incoming calls, in case of household emergencies say, like can you pick the kids up from school and is very closely monitored. Children do have accidents and with so many employees, they are quite a regular occurrence," she said.

"Thank you, you have been very helpful, but I need to check something so will you put me through to that phone please, or have me put through to it?" Julie asked.

She was transferred and the phone was picked up.

"Hello, Adam Schultz, please?" Julie asked the person who answered.

"He is on the shop floor, ma'am, please hold the line, and I will get him for you," they said and the line went quiet.

"Hello, Adam Schultz speaking," he said.

"Mr Schultz, I am Chief Inspector Ashton of the British Police and a Mr. Paul Simons suggested that I ring you to verify that he is employed by you as the overseas sales manager. Can you confirm that he is in the UK to open a new branch, please?" Julie asked him.

"Is he in any trouble? I sent him to the UK to open the new branch, as he told you, what has he done?" he asked.

"I suggest that you do not enter the UK, the least you can expect is the sack, the worst is a term in prison. It is an offence in the UK and America, to try to pervert the course of justice. You are not a manager and have no authority to send anyone to a foreign country to open a new branch. Therefore you could be charged with aiding and abetting a murder. This call is being recorded, good bye," Julie said and hung up.

"Ma'am, do you want me to send a copy of the telephone call to the Illinois Police?" Dan asked.

"Why not, mark it for the attention of Inspector Alan Jacobs, with my regards? My reach is far and wide," Julie said smiling, "Everet, what do we know about Paul Simons?" Julie asked.

"I have just received his details. he was born in the UK in nineteen eighty two in Little Hampton. He went to school at the local junior and then the local comprehensive. He went to work at the quarry as a trainee stone mason, in an apprenticeship. He qualified and rose to be the foreman on the night shift. Apart from watching over the men on the shop floor dressing the stone and the artists carving the stone, he was detailed to check the perimeter fence and the loads for delivery.

"He married a local girl and two days after the ceremony they emigrated to America, where they were divorced. He then became a salesman for a shoe company; we would call him a shop assistant. His ex-wife remarried, as we know. Last year he applied for and got American citizenship, which was also when he changed his name, no longer Walter Harrison, now Paul Simons," Everet informed Julie and Dan.

"Why change his name? Who paid for the trip? A shop assistant cannot afford a month in the UK, let alone two months, where did he work, or does he still work there?" Julie asked.

"Sorry, Ma'am, I should have said, he works for 'Shoes 'R' Us,' or did, I am waiting for confirmation that he still does work there, Ma'am," Everet said.

"Collins, we have searched both the hotel room where Simons is staying and the Ramashkin's place, but no .22 rifle was found. We need the one used to kill Sir Andrew. I want you to sit and think; the killer had the gun in the grounds of Sir Andrew's estate obviously. I want you to trace back, the movements.

"I am not totally happy that Ramashkin is innocent, I think she is involved in some way, perhaps not the murderer, but involved, so trace it back to her address and the hotel Simons was staying at. Once you are happy you have the most probably route, take a couple of officer, and search the route or routes," Julie said.

"Ma'am," he replied and got a map to start to trace the probable routes.

"Everet, get back in touch with Shoes 'R' Us and jolly them along. If they are being awkward, ring this number and ask him to pay them a visit. If he objects, remind him he owes me big time," Julie said with emphasis, yet light hearted.

"Ma'am, what about Simons?" Everet asked.

"Let him sweat, we have only ten hours left and we can hold him for another eighteen hours, so leave him. Dan, we are going to visit Mrs. Morris, I need clarification," Julie said and put her coat on.

They made to leave the office when the phone rang.

"Hey, what is all this about a debt?" a man with an American accent said.

"Helmand province, fifteen years ago. I have a very long memory, you miserable sod, don't tell me you have forgotten how I saved your life, carrying you two miles," Julie said, laughing with him.

"As I remember it was you who shot me in the first place," he said.

"When in a fire fight, it is a good idea not to jump up and shoot at friends," Julie replied.

"You mean when I shot the insurgent aiming for you from behind?" he replied.

"What the; *****were you doing on the wrong side of the fire fight anyway? We were facing north and you south. Anyway, it was only a shoulder wound. I winged you to make you duck so I could kill the insurgent behind you. You were spoiling my aim, typical American, always in the way.

"I was just about to go out, so make it fast," Julie said laughing with him.

"I thought you were a good Police Officer and knew the law, there is nothing in the call to prove he was involved in, the murders," Alan said.

"Correct, I know that as you do, but, does he? All I want you to do is frighten him. Bring him in and question him, make him believe he could be prosecuted and visit Shoes 'R' Us. We need to know if one Paul Simons is employed there, they are dragging their feet and we are on the clock, I need to know now not tomorrow," Julie said.

314

"Impatient as ever, you couldn't wait till I ducked to kill him; you had to shoot me," he said.

"I was not prepared to lose even a pain in my neck to the enemy; he had you in his sights. I did shout 'duck'; I had him in my sights before you jumped up. You never did explain how come you were in front of us and not guarding our rear, as you had been ordered to," Julie said.

"I'll tell you when you visit me, as promised. What was it, ten years ago?" he asked.

"Unlike America, where the crime rate is higher than in the UK, I am kept busy clearing up crimes and putting criminals behind bars, where they belong. Now I have to go, let me know how you get on, will you? a message will suffice," Julie said; she was smiling all the time she talked with her friend.

They went to Mrs. Morris's house and she invited them in.

"Mrs. Morris, I need clarification on one or two points. I appreciate that subsequent events can dim memories. When you bought the HP sauce, who was there and what happened exactly, please?" Julie asked her.

"The woman who handed the bottle to me," she said, and then went quiet, thinking back, "And now you ask me, there was a man, yes, Mr Croft. Now let me see, he handed her the bottle, sorry, I had forgotten that bit. I entered the aisle and the bottle was in her hand yes, it was in her hand and she handed it to him to put back on the shelf.

"He was being a gentleman to save her bending down, but I asked for the bottle and he passed it back to her, then she handed it to me. I seem to remember her holding her back, as if it was difficult for her to bend down so he took it off her," Mrs Morris said.

"That fits, with so many people handling the bottle we couldn't get a decent print to match, apart from yours. We got five different prints, but like I said four of them were smudged. We know that the shop keeper handled the bottle so that is two, now Mrs. Ramashkin and Mr Croft so that is four, but who owns the fifth set?" Julie asked.

"The man who didn't buy anything, perhaps; I felt I knew him, but can't put a name to the face," Mrs. Morris said.

Julie and Dan thanked her and then went to the shop.

"Hello, I need to ask you some more questions. You said that there was only Mrs. Morris and the big woman who we now know as Mrs. Ramashkin but they both say that there were more people in the shop. I need you to think back and tell me who was in the shop at the time Mrs. Morris bought the bottle of HP sauce," Julie told him, as a customer came to the counter.

"Hello Madam, allow me to help you," he said to the customer.

Julie put her hand on the basket and looked into the shop keeper's eyes, "We can do this down at the police station, if you like? Sorry, Madam, but this is very important. Now concentrate, who was in the shop?" Julie asked in a firm voice.

"As I told you, that aisle, is not covered by the cameras and mirrors, but now that I think back; Mr.

316

Croft was also in and the door did open and close, but I saw no-one. The big woman came to the counter and I was serving her when the door opened and closed," he said.

"You wouldn't happen to know if you say sold thirteen bottles of HP, when a case only holds twelve, would you?" Julie asked.

"No, I don't have that degree of stock control," he replied.

"So a person can enter the shop and leave and apart from the door ringing the bell, you would not know they had been in?" Julie asked in a shocked voice.

"Not now, then yes, I suppose you are right, but I have more cameras now and that cannot happen. I noted that as a possibility, and acted upon it," he said.

"Sorry to delay you, Madam, and thank you, the information is, a big help," Julie said.

"Dan, thoughts?" Julie asked in the car on the way back to the station.

"I think our mystery man is Simons and Ramashkin is involved. I suggest you ask your friend to get bank records for them both and credit card statements. I like the idea that she is paying for his trip. I don't like her for the murderer, but I do like her for the financials. Her win and the re-opening combined to make the motive and means," Dan offered.

"Great minds think alike and all we have to do is prove it," Julie said.

It had started to rain by the time they arrived back at the police station. Julie and Dan bent over and ran into the station.

"A summer shower like hell, a downpour more like, you are all right behind that desk," Julie said to the desk sergeant, who smiled at her.

"With age comes wisdom, Ma'am, I let the youngsters go out in all weathers now," he said.

The door opened and an officer brought in a man who stood at the counter and then for some unknown reason he kicked off and thumped the officer, bursting his nose. Julie just acted; she put his arm up his back and threw him to the floor all in one move. How, Dan and the desk sergeant didn't see, one minute he was punching the officer and then he was on the floor his arm up his back and he was complaining about her, telling her to get off him.

"Bitch, you're breaking my arm," he shouted.

"Then lie still, or I will break it," Julie said, "Dan, handcuffs," Julie added.

He bent down and took the other arm and pulled it behind the assailant's back and handcuffed him; Julie did assist by increasing the pressure to make him do as told.

"Go and get your nose attended to," she told the officer, "What is he in for?"

"Drunk and disorderly, probably drug abuse as well," he said.

"And now assaulting a police officer. Do you like eight by ten rooms with a bed and bucket? If not, get used to it. You will, be spending time in

318

one," Julie said to the prisoner and she lifted him up and stood him facing the desk.

Dan looked at the desk sergeant, "Don't ask, the chief inspector explains the moves to me and I still don't know how she does it," Dan said.

They stayed while he was booked in and then went to their office.

"Everet, get a court order to access Mrs. Ramashkin's bank records and credit card details, will you, and get them?" Dan asked her.

Dan went with Julie into the interview room where Paul Simons was waiting, agitated by the wait.

"Look, you have no right to hold me, I am an American citizen and I have rights," he said angrily.

"I agree and if you like I can arrest you on the evidence we have, but first I need to caution you," Julie said and read him his rights under English law.

"Then I want a solicitor present," he demanded.

"Do you have a solicitor, or do you want us to get one for you?" Julie asked.

"I have the right to a phone call," he demanded.

"Indeed you do, what is the number and we will make the call for you," Julie said.

"It is supposed to be a private call," he said.

"OK here, use my phone and we will leave while you make the call," Julie said, handing him her mobile phone.

Chapter 24 - Cracks

"Julie, haven't you just made it more difficult to get a confession, with his solicitor present?" Dan asked.

"Perhaps, but we will also have the number of the person he rings. I very much doubt it is a solicitor and when Everet has got the name of the person he rings, which I am assuming, it will be Ramashkin. We can have her brought in, as an accomplice, and with the bank records showing that she paid for his trip here. The pressure will mount; the icing on the cake would be the rifle. Poor Collins, he will be soaked to the skin in that downpour," Julie said, adding a smile.

"We have nothing on him, but that phone number is just the lever we need, clever," Dan said, "As long as it is Ramashkin's number."

"Who else would he ring? how many solicitors do you know in America?" Julie asked.

They entered the interview room and Julie took the phone off him.

"We will now have to wait until your solicitor comes," Julie said and they left the room.

"Everet, find out who he rang, will you?" Julie asked her, handing Everet the phone.

"Dan, we may need an extension; I think he will play the waiting game. His solicitor will arrive close to the time we need to release him," Julie said.

"On what evidence? we need to have a good reason to extend the holding time," He said.

"He seems placid enough, so assaulting an officer of the law is out and he still has five months before he needs to do anything about his visit. Americans can stay here for six months on just their passport. Come on, Dan, help me find an excuse?" Julie asked him.

"Apart from the fact that we only have eight hours left, before I go back, we need a confession, not an extension," Dan said.

"Contact Collins, we need that bloody rifle," Julie said, frustrated.

"It may be nothing, but wasn't that pond on the way to his hotel?" Dan asked.

"Yes, but none of the guns from it were the one that killed Sir Andrew," Julie said.

"Not when we checked it, but what if he has disposed of it after we searched it?" Dan asked.

"That does not make sense, why wait?" Julie asked.

"We searched it soon after Sir Andrew was killed, for a different reason, but soon after that, we spoke to Ramashkin. What if that made him dispose of the rifle and he would know the pond had been searched. It was on television, so an ideal time; why search a pond we have already searched?" Dan asked.

"OK, organise the divers, will you? You leave in a few hours, you can take the heat if it is futile," Julie said, with a comical smile.

"Ma'am, the phone number is a disposable one and it was bought in London at Heathrow airport. I have contacted the shop and they are looking up to see if it was bought with a credit card," Everet said.

"Just my luck, the only consolation is that they both landed at Heathrow, so the idea is still alive. A pity we can't search him, we have not arrested him, yet," Julie said.

"Julie, they all slip up at some point, sorry, Ma'am," Dan said, realising his mistake.

"Don't worry about it; I am more bothered about getting those two, than protocol. Are you ready to bluff it?" Julie asked, looking at Dan.

"Dangerous, you might give away the only card we have," Dan said.

"Everet, we are going to interview him, just a chat and I want you to wait a few minutes and then knock and come in with a piece of paper, and say 'the information you requested, Ma'am.' just that and hand me the paper," Julie said.

"What do you want me to write on the piece of paper Ma'am?" Everet asked.

"Nothing, it can be blank, it is a ruse, a bluff, but he will be led to think what I want him to think," Julie said.

Julie left with Dan and went to the interview room.

"I don't suppose you have heard from your solicitor, so we can't interview you, but what about a little chat? I mean a month in the UK, very nice. What have you seen whilst you have been here? A week in London is the usual and the countryside around here is well worth spending time here, isn't it?" Julie asked him.

"Erm, well, yes, I did spend a bit of time in London and I have been into the countryside around here," he said.

"How did you get into the country?" Julie asked casually.

"Erm, how, I well," he stuttered.

"You do not have a car, so how did you go into the country? A taxi for a day is expensive, perhaps you hired a car?" Julie asked.

"Y-yes, that is it, I hired a car for the day," he said.

"I have always found that the local car hire firms are the best," Julie said.

"I-I used a nationwide company, because I was thinking that I will hire one again to take me back to the airport," he said.

"Which one? Was the deal a good one?" Julie asked.

"Yes, very good it…" he was saying as there was a knock at the door and Everet entered with a piece of paper.

"Ma'am, the information you requested," she said and handed the paper to Julie, who looked at it and smiled.

"Do you know a, Mrs. Ramashkin?" Julie asked him, handing the paper to Dan who also smiled; it was the details they wanted from the shop.

"Yes, I-I was married to her," he replied.

"Of course, you took her to America with you, didn't you? When you married her?" Julie asked.

"Yes, what has that got to do, with you?" he asked.

"I," Julie began as there was another knock at the door and Everet entered again and handed another piece of paper to Julie.

"Ma'am I thought you would like to see this immediately," she said handing the paper to Julie, who now smiled and her eyes lit up.

"Why would you ring Mrs. Ramashkin when you need a solicitor? More to the point, why did you have her number, a number for a burner phone she bought at Heathrow airport, when she landed here?" Julie asked him.

"Like I said we were married and keep in touch," he said, but Julie knew he was ruffled.

"To have her mobile phone number for an American one would be acceptable, but a burner phone bought one month ago at Heathrow is stretching my imagination somewhat. Why did she give you that number?" Julie asked.

"W-we met at the airport and we were sat two rows apart on the plane, by pure coincidence, erm, and when we landed we decided to meet up for old time's sake. So she gave me that number to save paying the double charges of an international call," he said, but again Julie noted that he was not easy about the question.

"Wow, pure coincidence, two rows apart on the plane; just enough to make it look like you were not travelling together, but you were, weren't you?" Julie asked, pressuring him.

"N-No we met by pure chance, a coincidence," he said.

"Then why did Mrs. Ramashkin pay for your ticket?" Julie asked him, "You did not meet by accident or coincidence; it was arranged, why?" Julie demanded, banging down in front of him the credit card statement and the airplane seating confirmation.

"We-we were married and we are still friends, it was an amicable divorce and she knew I wanted to visit some old friends and having come into a lot of money, she asked if I would like to come. She was paying," he said nervously.

"So you lied before, when you said you met by chance at Heathrow, didn't you?" Julie demanded forcefully now.

"Y-yes," he replied.

"Why did you lie? What are you hiding?" Julie asked.

"W-w, erm, look does it really matter, how we arrived here? We are friends and my ex-wife is a very generous person and out of the kindness of her heart she offered to pay, but being a police person, you would not understand that, so I lied," he said but Julie noted he was ill at ease.

"We do understand; I am sure it happens all the time, where friends offer to pay for a good friend, but usually there is a reason, company, protection, and erm, to cover ones back, what was your reason?" Dan asked, being the calm one, now.

"Does there have to be a reason? Can't two friends just enjoy each other's company?" he asked.

"Then that would fall under company, you see, a reason, so why did they not take you to France and Spain with them?" Dan asked.

"P-Part of the reason was that I wanted to attend my cousin's wedding, which was while they were in France, so I stayed here to go to the wedding," he said.

"Now shall we get to the best part; where were you on the 6th June between two pm in the afternoon and six pm in the evening?" Julie asked.

"That's a few weeks ago, I will need to think about it. I have done so much whilst here," he replied.

"While you think, consider the next question, where were you between nine am on the eighth and ten am, and six pm and eleven pm on the tenth and between eight pm and ten pm on the fifteenth?" Julie asked and stood up, "Inspector, come on, we will allow Mr Simons to think about those dates and times," Julie said, and they left the interview room.

Chapter 25 - The Home Straight

Dan and Julie went back to the office and they sat down, looking glum.

"Julie, without something concrete, we have nothing to pressure him with," Dan said.

"I don't think he is as comfortable as he is pretending, he knows that we know he is the murderer and at the moment he is bluffing. He has disposed of the rifle, the one thing that would be irrefutable, but he is on rocky ground and knows it," Julie said.

"Mrs. Ramashkin, where is she?" Dan asked.

"Just where I want her, in Interview Room 3, she is not sweating as yet, but she soon will be, if you are ready?" Julie asked, smiling at him.

"Mrs. Ramashkin, several anomalies have come to light and we need your confirmation as to why certain things have happened. We have Mr. Simons in the other interview room and he is helping us with our enquiries. What a coincidence it was meeting him at Heathrow Airport and being sat just three rows behind you on the plane, wow," Julie said, adding a broad smile for effect.

"Yes, I used the toilet at the front of the plane, had I used the one at the back then I would probably have seen him," she said.

"So you didn't know he was on the same plane, as you?" Julie asked.

"No, it was a complete surprise," she replied.

"I do this usually to assess the honesty of the person before us and it never fails to surprise me that everyone, fails. We know you bought the tickets for Mr. Simons and we now know you lie, so shall we begin again? I know the answer to most, if not all, of the questions I am going to ask, so please, do not waste my time. Now in the shop you told us that Mr. Croft handed you the HP sauce off the shelf; that was not correct, was it?" Julie asked her.

"I didn't say he handed it to me off the shelf, just that he handed it, to me," she replied with a smile.

"Then where was the bottle, prior to him handing it to you?" Julie asked.

"It, well, it was, well Mr Simons handed it to him and he took another bottle. To save me and Mr Croft, bending down, he was already bent down," she said.

"I see, another coincidence, meeting him in the shop, was it?" Julie asked.

"Yes, it was," she replied.

"You say you saw him take another bottle, after handing you the one in his hand?" Julie asked.

"Yes, he always was a kind person," she said.

"And a thief, I presume you will testify in court that he took another bottle?" Julie asked.

"Why?" she asked confused.

"He left without paying. The shopkeeper hadn't seen him in the shop; that aisle was a blind spot and he left without paying, which is a crime," Julie said.

There was a knock at the door and Collins entered smiling a very broad smile.

"Ma'am sorry to interrupt you, but it is important; can I see you, please?" he asked.

Julie got up and left the room after announcing his entry and their exit to the tape recording.

"Ma'am, one .22 rifle, found in the pond, now being examined by forensics," he said as if bragging.

"Well done, Collins," Julie said, adding a broad smile to show him how pleased she was.

Julie re-entered the room and announced it to the tape.

"Mrs. Ramashkin, I am arresting you for conspiracy to pervert the course of justice by withholding evidence," Julie said and told her, her rights and then added, "A bit thin, too weak to get a conviction, but enough to hold you while we test the rifle we found and expect to find his fingerprints on it. He is not as tough as you, so he will tell us that you paid for his trip, so that he could kill the people responsible for the death of your brother and then that will stick, Mrs. Ramashkin. It will be a long time before you go back to America," Julie said and walked out with Dan, telling the officer to put her in a cell.

It was late afternoon when the results came back and Julie smiled, she had Simons brought back to the interview room and entered with Dan. She slammed the rifle on the table, smiled at him then sat down.

"I like initiative and it was; I mean you saw on the television that we had searched that pond, so you assumed that we would not search it again,

329

once it was getting rather hot for you and Mrs. Ramashkin. The ideal place to throw the rifle to hid the evidence and after wiping it clean, you tossed it away. There is just one thing, you see as a sniper, I know how much you sweat on a warm summer's evening lying prone, waiting for the ideal shot and because of gravity, the sweat always drops down and, being liquid, it goes into the joints of the rifle. This was why I asked the forensic people to break down the rifle and test for DNA in the cracks, between the stock and mechanism, the minor crevasses around the mechanism, hard or inaccessible places. Places you would not think to clean and here are the results.

"The rifle is the weapon used to kill Sir Andrew, ballistics confirm it is. Inside the joint between the stock and mechanism, traces of DNA were found and it is your DNA. Partial fingerprints found on the bottle of HP sauce, not enough to confirm anyone's identity, but they are or do match partial ones, found on the rifle. You see when you threw it into the pond never to be seen again, you were confident that it would not be found, because we had already searched the pond. You failed to use gloves and left some partial prints on the barrel, it is difficult to throw the rifle far enough wearing gloves, they tend to slip," Julie said.

"You have two options; you can argue and hope that Mrs. Ramashkin does not sell you down the river or tell us what happened and because you helped us, we can ask the judge to take it into consideration, when sentencing," Dan suggested, "I mean, you have murdered four people, so arguing and upsetting us would mean that we demanded the most severe imprisonment, thirty years perhaps, without parole," Dan said.

"And if I helped you?" he asked.

"We would need to know who organised the murders, who paid the expenses and who was meant to be killed and, as we said, we would put a good word in for you with the judge. This is not America where they plea bargain, you will be charged with four murders, but a good word from us would help you," Julie said.

"That is if you can make the charge stick?" he asked.

"One rifle with your D.N.A, on it and partial finger prints use to kill Sir Andrew. Being a sniper is not the most enjoyable of jobs, there is never a toilet when you need one and to move means that you miss the shot; wet underwear is just a minor inconvenience. Then again your D.N.A was found in the soil we dug up.

"Partial fingerprints on the HP sauce bottle and the rifle links you to both murder weapons, I admit there are blanks, but not enough to get you off. How on earth did you get the poison in the wine for Lady Sophie?" Julie asked.

"I-I don't think you will get a conviction, you-you can't put me at the scene," he tried.

"Mrs. Morris remembers you handing the bottle of HP to Ramashkin and her handing it to you so we can put you at that scene and the DNA found at the scene of Sir Andrew's murder puts you there, so do not get too confident.

331

"I can put you handling both weapons and at the scene and you will not be able to argue the point, they are forensically proven," Julie pushed.

"If I confess, you will put a good word in for me?" he asked.

"I need the confession, and your accomplice, and then I will put a good word in, for you," Julie said.

"We will leave you to think the offer over, but remember it is time limited, once we charge you, the offer is off the table," Julie said and got up.

They turned the tape off and left the room Dan turned right for the office, Julie turned left and he joined her.

"Well, we have a confession from Simons; he told us everything like you opening the door, so that he could enter to poison the wine. Sir Andrew had put the bottle to one side to allow the sediment to settle, before decanting it. He told us how you made sure Mrs. Morris was where you wanted her. Having overheard her telling her husband that she would need to get a bottle of HP sauce from the shop, in the high street, the night before in the pub and how he waited, bottle in hand.

"Then Croft showed up, a problem, but how lucky you were because he thought you were going to buy it and picked another bottle up, but then you used him to hide fingerprints by passing it to him first. Five sets of fingerprints overlapped and hard to discern one from the other.

"I mean finding the rifle in the pond was the clincher, we had his DNA on the rifle and partial fingerprints; he is going down, like he said, why go down alone when the sentence can be shared? By implicating you as the organiser, he is just your puppet so he said then you get the big sentence and he just gets the assistant's sentence. Do you have anything to say?" Julie asked her.

"He is the murderer, wow, I would never have believed it; he was always so kind, and thoughtful. As for me and your implication prove it, you cannot put me with him, so I paid for his plane ticket, sue me, bitch.

"Apart from her saying that he was in the store, which I can refute - her word against mine, you have nothing, now I want a lawyer. I am saying nothing until they get here," she said and folded her arms.

Julie left her with Dan and went back to Simons.

"Julie, I didn't know you could get DNA from soil, especially after heavy dew," Dan said.

"Neither do I," Julie said, as they reached the interview room.

"This is getting very awkward, I mean we said that we would put in a good word for you with the judge, but she is willing to tell us everything. How you suggested that she buy the tickets to hide the fact that you were together and made her believe that they had to die because of her little brother's death. The tears were very effective and in front of a judge, well they could just be the final straw, or nail in your coffin, thirty years without parole. What are you now, thirty five; you will be out just in time for your pension, won't you?" Julie asked him.

333

"OK, OK, it was all her idea. She planned everything; she bought my ticket and paid for my hotel. Three months in the UK, not that I relished the idea, but she said it would take time, as with each murder a new suspect would be sought. She opened the back door for me to enter and poison the bottle of wine on the side table, resting, she thought Sir Andrew would taste it, but when Lady Sophie did, that changed everything, but it helped us because it started the confusion we wanted.

"Then it was Morris, a change of MO to add to the confusion and then Tindall, that was the easiest, I knew him and he opened the door for me to enter. She got the gun from Bancroft, she had found the key before we left and used it. Then it was Sir Andrew, he should have been first and finally, Underwood, but Croft getting shot delayed that one. I was in the woods with the rifle and I was aiming it at him, but the shot rang out and all hell broke loose, so I split," he said.

"Thank you, all we need now is for you to write it down for us, with perhaps a little more detail. Officer, get Mr Simons a cup of coffee, will you?" Julie asked, and got up, switching the recorder off and leaving with Dan.

Back in the office she smiled at Everet and Collins. "We have the confession, all you two have to do is get it in writing and then push Mrs. Ramashkin to confess, so that it is all neat and tidy. Even without her confession we have her, but it would be nice to dot all the 'I's and cross all the T's.

"Dan, it has been wonderful seeing you again and I thank you for all the help you have given us. Should you want a quieter life than that metropolis, I can always use a good Inspector. I have two very good detectives who would benefit from a good, solid Inspector, while I learn how to be politically correct, sorry, political," Julie said and smiled.

She showed Dan to the car park at the rear of the station; she gave him a hug and a peck on the cheek and waved good bye to him.

THE END